The Haunting
of Mount Cod

Nicky Stratton

Clink
Street

London | New York

In memory of Mark

Chapter one

Lady Laura Boxford folded the *Telegraph* obituary page, put it back in the drawer of her desk and took out the local paper.

"Spectacular Death of Heroic Military Gentleman," stated the *Woldham Herald*.

She sat down on the sofa next to Parker, her old grey pug and began to re-read the article.

'Dear Arthur, what a way to go,' she said, as Parker began to snore. She patted him, noticing the rich patina of age spots on her once elegant hand and then the glint of the slightly insignificant ruby and diamond ring on her finger.

Laura Boxford had only been engaged to Brigadier Arthur Stanway for three weeks when he was killed at Woldham's annual Spring Agricultural Show and "Spectacular," was not a word she would necessarily have chosen to describe her late fiancé's fatal encounter with the marauding Limousin bull. It had broken loose from the young farmer who was handling the beast as they made their way to the main arena for judging.

'Christ Boxford, that brute's going to stampede the children's play area,' were the Brigadier's last words to her before he had removed the red silk spotted handkerchief from the pocket of his tweed jacket and waved it at the bull. At eighty-six, he did not have the agility of a Spanish matador and that was that. Children saved, Brigadier trampled to death.

'I wonder if he'd have stopped calling me Boxford after we were married?' Laura pondered aloud.

Parker looked up at her momentarily and went back to sleep.

She checked her watch. It was three-thirty – that sort of noncommittal time of the afternoon when one had almost forgotten what had been for lunch and one wasn't quite hungry enough to wonder what was for dinner.

Life at the residential care home of Wellworth Lawns, that had formerly been Laura's own family home, Chipping Wellworth Manor, was, she thought, merely a matter of waiting for the next influx of food. Well, obviously there was drinks time to look forward to, and the possibility of joining in one of the evening activities, but she had tended to avoid these occasions since the arrival of the new manager, Edward Parrott. There was a limit to the amount of inheritance tax seminars a person could stomach.

She decided to ring for a cup of tea.

Mimi, the Bulgarian maid answered the phone. 'Hello there Ladyship, you not coming down? Alfredo making special Black Forest cake, cherries and all.'

Laura declined the chef's gateau and said she'd prefer to remain upstairs.

Some minutes later there was a knock and Mimi popped her head round the door smiling prettily, her lips coated today, Laura noticed, in an iridescent apricot colour.

'I bringing tray in?' she asked.

'Thank you Mimi; put it over there would you?'

Mimi placed the tray on a small round table by the window and turned to Laura. 'You needing get out more, Ladyship. No good sitting up here all on the tod. You not still thinking poor old Brig?'

'I feel he should be commemorated.'

'But you already collecting his ashes.'

'There should be something to remember him by. A gravestone, if he had been religious.'

'Ah, I getting it.' Mimi smoothed her sleek dark ponytail. 'How 'bout nice park bench. Brig's name on type thing.'

'There are more memorial benches in the garden than at Woldham Bowls Club. The last thing we need is another.'

'Maybe making nice photomontage?' Mimi's voice lilted up at the end of the sentence as she stretched out her arms to indicate the size of the tribute. 'I see something like this when my Tom is taking me to Tate Modern, London time. Maybe Mr. Parrott letting you put it at the reception desk?'

'That's certainly an idea. But then I have a feeling Mr. Parrott's not much of a one for ostentation.'

'Him that too?' Mimi tutted. 'I know he having arthritis.' She picked up the little chrome teapot and poured.

'Yes, it's jolly bad luck,' Laura said. 'You expect it at my age but he can't be more than fifty.' She thanked Mimi as the maid handed her the cup and saucer.

'No probs Ladyship, I see you dinner time.'

As Laura sipped the tea she mused on the idea of the Brigadier's memorial. Thinking that perhaps her friend Venetia Hobbs might have some input, she replaced the cup and rose from the sofa. 'Come along Parker,' she said, making for the door. He leapt down onto the carpet, bounding after her and together they took the few short paces along the corridor to the room next door.

Venetia was on the edge of her chair, watching afternoon TV. 'Come in, come in,' she said, beckoning Laura over with a wave of one frail arm. 'It's such a good programme; all about redecorating on a shoestring.' She gave a little shiver of excitement, her face radiating a childlike exuberance. 'I'm thinking about turning this into a lampshade.' The lime green plastic earrings dangling from her somewhat sagging lobes swung as she leant over, picked up her raffia wastepaper basket and turned it upside down.

'Don't you think it's more useful in its present form?' Laura said, collecting up the used tissues and Venetia's glasses that had fallen onto the floor.

'What about upholstering this Zimmer frame to match

3

the soft furnishings?' Venetia jumped up with surprising agility for one whose delicate frame could have disintegrated at any second into a pile of brittle bones. She pulled the appliance to the window, draped the hem of a chintz curtain over the tubular steel and reflected on the effect.

'Perhaps not, but you see, I'm keen to be creative.' She let the curtain fall and stared out of the window. 'Who's this arriving, I wonder?'

Laura walked over to join her and they watched as a burly middle-aged man with dishevelled blond hair, wearing a checked shirt got out of an old Land Rover in the driveway below. He walked round to the passenger door, opened it and pulled an aged figure in a dark blue blazer and grey trousers out of the vehicle by one arm. As the younger man let go, the gentleman, clutching something to his chest with his other arm, swayed back and forth as he fought for his balance.

'Unless I'm much mistaken, that is my cousin Repton Willowby,' Venetia said.

'Sir Repton Willowby, the actor?' Laura focused more closely. 'Goodness I believe you're right. I remember seeing him in *Hamlet*, at least forty years ago. But what do you mean your cousin?'

'By marriage.'

Laura turned to Venetia. 'Your cousin by marriage? You are full of surprises.' She returned her gaze to the scene below. 'He used to be so good looking, of course his nostrils let him down – too wide for my liking. But would you look at him now; he's positively haggard.'

'That's guilt for you; the murderous psychopath.'

'What are you talking about?' Laura asked.

'He drowned her in her bath.' Venetia crossed her arms and gave a little shudder. 'Must be six months ago now. I hadn't seen or heard from her in ages, but I remember clearly because she rang me out of the blue just before Christmas and asked how much my room cost and shortly afterwards I heard she was dead.'

4

'Hold on a minute. Who?'

'His late wife; my cousin, Matilda Laverack, that was. She had diabetes – who doesn't by the time they get to eighty – but she sounded perfectly all right on the phone.'

Laura watched as Sir Repton Willowby brushed something from his lapel with his one free hand and then she noticed that underneath his other arm he was carrying a small brown dog. She sighed in disgust; there was no breed worse that the silk coated dachshund.

'She was thinking of leaving him, I'm sure,' Venetia continued.

'Did they have marital troubles?'

'Inevitable at their age I'd have thought. Anyhow he convinced the police she had died of natural causes and the post-mortem showed up the diabetes so the silly fools said she must have fallen asleep.'

'It sounds fairly plausible. What makes you so sure he killed her?'

'To get his hands on her money of course.'

'Did she have a lot?' Laura knew Venetia was careful with her limited resources.

'Matilda came from the rich side of the Laverack family; the Yorkshire branch. They know how to hold on to it up North and she kept Repton on a tight rein.'

'Surely he has money of his own? He is, or was, famous after all.'

'Spent it all I assume and he hadn't had a part in ages. Not since Matilda refused to back any more of his duff vanity projects. *Under Milkwood on Ice* was a disaster. Heaven knows how much she forked out for his skating lessons.' Venetia huffed. 'Then he tried reinventing himself and ended up making a complete hash of it doing that silly washing liquid advertisement on TV.'

'I remember.' Laura laughed. 'Dressing up as a plastic bottle was not a good career move.'

'And the strange blue beak thing on his head that was meant to be the dispenser.'

'Preposterous,' Laura said. 'But what's he got on his head now?'

They pressed their noses back to the window. Sir Repton stood waiting as the driver went to the back of the Land Rover.

As Laura wiped the condensation from the pane with her shirtsleeve she noticed ink on the cuff. How did it always manage to happen to her? 'Have you any binoculars?' she asked.

'I think I may have left them in the pub after the Horticultural Club outing,' Venetia said. 'I remember having them while I ordered the chicken liver pate. It was £8.95, rather dear I thought at the time. Topsy Reynolds agreed with me.'

Laura strained her eyes. In what remained of the hair around Repton Willowby's almost bald head she could see small coloured bits of paper. 'Has he just got remarried?' she asked.

'I knew it. He's no sooner got his hands on Matilda's money and he's found a newer model, some brainless teenager in all likelihood. But what makes you think he's married?'

'Because, if I'm not mistaken, he's got confetti in what's left of his hair.'

Venetia peered back down at Sir Repton. 'Well there's no sign of the bride...unless...?'

The younger man was busy unloading a small suitcase and a large pink and grey checked dog bed when they saw the manager of Wellworth Lawns run down the steps from the house and greet Sir Repton.

'Did Edward Parrott just kiss him?' Laura said.

'This is all too much for me.'

They watched as the younger man handed over Sir Repton's possessions to the manager. He returned to the vehicle and drove away as the other two walked slowly up to the front door and out of sight.

'Well, it looks like Repton's come to stay either way,' Venetia said. 'But leaving Mount Cod? I'm surprised.'

'Mount Cod?' Laura remembered the rambling, turreted Edwardian pile, from her hunting days, when her first husband, Tony, was briefly Master of the Vale of Woldham. Mount Cod had its own railway halt just outside the village of Chipping Codswold and once on the morning of the lawn meet at Mount Cod, their horse box had broken down. It was particularly foggy, and they had ended up sequestering the goods train from Woldham station. The journey was only about twenty minutes but Laura could still remember the sound of the horses hooves stamping and Tony's pack of hounds baying wildly from the end carriage. Other than that, it was not a part of the Cotswolds that they visited much, being situated on a small hillock in an otherwise boggy area intersected by the river, roads and railway. Rumours were rife when it came on the market in the late 1980s and was sold for what was said to be an absurd amount of money.

'Of course, I'd forgotten the Willowby's bought Mount Cod,' Laura said. 'Mind you they never really mixed did they? I mean it was more of a weekend place.'

'As they got older, they were less and less in London. Then they became quite reclusive. That's when the marital rot must have set in.'

Laura cast her mind back to the day's hunting. The fog hadn't lifted even by mid-afternoon. No scent, entirely fox-free. She had been pleased to get back home for dripping on toast and a hot bath. 'So, Sir Repton owns Mount Cod,' she reiterated.

'He does now. The house was Matilda's.'

'But are you really so sure he murdered her?'

'Undoubtedly. Matilda would never have drowned; she had the lungs of a walrus. As children we spent summer holidays with her family at Whitby. She was a very strong swimmer; she could breaststroke across a riptide like a frog through porridge. Besides that, her last words to me were, "If anything happens to me Venetia, you'll know it was him. But if he does bump me off, one thing's for sure he won't rest easy."'

'You're making it up,' Laura said.

'Well, those may not have been her exact words, but something like that anyway.' Venetia returned to the little round table on which stood her TV; the 42" inch flat screen like a huge oversized sail on a dinghy. She picked up the remote control. 'Is it time for Judge Rinder d'you think?'

Chapter two

Laura was keen to meet Venetia's murderous cousin by marriage but by the time they got down to the dining room for dinner, Gladys Freemantle had already bagged Sir Repton. Sitting beside him, Gladys' generous frame accentuated his lack of physique. Sir Repton was putting on the half-moon glasses that were dangling from a thin gold chain around his neck as, Laura noticed with disquiet, Gladys undid the top two buttons of her normally prim white shirt and began fiddling with the one below. As it happened, the table was laid for four so she and Venetia made their way over to join them.

Parker sniffed the air and rushed ahead towards the table. From underneath, a high-pitched yapping could be heard. The white tablecloth fluttered and Sir Repton's dachshund appeared, its teeth bared. Parker whimpered and trotted back to Laura's side.

'Have you met Sir Repton Willowby and his delightful dog?' Gladys said. 'She's called Sybil Thorndike. Isn't it charming?' Gladys giggled and leaned towards Sir Repton with an unsubtle hint of intimacy. It was out of character from the serious minded stalwart of the Horticultural Society. Apart from Parker, who she tolerated, Gladys was normally averse to dogs and complained that their urine ruined the lawns.

Sir Repton, who had brushed his hair free of the confetti, bent down and picked up the dog. Then he got up and shook hands first with Venetia – he appeared confused as to why she was present until it was explained that she lived at Wellworth Lawns – and then with Laura, who put Parker on his lead as the dachshund growled.

Sir Repton sat back down and put the dog on his lap. It wriggled, put its front paws on the table and ate a slice of bread and butter from his side plate.

'Sybil Thorndike,' he intoned with Bardish grandeur. 'You are a most vexatious creature.' The dog swallowed hard and turned its attention back to Parker, eyes ablaze with vicious intent.

Laura said she'd take Parker back upstairs.

'It's most unfair,' she said to him, as she pressed the button for the lift. 'Fancy having to take my own dog out of my own dining room, all for an ill-tempered dachshund.'

The lift door opened and Edward Parrott got out.

What was it about him that was so unappealing? She had nothing against short stature in a man – in fact she was used to looking at men directly in the eye, being tall herself. And again, many people had broken blood vessels around the nose and pockmarks and it had never bothered her. She supposed it must be the combination of these things and the fact that he always seemed to have had some sort of shaving mishap.

'Good evening Lady Boxford,' he said. 'Leaving dinner early?' He took a tissue from his pocket and held it over his mouth as he sidled round her, his flat feet shuffling on the carpet. 'Not ill I hope?' he mumbled.

'Me? Never.' Laura carried on into the lift.

Returning to the dining room some minutes later, Laura saw her friends Strudel Black and Jervis Willingdale who, amongst other things ran ballroom dancing classes and the dating agency, Ancient Eros, that had been so instrumental in her courtship of the Brigadier. The unmarried couple were a decade or so younger than the average residents of

Wellworth Lawns and lived in one of the newly built bungalows in what had been the old kitchen garden. She greeted them and complemented Strudel on her pink organza dress and latest striking hairdo, before re-joining her table.

Sybil Thorndike was back on the floor and Venetia and Sir Repton were chatting to one another over their bowls of tomato soup. Venetia seemed to have forgotten about him murdering her cousin and was discussing the latest episode of *Who Do You Think You Are?* that had featured an actress Sir Repton claimed to know.

Laura noticed Gladys was looking put out. Failing to get a word in, she dipped and lifted her spoon with exaggerated pomp, her large manly hand gripping the utensil. A drop of soup fell and landed on the tablecloth. 'Silly me,' Gladys said, picking up her napkin.

Sir Repton removed his glasses 'Out, out, damn spot,' he declared, as Gladys tried rubbing the stain.

At that moment Mimi came to take away the bowls. 'No prob, Mrs Free,' she said, placing a clean napkin over the stain. 'I taking laundry time.'

'You are too kind.' Gladys grinned up at Mimi.

Laura had often wondered why Gladys' parents had never taken her to an orthodontist – she was good looking as long as she didn't let her teeth out.

'I can't imagine how I can have been so clumsy,' Gladys continued.

The incident had the effect of putting her back in the driving seat and it was not long before she had steered the conversation round to the subject of herbaceous borders. Sir Repton said it was not an area of garden culture he had given a great deal of thought to but that he would be keen to learn more.

She was busy telling him about the benefits of early flowering lupins when Mimi returned with the main course.

Sir Repton replaced his glasses. 'Sole bonne femme, how delicious,' he said, looking at the steaming plate that Mimi

11

had placed in front of him 'I haven't had it in years. Not since we used to go to Wheeler's after a performance.' He picked up his knife and fork.

'We are very lucky, Alfredo, our chef here, is a superb cook.' Laura winked at Mimi.

'I think it's going to rain tomorrow,' Gladys said. mashing a potato into the fish sauce. 'It always does the first week of Wimbledon.'

'Very bad for business,' Sir Repton shook his head.

'What business is that?' Laura asked.

'I run a wedding concern from my home at Mount Cod.'

Laura remembered the confetti. 'It must be the height of the season now, I should think.'

'Ah, heaven's drowsy with the harmony. Simply nonstop nuptials, I really should be there. I've recently had the chapel re-consecrated by Canon Frank Holliday, such a very dear friend and such a comfort since...' He put his knife and fork down as his voice trailed off.

Laura sensed self-pity. 'So why aren't you there?' she asked.

'Yes.' Venetia pushed the last of the sauce round her plate with one finger. 'What are you doing here?' she said, licking it off.

'Alas, I had to get away.' Sir Repton leant sideways and picked up Sybil Thorndike by the scruff of her neck and put her back onto his lap. He stared morosely at the dog, tapping her birdlike scull with one bony cadaverous hand but he did not elucidate further.

'Shall we take our coffee in the lounge?' Laura suggested, thinking of Parker's stolid, sensible rounded head.

'But we haven't time,' Gladys said. 'You can't have forgotten, it's the Horticultural Book Club.' She turned to Sir Repton. 'It's my latest venture, purely plant-based literature. No more messing around with novels. I've always thought life was far too short for fiction.' She appeared not to notice Sir Repton's furrowed brow, and carried on regardless. 'We've been reading Reggie Hawkesmore's friend's book,

The Edible Tree. Reggie lives here at Wellworth Lawns you know. His friend has written about an explorer who survived for ten years in the jungle eating only bark. *The Edible Tree* is a fascinating and informative travelogue.'

'Well Repton won't have read it and I haven't had a chance either,' Venetia said. 'You must tell us all about it tomorrow, Gladys.'

'You watch too much TV, that's your problem Venetia. Laura what about you?' Gladys appealed.

'I'm sorry, I'm really not feeling up to it but I know it will be a popular evening.' Laura felt guilty for not supporting her friend but she was thinking about the Brigadier's diaries that she had discovered in an old tin trunk along with his service revolver.

'Oh, but now I'm torn... Perhaps I could postpone the meeting.' As Gladys squeezed her napkin into a ball, Strudel Black and Jervis Willingdale walked over to join them. Gladys introduced them to Sir Repton.

'Lovely beehive,' Venetia said, admiring the golden coloured creation on top of Strudel's head.

'Thank you dear,' Strudel said. 'I have discovered a new hairspray with lasting effect, but backcombing is the key. You should try it. Come over one afternoon and watch my video on Youtube.'

'What a good idea.' Venetia tucked the thin grey strands of her bob behind her ears as Strudel turned to Gladys.

'We are very much looking forward to the book club,' she said.

'And I've had an idea for next month.' Jervis tapped his nose with one finger. 'There's an excellent little book all about the meaning of flower species as tokens of affection.' He put his arm round Strudel's shoulder. 'I can't get enough of that scent of lavender.' He plunged his nose into her hair, then adjusted his blue and white striped silk tie and turned to Gladys. 'Come along, I'll tell you all about it on our way to the recreation room.'

As Gladys got up to go, she leaned over to Laura and whispered, 'You'll have to fill me in in the morning.' Her warm breath tickled Laura's ear. 'I want nothing held back, and remember, I got here first.'

Laura, Venetia and Sir Repton retired to the lounge and ordered coffee. It was unusually quiet as nearly all the female residents, who made up the majority of inmates at Wellworth Lawns, were attending the book club meeting. Laura had been once, granted before Gladys had taken charge and become so prescriptive in the reading list. She had been surprised at how quick the leap was from discussing the main tenets of the central character – in this case, Lawrence in *Seven Pillars of Wisdom* – to the merits of using unsalted butter in the making of a lemon drizzle cake.

'Fearfully hot in the desert,' someone commented.
'Personally, I'd miss the rain,' someone else had said.
'Dry as a bone.'
'No even a light drizzle.'
'Mind you there's nothing worse than a heavy drizzle...'

By the time the coffee arrived, Venetia was looking precariously close to sleep and Laura was aware of leaving Parker alone upstairs for too long on his own. This could often lead to small acts of vengeance, the chewing of a slipper and suchlike. She decided not to beat about the bush.

'So Repton, why have you left Mount Cod in the middle of the wedding season? Do they have very noisy parties?' she asked.

'Oh yes, but I love to listen to the Tom Jones tribute act when he is booked. Jez Abelson is truly magnificent as the crooning Welshman. Such a charming young man – he almost reminds me of my youthful self.' Sir Repton sighed. 'The discos are another matter,' he continued, 'but I've learned to sleep through them.'

His hand began to shake as he picked up his cup. 'My

housekeeper furnishes me with an excellent sleeping draught.'

He tried to get the cup to his lips but failed.

'No, that isn't it,' he said, putting the cup back in its saucer. 'The problem is that I am being persecuted.'

He looked up, his eyes wide and fearful. 'A phantom by the name of Rosalind has come to haunt me.'

'A ghost called Rosalind?' Venetia brightened visibly.

'An eighteenth-century serving wench; Canon Frank Holliday found evidence of her untimely death in the parish records. She fell from a window in the servants' quarters on the third floor.' He picked up the cup, but again his hand was shaking and he abandoned the idea. 'A horse's bit – a Pelham I believe the Canon said – and reins around her neck hastened the plummet. It was 1752.'

'But surely Mount Cod isn't that old,' Laura said.

'It was rebuilt in 1910, after a fire destroyed the original Elizabethan house.'

'How thrilling.' Venetia was quite alert now. 'I saw a most enjoyable American documentary about ghosts the other night. *Paranormal Activity*, I think it was called.'

'I can assure you this is a far from entertaining experience.' Sir Repton shook his head and stroked the sleeping Sybil Thorndike on his lap.

Laura looked out of the window behind him. It was getting dark outside and she could see the outline of the magnolia tree looming against the house. It's glossy leaves trembled in a light breeze as dusk descended.

'So what form does this persecution take?' she asked, getting up to draw the curtains.

'She inflicts unmitigated terror upon me.' Sir Repton shifted in his chair. 'Often in the middle of the night.'

'I thought you said you took something for insomnia?' Laura said.

'Rosalind can penetrate the deepest slumber, but it is not only at night.' He pulled out a handkerchief from his pocket and wiped a drip from his nose. 'I have found bloodstains on the carpet in the library. And then, alas poor Yorick…'

Venetia and Laura stared in anticipation.

'Yorick?' Laura asked.

'Our saluki had gone missing – I had even put a poster in the village shop before we found him dead in the billiard room.'

Laura picked at one of Parker's short grey hairs that was caught in the dark wool of her skirt. 'Was the dog old?'

'Of a certain age, but he had been purposefully shut in. He never was a one to whine or bark and had quietly passed away from dehydration.'

'Surely it must have been some sort of unintentional oversight.'

Sir Repton's nostrils flared. 'It was the hand of Rosalind I can assure you; she knew I never went in there. My late wife Matilda was not overly fond of the dog; granted he never quite got the hang of house training, but it was not an end he deserved, even she would have seen that.'

'I remember so clearly the last time I saw Matilda,' Venetia said. 'She was wearing a lovely oatmeal coat. I saw one like it the other day on the shopping channel.'

'How long ago did your wife pass away?' Laura asked. 'You see I myself have recently lost the man I was to marry and find I often have vivid memories of our days together. So vivid in fact that at times I think I may be hallucinating.'

'Oh Laura, the Brigadier, he was so… masterful. The tragedy of it.' Venetia sank her head into the back of her chair.

'But to get back to the story, what possible reason could this serving wench have for killing the dog?' Laura asked.

'I believe it to be part of her plan.'

'That is?'

'I have yet to ascertain her true motivation. My bowels are aquiver just thinking about it and I feel I may have missed some signs. A dampness in the air. The lingering waft of ale. An unexplained hint of corsetry. These all may have been clues.'

Laura frowned. This was too much. 'The lingering waft of ale?'

Sir Repton delved into the breast pocket of his jacket and took out a battered photo. 'A simple aroma could be a portent. I feel it in the hinterland of my digestive organs, that Rosalind is now threatening me and that I am in mortal danger.' He handed Laura a picture of the saluki. 'Being alert at all times is exhausting.'

'And how long has this been going on?' Laura handed the photo to Venetia.

'Longer than I at first imagined I believe. I can recall an unexplained smell of rosemary in the dining room over a year ago. She may well have left a tussie mussie.'

'A what?' Laura asked.

'A nosegay.'

'A nosegay?' Venetia looked mystified.

'And recently I have cast my mind back to the day of my wife's passing and I distinctly recall a strange smell emanating from her bathroom. Carbolic soap was not a cleaning agent she ever used. Of course at the time I was preoccupied with the tragedy that had occurred.'

'You mean the ghost had been in the bathroom with your wife?' The man was without doubt, deranged. Laura turned to her friend for support.

Venetia had a far-off look in her eyes. 'This is all too much for me.' she said, handing the photo back to Sir Repton. 'Have we missed the darts do you think?'

Ignoring Venetia, Sir Repton leant forward towards Laura. 'That is exactly what I mean,' he said. 'Rosalind, one way or the other, was instrumental in Matilda's drowning in her bath. Then she killed the dog and now she's after me.'

Chapter three

Laura was sitting up in bed eating breakfast whilst reading the Brigadier's diary when she heard a knock on the door. She was half way through 1939 – he must have been about ten. The black ink of the Brigadier's childish writing stared out at her as she read the only entry for that week, "Mummy put olive oil in my ears." Poor chap, his hearing was no good even then.

She heard another knock and Venetia came rushing in.

'We must go to poor dear Repton's aid,' she implored. 'He is being tormented by this awful creature Rosalind. She is hellbent on evil.'

Parker snuffled out from under the bedclothes and bounded over the pink satin eiderdown to her as she perched on the end of Laura's bed.

'You've changed your tune in a week,' Laura said. 'I thought you'd be pleased after what he did to Matilda; drowning her in her bath like that. What did you say he was, a murderous psychopath?'

'That was before.'

'Before what?' Laura put the diary down on top of the morning's paper that lay open beside her. 'You know he's making it up. The ghost is pure fabrication and if it isn't, he's only getting a dose of what you said Matilda predicted would happen if he bumped her off. No rest for the wicked and all that.'

Venetia patted Parker's head. 'I think I may have got it wrong about that. It's as Repton says, the ghost is the one who is responsible for Matilda's death.'

'You mean he didn't murder her?' As Laura pulled at a piece of croissant, Parker abandoned Venetia and trampled over the newspaper to beg for a morsel.

'Now I think about it, it was my daughter who told me Repton did it and you know how unreliable she can be.'

'But Angela's a vicar isn't she? Why would she lie?'

'She can be prone to exaggeration...'

Laura drew in a deep breath. Dear Venetia, her mind wandered in any direction it felt like, often new theories on almost any subject formed by the last TV programme she had been watching. 'Well this is a turnabout to be sure but I'm not convinced. I think there's something very fishy about Sir Repton.'

'You're talking about my cousin, Laura.'

'He's not your cousin, Matilda was.'

'He told me to think of him as my cousin, now that we are all alone in the world.'

'You're not all alone in the world. You've got me and your daughter Angela for starters.'

'But aren't you the least bit curious about his spectral experiences?'

'I don't believe a word of all that nonsense and I'm beginning to find his histrionics mildly irritating. He's just a lonely old fool using the idea of a haunted house as some sort of ridiculous seduction ruse.' Laura gave Parker a piece of the pastry. 'A serving wench somehow killing Matilda, not to mention the dog, I ask you? You and he are both as bad as each other. If it weren't for the fact that you are only related by marriage, I'd say it ran in the family.'

'Don't be unkind Laura, it doesn't suit you.'

'Well, I don't know about him but with you I fear it's as Gladys says, you watch too much TV. It overexcites your imagination. Anyway his supposed mental torture isn't enough to stop him chatting up Gladys and myself, if I'm not mistaken by his dubious technique. Have you forgotten that bit as well? Murdering his wife so he could find a younger model. Not that Gladys and I are exactly brainless teenagers.'

'I think you and he would be very well suited. Oh wouldn't it be lovely! Never forgetting the dear Brigadier of course.' Venetia lay back on the end of the bed and closed her eyes.

'What an old romantic you are,' Laura said. 'But really, I can see straight through his ludicrous pigeon-chested soliloquies, pretending to direct them at that dachshund of his.' Laura was reminded of the afternoon that she and Gladys had been walking back down the hill past the larch spinney where the family pets of Chipping Wellworth were buried. They had been discussing *The Edible Tree*. Gladys was explaining how the explorer had eventually died of, in effect, self-mummification due to the extreme cleansing nature of the forest tree bark, when from behind a hedge Sir Repton had appeared clutching the dachshund in his arms. He had attempted to engage them with the rendition of a Shakespeare sonnet.

'Mind you,' she continued. 'I've never seen Gladys behave like such an idiotic schoolgirl. She's quite beguiled by the old charlatan.'

'But Laura, I sat with him in the garden yesterday. He's so afraid. He knows he must go back to Mount Cod.'

'Why does he have to go back? He's not short of money now is he? I thought you said Matilda was loaded?'

'I always thought she was, but perhaps I was mistaken about that too. Perhaps he needs the money from his wedding business. Whatever it is he feels he must be there. He's asked me if I can persuade you to come with us and see that he's not making it up about the ghost. Then at least we can tell the police or something.'

'You haven't said you'd go have you?'

Venetia's bottom lip quivered.

Laura sighed. 'If he's so convinced the ghost is putting him in mortal danger, you might be putting yourself in harm's way too. Have you thought of that?'

Venetia's lip quivered further.

Laura laughed and reached for her friend's hand. 'Really, he's making it up.' She gave it a friendly squeeze. 'There must be someone else who can look after him.'

'There's Angela, I suppose. She's living with a group of friends in Woldham at the moment. Actually I almost forgot, she calls herself Angel now. Perhaps I should ask her; she will inherit Mount Cod after all.'

'Angela?'

'Angel.'

'Will inherit Mount Cod?'

'Angel and I are his only surviving relatives.'

'But this puts a very different light on the situation.' Laura let go of Venetia's hand and got out of bed. 'How old is Angela – Angel now?'

'Goodness, she must be in her sixties, but will you think about it then? He really does need help.' Venetia checked her watch. 'Look at the time,' she said. 'Can I turn on the telly?'

While Venetia went into the sitting room, Laura got dressed. She put on a blue cotton shirt from the drawer. 'You know Parker, perhaps a few days away would be a good idea,' she said, as the dog lay snoring on her bed. 'There's something very odd about Sir Repton and his ghost. A hint of corsetry, I ask you.' She opened the cupboard and took her lightweight Cameron Hunting Tartan shift dress from its hanger.

'Battle gear in order,' she said, pulling it over her head. 'We need to scotch his pack of lies once and for all before he gets Gladys or any other prospective wife hooked.' She walked to the bathroom and ruffled her short blonde hair in front of the mirror. 'Then all he has to do is orchestrate a fake exorcism and Bob's your uncle, ghost gone. New wife in and bang goes Angela's long awaited prospects.'

Laura took a new contact lens from its sealed pouch and, looking in the mirror, lifted the lid of one eye and placed it on her eyeball. 'That poor dear child – she must be a bishop by now.' She put in the second lens. 'Bishop Angel, funny that doesn't sound quite right.' She opened her compact and dabbed some powder on her nose. 'And Venetia, bless her, she just hasn't the mental agility to safeguard her daughter's inheritance.' She applied some lipstick and stared at her image squarely in the glass. 'And what if Angel was right? What if he had killed Matilda? Why would a bishop make that kind of thing up?'

Laura returned to the bedroom, picked up her silver and turquoise Navajo bracelet from the dressing table and called for Parker.

The dog woke with a start.

'This is a matter for urgent investigation. Perhaps he is short of money. Mind you he's barking up the wrong tree with Gladys there.'

Like Venetia, Gladys often worried she'd live too long and wouldn't have enough money to pay the care home fees.

'Barking up the wrong tree...' Laura thought back to the first evening Sir Repton had arrived at Wellworth Lawns and Gladys' book club choice.

She was reminded of Gladys and the tomato soup.

"Out, out, damn spot." Those were Repton's words. Was he, like Lady Macbeth, racked by guilt as Venetia had first intimated?

Chapter four

As Laura drove Venetia and Sir Repton through the dappled shade and over the bridge leading to the gates of Mount Cod, she noticed the lodge on their left. Outside it, the old Land Rover that had brought Sir Repton to Wellworth Lawns was parked untidily at an angle by the front door, the tailgate down.

'Who lives there?' she asked.

'My general factotum, Lance Wilkes.' Sir Repton turned to Laura. 'A man of inestimable value; absolutely indispensable.'

'General Factotum,' Venetia said, from the back seat where she was acting as a barrier between Parker and Sybil Thorndike. 'That could be an excellent title for a reality show. I can see it now. A knockout competition based on valeting skills; starching collars; boot polishing; wet shaving... that sort of thing.'

'Lance is more of an all-rounder; some household chores to be sure, but gardening too and general outdoor maintenance. He keeps the chickens in the back garden at the lodge. Wonderful fresh eggs when they are laying. But really there's not much for him to do these days,' Sir Repton continued. 'Kevin and the other gardeners employed by the wedding team have all but taken over, what with creating photo opportunities and suchlike. I mean just look at that.' He pointed one stick like finger at the parkland to his left.

Amidst the majestic oak trees dotted around the landscape, a balloon basket sat empty, the canopy spread out beside it like a small crimson lake.

'The vintage car has had its day.' Sir Repton shook his head. 'Now, every bride and groom must be transported away by some form of aerial device. Helicopters are quite the norm.'

As they continued up the short incline and parked outside Mount Cod, he explained that he had phoned the live-in housekeeper to expect their arrival. 'Mrs Varley, Cheryl, came as the cook but latterly she also cared for Matilda,' he said. 'Such a nice woman, I don't know what we'd have done without her. But here we are, home at last.' He looked up at the house. 'How I adore the perpendicular.'

It was not a piece of architecture that one would automatically associate with romance. The mock-Gothic monstrosity had a distinct air of dilapidation. Laura wondered why anyone would want to get married there. A pillared porch with steps splayed out to meet the gravel. Huge Edwardian sash windows dominated either side and overhead four stone eagles perched menacingly on the battlements, above which, roofs steepled into the cloudless sky.

From the back seat Venetia let out a small shriek. 'I saw a figure at the upstairs window. I think it could have been Rosalind.'

'Don't be silly; it was most likely what's her name? Cheryl.' Laura said.

'With a veil over her head?'

'Probably a duster.' Laura got out of the car.

'Your psychic powers are indeed acute cousin, for I have never actually seen "her". I knew it was a good idea to bring you here.' Sir Repton helped Venetia out of the car. 'I have taken the precaution of asking Cheryl to make up beds in adjacent rooms for you ladies. There is an interconnecting door between the two. But I'm sure it is only me that Rosalind is seeking.'

'Is Cheryl not bothered by the ghost?' Laura asked.

'She has not to date been a recipient of Rosalind's presence, besides which Cheryl has a self-contained apartment with its own entrance.'

'Why should that make a difference?'

'I don't believe Rosalind can be aware of it.'

'That's a relief for Cheryl then,' Laura said.

They walked from the warm sunshine into the cool shade of the porch and waited as Sir Repton staggered back from the car with their bags.

'He looks like he's going to have a seizure,' Laura said, and went to help him. Together they put the bags and assorted dog beds down outside the front door and as Sir Repton was putting one hand out to turn the great brass handle, it opened. From the deeper gloom within, a middle-aged woman with dyed blonde hair wearing jeans and a grey sweatshirt appeared.

'Hiya Repton. Got your reinforcements with you?' she said with surprising familiarity as she tied back her hair with an elastic band. The roots had obviously not been attended to for some time and the result was that she now looked as if she had dark hair.

'Hello Cheryl, meet my friends, Lady Boxford and my cousin, Mrs Hobbs. Would you be so good as to take their cases up and show them where they are staying.'

'You what?'

'Show them their rooms.'

'Sure, this way ladies.' Cheryl bent down and took the umbrella Laura had put beside her case and shoved it in the stand beside the door. 'You won't be needing that upstairs will you?'

Laura said she'd carry their cases if Venetia brought the dog bed and so they followed Cheryl across the dusty marble hallway and up a dark oak staircase.

Venetia nodded her head at various portraits of red-faced "Willowby" ancestors lining the staircase. 'All quite bogus,' she whispered. 'Probably a job lot from that London auction house I've seen featured on Channel Four.' She stopped and held the bannister rail for a moment. 'I wonder if there's a telly in my room?'

At the top of the stairs, they turned right and walked along a landing strewn with misshapen threadbare Persian runners until Cheryl halted between two open doorways and pointed up at the names painted in black-edged plaques above them. 'You're in Bridlington and Grimsby. Bridlington's got a better bed but Grimsby's got more room, what with only having Matilda's single in it. And of course, it's got the en suite.'

'Matilda's bedroom?' Laura was faintly shocked.

'Don't worry I've been over it with a fine toothcomb. Not a trace of her left in there.'

'I didn't mean...' Laura started to say.

'Perhaps as you've got Parker you'll need the extra space,' Venetia said. 'But then again I wouldn't want you to be uncomfortable in Grimsby. There's nothing worse than a lumpy bed.'

Cheryl coughed. 'I'll leave you to sort yourselves out.' She turned and retraced her steps back down the landing.

'I sleep like a log wherever I am,' Laura said. 'So I'll take Grimsby and hope it doesn't live up to its name.'

'Whatever you think best dear.' Venetia disappeared into Bridlington.

The single bed in Grimsby seemed out of place in such a large room. Around it Laura saw that the carpet had faded revealing that a much larger bed had previously been there. She pulled back the overly large beige candlewick bedspread and noticed with relief that the sheets appeared freshly laundered. Dangling down beside the pillow was an electric cable with a control attached. Laura pressed one of the buttons and the bed began to vibrate. She turned it off and sat down to test the springs. It was rock hard. She wandered round the room, peering at small oil paintings dotted about – mainly shipwrecks as far as she could tell. A writing desk, chair and an overbearing oak cupboard made up the rest of the furniture. The curtains at the window were of pale blue silk but had faded and frayed at the edges from the sun. At least the room faced south, she thought, as she looked out. The wedding venue made more sense from this side of the house; an ornamental pond stood as the centrepiece to the formal garden – more photo opportunities, no doubt.

She tried the bathroom door but found for some reason it was locked, so she walked back out onto the landing and found another door that opened into the bathroom. The pink suite smacked of the 1970s except that it had been adapted with modern disability aids. A white rail had been attached to the wall beside the bath and a sort of plastic booster seat sat on the loo. She crossed the room and, finding the key in the door, unlocked it and re-entered the bedroom.

Thinking she would go and find Venetia, she went to open the connecting door to Bridlington, but it was also locked with no key on her side so she returned out onto the landing again, knocked briefly and let herself in. Parker rushed ahead and started snuffling under the double bed on which Venetia lay on top of another beige candlewick bedspread.

'Do look at that.' Venetia motioned with her head.

Laura's attention was caught by a square protrusion in one corner of the room.

'Do you suppose his eighteenth-century serving wench knows how to use a lift?' Laura laughed.

'Laura please don't frighten me! But I didn't mean the lift.' Venetia waved one arm wanly in the direction of a mirror framed in a curious mix of seashells and shards of black jet. 'Isn't it wonderful; Matilda liked to remember her Whitby roots. Her father owned a fishing fleet.'

'So that's why the rooms are all named after ports.'

'It's what attracted Matilda to Mount Cod.'

'They bought the house, for its name?'

'One of the reasons.' Venetia drew the bedspread around her. 'Matilda was not only rich but also nostalgic. But Repton wasn't keen on the north; he'd spent such a lot on elocution lessons. I do hope I'm going to be warm enough.'

'Chip on his bony old shoulder?' Laura walked over to the wall beside the lift and inspected a small watercolour of a sandy cove. 'So he had a Yorkshire accent?' She turned back to her friend but Venetia had fallen asleep.

Laura thought it best not to disturb her so she went in search of Sir Repton. Despite the sound of clanging coming from downstairs, she was deep in thought. A lift for Matilda – she was obviously more incapacitated than Laura had suspected. This incapacity precipitates her need to be moved out of the matrimonial bedroom. Cheryl Varley, put in charge of caring for Matilda would need access to the bathroom at all times. Instinctively she felt for the warm silver of her bracelet. But why was the door locked from the wrong side?

Chapter five

As she reached the bottom of the stairs, Laura saw the reason for the clanging as Sir Repton, in his shirtsleeves, tossed another log of wood from a wheelbarrow at his side into a monumental copper tub. He was breathing heavily and one of the few strands of hair on his head had fallen over his damp brow. Beside him, a man in a checked shirt and combat trousers stood watching, his arms folded. Laura recognised him as the driver who had delivered Sir Repton to Wellworth Lawns.

'Just a couple more to go now Repton,' he said, scratching his untidy mop of matted straw-coloured hair.

'That looks like hard work,' Laura said.

Sir Repton glanced up from the wheelbarrow. 'There you are, Laura. Everything to your satisfaction upstairs, I hope?' He put the final log in the tub.

'Yes thank you, but should you be doing that?'

'Needs must; Lance here, has most unfortunately sustained a spinal injury.' Sir Repton gestured in the man's direction then smoothed back his hair and slumped down on a small oak hall chair on the back of which his dark blue blazer hung. He loosened the silk paisley cravat around his neck.

'Done my back in,' Lance said. He arched at the waist in exaggerated discomfort. 'Doctor says I mustn't lift a thing. Lucky old Repton here's still up to the job.'

'That is most unfortunate.' Absolutely indispensable; weren't those Repton's words? Laura didn't care for Lance's tone and now she was surprised to see him undo the button of one of the bulging pockets half way down the side of his baggy trouser legs and take out a pouch of tobacco and some cigarette papers.

'Still I should think there are plenty of things to do that don't require lifting. That copper could do with a good polish,' she said.

Lance frowned and shook his head. 'Even the smallest wrong movement could tweak it. Shall we take the barrow back?' He returned to the business of the roll-up.

Sir Repton heaved himself up from the chair. 'Laura, this is very dull for you. Where is Cousin Venetia?'

'She's having a nap. I thought I'd take her a cup of tea in a while.'

'Of course. Now why don't you make yourself comfortable in the sitting room while I get rid of this wheelbarrow.'

'I'll come with you. I'd like to see around the place.'

'Sure.' Lance struck a match and inhaled deeply on the cigarette. 'Let's show Laura the gaff.' He sauntered on ahead and pushed through a green baize door in the far corner of the hall. Laura held the door open for Sir Repton and he pushed the barrow through.

The first thing she noticed was the lift door to her left. She made a mental note as to the layout of this part of the house. They followed Lance down a long servants' passage flanked by closed doors. Along one side, a row of tarnished brass bells hung like oversized quotation marks. The names of rooms were painted below them, a reminder of times gone by. At the far end they could hear music blaring from a radio. 'Coming through,' Lance shouted.

Bright sunshine streamed in as he opened a door at the end of the passage. Before Laura and Sir Repton had reached it, Cheryl appeared from another door to the left. 'There you are Repton,' she said. 'I was just coming to find you. Now listen, I've put a chilli con carne from the Co-op out for you. Just pop it in the Aga forty minutes before you want your tea. There's a can of grapefruit segments in the fridge for afters.'

'But I thought you might…' Sir Repton stood holding the wheelbarrow.

'Sorry, pub quiz night.'

'I see. Well, could you make us some tea before you go? I thought we'd have it outside in the summerhouse.'

'Honestly I would if I could but I haven't a spare minute. I've got my "Sun-in" to do.' Cheryl adjusted her hairband. 'You know where the teabags live. I've got some more of the posh ones. Oh and that reminds me, you owe me fifty quid.'

Sir Repton put the wheelbarrow down and they followed her into the kitchen. It was a huge old-fashioned room. In the middle of the black-flecked green linoleum stood a solid looking pine table with an assortment of chairs around it. Next to a high window hung with thin cotton curtains, a white painted dresser displayed a mass of mismatched plates and dishes. Whatever Venetia thought about her cousin's finances, it seemed plain to Laura that the Willowby's hadn't had money for some time. Perhaps Matilda had a life insurance policy? She looked at the Belfast sink. An attempt had been made to 'fit' a stretch of Formica on either side of it but there had obviously not been enough to cover the washing-up machine.

'I thought I had given you enough for the month?' Sir Repton said.

'Repton, Earl Grey's not cheap you know,' Cheryl admonished. 'And you've no idea what it's been like since Lance did his back in. I had to pay a man in the village to put the bins out while you were living it up with your mate Eddie Parrott at Wellworth Lawns.' She flicked the radio off and folded a copy of the *Daily Mail* that was lying open on the kitchen surface. 'I took the liberty of cancelling the *Times* while you were away. But I'm sure your guests would prefer the *Mail*, wouldn't you Mrs Boxford? Matilda did.'

'Lady…' Sir Repton attempted to correct her.

'There's an article about fascinators on the fashion page,' she said, handing Laura the paper. 'Personally I've always thought they were stupid, but there you go.'

There was no sign of Lance when Laura and Sir Repton deposited the wheelbarrow in the woodshed. The woodshed was situated in one corner of the large cobbled square that made up the old stable block. An imposing arch topped with a scrolled pediment in the centre of the far end framed the parkland beyond through which the back drive led towards the village of Chipping Codbury. In the distance they could just make out a Land Rover bumping along.

'I expect Lance has gone to collect more feed for the chickens,' Sir Repton said. 'He was inclined to give them scraps but Matilda was insistent he use only the best layers' mash.'

Laura refrained from adding her surprise that Lance would risk his back condition on such rough terrain in a vehicle renown for rudimentary suspension.

'But let me show you this, it used to be the tack room,' Sir Repton continued.

Next to the woodshed was a door with a sign on which Laura read, "State of the Union".

'It's the wedding planner's offices.' Sir Repton turned the handle. 'We had it converted last year. It has its own kitchen – Matilda was quite envious of the gas hob.' He pushed against the door. 'It seems to be locked. Oh well, it's not that interesting. They complain the facilities aren't up to scratch of course but for canapés it's serviceable enough and for the rest Robert tends to favour outside caterers.'

'Who's Robert?'

'Robert Hanley Jones. State of the Union is his baby. He was once my protégé.' Sir Repton gazed vacantly at the door for a moment, a wistful smile on his thin lips. 'Those were the days; when we had the Bristol Old Vic.' He gave the handle another rattle. 'Well, to be precise when Matilda had the Bristol Old Vic.' He turned to Laura. 'Sadly the actor's life was not for

Robert, Matilda was right about that. It took him some time to realise the truth of her words, and they were harsh believe me, but he's found his niche now. The two girls, Tam and Pom, who run the Mount Cod operation for him are first rate.'

'Tam and Pom? Sounds like a pair of chihuahuas.'

'Very amusing.' Sir Repton gave a weak titter. 'Let me show you the stables.'

They went through a door on the other side of the archway. A shaft of light from a hole in the roof illuminated the internal stalls, each separated by wood panelling. Empty metal hayracks hung on the whitewashed walls and the floors sloped down to a gulley leading out into the yard. It all made Laura feel nostalgic and she was reminded of the fun she and her first husband Tony had had in amongst the straw bales with their wonderful head groom, Barry.

'We've work to do here.'

Sir Repton's voice brought her back to reality.

'Roofs are the bane of my life,' he said.

They moved on to what Laura assumed were once the carriage houses on the third side of the square. They now acted as a garage for an aged dark green Bentley, a miniature volcano of swallow droppings plastered to its bonnet.

'Oh dear, Matilda's car. It hasn't been driven since...' He tailed off.

Laura looked at him as he placed one hand on the wing mirror. Was this a sign of remorse for his sins? 'Do you think it would be too much to ask Lance to clean it?' she asked.

'I'd like to have been able to take you out for a ride.'

'Are you flirting with me Repton?' If he was feeling guilt, it was short-lived to be sure.

'Were I so bold. I had thought it might be useful for the weddings but as I said, the days of the vintage car are dead. I should get rid of it.'

'You can't sell it as it is.' Another sign of financial troubles? 'You'll have to wait until Lance recovers his strength, which I'm sure he will do in his own good time.'

'I have every confidence in him.' Sir Repton gave the wing mirror a pat. 'Shall we carry on?'

They walked out into the sunshine and made their way back towards the house. 'That's Cheryl's flat above the garage.' Sir Repton pointed to a stone staircase as they passed a double doorway to their left.

'Very handy.' Laura said. 'Shall we go and make tea?' I'm looking forward to the experience. One gets so used to never having to lift a finger at Wellworth Lawns.' As she climbed the steps to the backdoor, she was reminded of something the housekeeper had said. She turned to Sir Repton. 'I didn't know you knew Edward Parrott.'

'Small world isn't it. He was our stage manager for a time at the Bristol Old Vic.'

Laura was thinking about this coincidence as she put the kettle on the Aga while Sir Repton opened the packet of teabags, but she was distracted by the sound of someone clearing their throat. She turned to see a deeply tanned middle-aged man in sunglasses and dark slicked back hair peering round the kitchen doorway.

'Hello Repton.' he said. 'Look what I've got here.' He walked in and beside him, clutching his arm and looking up at him adoringly was Venetia.

'I parked at the front,' he continued. 'Cobblestones are no good for the springs on the Mazzer. That's when I found her wandering about in the drive.'

Venetia giggled, dropped her tapestry bag on the floor and sat down at the table. 'I mistook him for the antique dealer on *Flog It.*'

Laura noted the man's crumpled blue linen suit worn without a tie. The top button of his white shirt was undone revealing a cheeky clump of chest hair.

'But who have we got here?' he said, looking directly at Laura. 'Fast work, Repton, I like it.'

'Robert, my dear fellow,' Sir Repton dropped a teabag

into an old brown teapot. 'This is indeed a coincidence. We were just talking about you.' He introduced Laura. 'But what brings you to Mount Cod?'

As Robert Hanley Jones lifted his sunglasses and perched them on his wavy hair, Laura saw the glint of a chunky gold watch at his wrist.

'I was delivering mushroom spores from Andalucía,' he said, adjusting his shirt cuffs. 'The girls want to grow them in the cellar here. I've just taken them down. Ideal conditions. Dark and damp. I was on my way back to my car when I bumped into your friend.'

'We must have just missed you.' Sir Repton dropped another teabag into the pot.

Laura carried the boiling kettle over. She had seen steps leading down just outside the backdoor. The cellar must have been right below them here in the kitchen. 'Mushroom spores?' she asked.

'A new culinary delight the girls want to try out. State of the Union has to keep one step ahead of the game when it comes to vol-au-vents.' Robert Hanley Jones eased his head from side to side. 'Exhausting drive down from London, neck's stiff as a backgammon board, and now I've got to go all the way back. Still, lovely to have met you all; I won't stay for tea. Cheerio!' He waved as he sauntered off.

Laura pulled out a chair and sat down next to Venetia. 'Well that was a turn up for the books.'

'I didn't understand a word of it. Is he some sort of gambler?' Venetia asked.

As Laura poured the tea, Sir Repton explained to Venetia about the weddings and the two girls employed by Robert Hanley Jones.

'Tam and Pom?' Venetia said. ' Sounds more like a couple of poodles.' She took a sip of tea. ' And talking of dogs, I thought you said your saluki had died.'

'Don't remind me.'

'But I saw him.'

'Yorick?' Sir Repton stared at Venetia.

She nodded. 'He bounded up the steps into the house just as I was coming out.'

'Robert Hanley Jones must have a dog,' Laura said.

'He's got a saluki too?' Venetia sounded unconvinced.

Sir Repton shook his head. 'I'm sure he doesn't; a saluki would never fit in the back of a Maserati. No. I see it now.' He put his cup down. 'Rosalind has taken Yorick to the other side with her.'

'You mean I saw the ghost of Yorick?' Venetia reached for her bag and began to rummage through it. 'Where is my Rescue Remedy? I can't believe I've left it behind. Repton, I may have to have a thimble of brandy in my tea.'

'Right with you, dear cousin.' Sir Repton opened a cupboard and took out a bottle. 'Matilda kept it for Christmas pudding. Will you?' He gestured to Laura as he poured a good slug into Venetia's cup. Thinking it was better to ignore their childishness, Laura declined the offer and watched as Sir Repton fortified his own brew.

After tea, they resume their tour of the house. First they went back through the hall from where Sir Repton opened a pair of double doors that revealed the ballroom.

The interior was something of an anti-climax.

'The girls didn't care for the oak panelling; they wanted a more minimalist look,' Sir Repton explained. 'They say they will finish the plasterwork soon. It looks very different at night; you'd hardly notice. The chandelier, too, they thought was out of keeping.'

Laura surveyed the badly filled cracks and the disco ball overhead as they moved on to the next room.

'Here we are.' Sir Repton opened another set of double doors leading to a high ceilinged glass house. 'The Orangerie is where the daytime receptions take place. This is really the extent of the wedding venue – apart from the old gunroom etcetera that is now the greeting area and home to the cloakrooms – I don't think we need inspect them, do you?'

Laura and Venetia shook their heads and they retraced their steps.

'The gunroom has its own covered walkway and entrance, so you can see it hardly affects me in the rest of the house,' Sir Repton continued, as they returned to the hall.

He showed them the sitting room. It was a cosy jumble of furniture. A broad cushioned window seat overlooking the driveway, an armchair and a pretty rosewood tallboy stood at one end and in the centre of the room, two battered pink sofas and a dark red velvet tub chair surrounded a low table in front of the fireplace. At the far end bookshelves lined the wall in the middle of which was a door leading to the dining room. Sir Repton led them through.

Laura considered the bare mahogany expanse. 'Did you have large dinner parties?' she asked.

'I remember Matilda's birthday here one year.' Venetia gave a hiccup. 'She got on the table and danced after dinner. She used to be so athletic.'

'You have a good memory cousin. That was a long time ago. Come I will show you the drawing room.'

White blinds were drawn to protect the sparsely furnished and uncomfortable looking Sheraton suite from sunlight. The Chinese rug on which it stood looked like a modern copy to Laura and she had never been fond of parquet flooring. They didn't linger but carried on down another passage and reached another door. 'Billiard room,' Sir Repton said curtly. 'I don't think we need look in there.'

They carried on and somehow ended up back in the hall through another door Laura had previously not noticed adjacent to the green baize one leading to the kitchen.

'Goodness, it's quite a maze.' Laura turned as the grandfather clock beside her began to chime. 'Seven o'clock already; I think we should get supper on, don't you?'

While Laura read the instructions and put the chilli con carne in the Aga, Sir Repton busied himself opening the wine.

'I think we might eat in the dining room,' he said.

'Then we must have candles,' Laura said.

The Mount Cod silver candelabra were kept in a safe that was in a cupboard in Sir Repton's office – another hitherto unseen door opposite the billiard room. This meant finding the combination that he kept written down in a drawer of his desk. He held the piece of paper to one side and began to turn the dial. He pulled the handle.

Nothing happened.

Laura stood patiently as he began muttering and tried again. As she leant on his desk and waited, she glanced at a short letter lying on top of a pile of correspondence. It came from an address in Fulham and was a request for an interview. Was Sir Repton looking for new staff members? He certainly needed them from what she had seen so far. She noted the signature at the bottom. "Ned Stocking," the bold flourish read.

Her thoughts were broken as Sir Repton stamped his feet petulantly.

'I can't get this to work,' he huffed.

Laura took the piece of paper from him. 'Let me have a look.' She read out the instructions. 'Clockwise to seven. Anticlockwise to five...'

'That's what I did,' Sir Repton said.

'Did you hear the click? Here, mind out, I'll have a go.'

Within a few minutes Laura had it open. Sir Repton jostled her out of the way. He was stronger than she had expected and with a deft manoeuvre, he grabbed a large branched candlestick and closed the door.

Having placed it on the table and found some candles, they returned to the kitchen and deliberated as to whether they should decant the meal from its foil container.

'It'll be cold by the time we do that,' Venetia said.

So they took it as it was into the dining room on a

wooden trolley with some peas they had cooked, still in the saucepan, and three warm plates. After several journeys back and forth to the kitchen as they remembered knives and forks and salt and pepper, and more importantly, the wine, they finally sat down to eat.

'How far that little candle throws his beams,' Sir Repton said, a forkful of Chilli poised mid-air as he stared at the majestic flaming centrepiece.

'Really Repton, sometimes your quotes are quite out of place,' He must be drunk, Laura thought. She took a sip of claret. But was it out of place? 'Jolly nice bottle of Pomerol.' Laura raised her glass thinking about the quote. In his mind were the candles a metaphor for Matilda's domineering character? Or did the flames represent her radiating saintliness? Or was she, Laura, a little tipsy? Still she made a mental note to watch out for further Shakespearean clues.

'Mind you, one chilli con carne is pretty slim for three,' she continued.

'Oh but frozen peas,' Venetia raised her fork, 'are such a treat.' A number of them didn't make it as far as her mouth, but Parker and Sybil Thorndike, affecting a truce at her feet, were there to catch them as they bounced off the table onto the floor.

They decided against the grapefruit, so when they had finished, they blew out the candles, turned off the lights and trolleyed everything back to the kitchen.

'Shall we try our hand at coffee?' Laura suggested, as she haphazardly loaded the dishwasher.

'Any biscuits?' Venetia said with plaintive longing.

Sir Repton went to the dresser and picked up a battered tin with a picture of the Queen on it. 'I believe Cheryl keeps some in here.'

Venetia hurried over as he lifted the lid.

'Bourbons.' Her eyes lit up.

It was only instant coffee but the sense of accomplishment that the three of them had made it together, gave

Laura a feeling of camaraderie. He's not a bad old stick, she thought. Too much Shakespeare over the years has obviously addled his brain to the point that he sees the likes of Banquo round every corner, but as long as he doesn't inflict any more supernatural nonsense on us we should be able to get through until the morning, make our excuses and get back to the normality of Wellworth Lawns.

She followed him as he carried the tray into the sitting room and she and Venetia sat down, one on each of the sofas.

'I'm feeling so much better now I know we've got some biscuits,' Venetia said.

Sir Repton put the tray down on the low table in front of Laura and sat down beside her.

'Who needs home help?' he said.

Laura watched as he spilled coffee on a pile of magazines as he poured from the pot. Venetia was right; her daughter Angela, or Angel or whatever she called herself must have got it wrong. Doddering old Repton couldn't possibly have murdered his wife.

The coffee began to drip onto the moss coloured carpet. Sir Repton took out a handkerchief, lurched forward and dabbed at it.

Laura looked at the stain. 'You must ask Cheryl to clean it properly in the morning,' she said. 'Mind you, you've got your work cut out with her. I'm afraid you've let her get the upper hand.'

'Alas, I know it.' Sir Repton sighed. 'But what can I do? Help is almost impossible to find.'

'Domestic engineers, that's what they're called,' Venetia said. 'I saw a frightening programme the other day. A pair of them went into an innocent woman's home and proceeded to verbally abuse her about how untidy the house was.' Venetia took a bite from her biscuit. 'Then they demanded she put her treasured possessions in a car boot sale and wash the kitchen floor, while they stood around drinking cups of tea. I expect there were a lot of complaints on *Watchdog*.'

'It is a terrible thing to be old and alone and at the mercy of others.' Sir Repton stuffed the handkerchief back in the pocket of his blazer. 'I'm so grateful to you both for being here with me.' He leant sideways and patted Laura's knee. Her muscles tensed and he hastily retracted his hand.

Venetia pulled at her cardigan and gave a little shiver. 'Has it gone cold in here?'

'I should have lit the fire,' Sir Repton apologised.

'We're too used to central heating at Wellworth Lawns, that's the trouble.' Laura was about to add that actually it might be nice if he could crank the temperature up a bit, when they heard a thud and Parker ran forward and cowered at her feet.

Venetia jumped up. 'What was that?' she gasped.

Laura looked round and saw a small tripod table beside the tub chair. Beside it on the floor was a lead tea caddy, the lid lying a foot or so away.

'It is her.' Sir Repton's voice trembled. 'She is amongst us.'

'Don't be silly.' Laura got up and went to pick up the caddy. She placed it back on the table. Then she reached for the lid and inspected it. The knob in the middle of it depicted the head of a miniature sculpted Buddha. 'Charming workmanship,' she said.

'Was it Rosalind? Oh dear, I don't like this.' Venetia sniffed the air and laughed nervously. 'Perhaps she was trying to do some dusting.' And then, her voice now staccato, 'I think I smell Pledge.'

'Her nosegay. My God.' Sir Repton held his head in his hands. 'Sweet Jesus, my nerves are shot to pieces.'

'Really you two, you're winding each other up. Parker bumped into the table, that's all, and you can probably smell his shampoo. He had to have a bath yesterday – my own fault for letting him off the lead near the badger's sett.'

'But if he knocked into it, why didn't the table fall over?' Venetia said.

'I don't know,' Laura said. 'It just happened that way.'

Sir Repton leapt up and staggered towards the drinks cupboard. 'She's canny, oh but she's canny. I feel the need of a digestif.' He pulled the door of the glass-fronted cabinet open and grabbed at a bottle. 'Will you ladies join me in a cognac?'

'Yes please,' Venetia stammered.

Laura replaced the lid of the caddy. 'I'd love a drop if you're offering.' He was a good actor that was for sure.

Chapter six

'Sepulchral chill, I ask you. Venetia's worked herself up into complete state over nothing,' Laura said to Parker, as they went downstairs the next morning. 'Fancy trying to get into my bed in the middle of the night.' She tutted. 'Lucky we found that extra blanket from the cupboard.' Parker's toenails clattered on the wooden boards beside her. 'But this, on the other hand...' She brandished the small piece of paper she was holding '... is much more interesting. I'm afraid we may have to stay another day and see what we can unearth.'

While she and Sir Repton had taken the dogs out the night before, Venetia had taken the lift up to her bedroom. She had seen the slip of paper on the floor when the lift doors had opened.

'It's Matilda's writing, I remember it from Christmas cards,' she said when Laura came in to say goodnight. 'I don't suppose anybody's been in the lift since she died. It's rather sad; she obviously suffered from dry skin.'

But Venetia was wrong, it didn't say E45, it said P45. As Laura walked across the hall, she read it again. Along with needing matches and more granola, Matilda was going to sack someone.

Sir Repton was in the dining room and Laura had sat down beside him when Cheryl appeared, her hair covered by a blue beret and wearing a grey jogging outfit and trainers.

'Chickens are on go slow according to Lance,' she

said, splattering a small dollop of scrambled egg onto Sir Repton's plate from the saucepan she was holding. She turned to Laura. 'Where's your friend then?'

'Mrs Hobbs tends not to get up early. But don't worry, she took the precaution of taking some chocolate biscuits up with her last night,' Laura said.

'My Bourbon creams, I wondered where they'd gone.' Cheryl scooped into the pan and held out the wooden spoon in Laura's direction. 'Want some?'

'I'll stick with toast, thank you.'

'So Repton, quiet night was it, no spooky doings?' Cheryl lifted the spoon to her lips and started eating from it. She put the spoon back in the pan and gave his sagging cheek a friendly pinch. 'You're looking pretty chipper.'

'A minor incident, but I think Rosalind may have been caught off guard by my guests. I did note that a chill descended at about four-thirty.'

'What a shame.' Cheryl scratched her neck with one varnished nail.

Sir Repton nudged the lump of egg onto his fork and turned to Laura. 'It did not affect you I hope?'

'I slept like a log.' Laura omitted to tell him about Venetia's disturbance and buttered her toast. 'And now I'm feeling full of energy.' She reached for a pot of marmalade. 'Have we got a plan for the day?'

'I'd make yourselves scarce if I was you,' Cheryl said. 'Tam told me they've got some film thingy going on in the ballroom.'

'Will that affect us?' Laura asked.

'I can't see why,' Sir Repton said.

'I wouldn't be so sure. You know what happens if you get on the wrong side of Tam, that's all I'm saying. Now, I can't stand around here all morning chatting, I've got the gym to get to.' Cheryl slapped her thigh with her free hand and walked to the door. 'Cellulite doesn't shift on its own. Leave the plates, I'll be back later.'

'But what about…' Sir Repton attempted to interject but she had shut the door behind her. '… lunch?'

'Standards, Repton, Standards.' Laura eyed the layer of grey bristling beard on the top of the marmalade. 'If you can't get a grip on Cheryl, she will have to be replaced, however onerous it may seem.' She thought of the P45 as she dug her knife into the jar and flicked a gobbet of mould onto the side of her plate. 'I mean, would Matilda have put up with this kind of thing?'

Sir Repton shook his head and stared disconsolately at his empty plate.

'You might have to spread your net wider. Have you thought of trying a London staffing agency?' Laura was thinking of the letter she had seen on his desk.

Sir Repton shook his head again.

'Well at least have some more toast,' Laura said. 'That amount of egg's not going to keep you going. That's the reason you feel the cold so much.'

'Ah, but they are sick that surfeit with too much.'

Laura was alert for the warning sign. Was guilt kicking in again? 'Nonsense. What I mean is that woman's trying to starve you.'

Sir Repton sidestepped the issue. 'Shall we adjourn to the sitting room and read the morning paper? Cheryl tends to put it out for me there,' he said. 'Do you care for the sports section?'

Laura might have taken this the wrong way but she was busy mulling over the scene she had just witnessed. 'I'm always interested in the racing,' she said. It wasn't that Cheryl was actually trying to starve him. It was the hold she seemed to have over him and her lack of respect, tempered with overfamiliarity that was definitely out of order. Laura followed Sir Repton from the dining room. Was it her that Matilda was going to sack? Laura's suspicion level rose.

They found Cheryl had reinstated the *Times*, which she had left on the low table in front of the sofas along with a crumpled copy of the *Daily Mail*. While Sir Repton attempted to get the pages back in order, Laura sat on the window seat and watched as a blacked out 4x4 followed by a pantechnicon wound their way up the drive and parked outside the front door.

'The wedding planners I presume?' she said, as Sir Repton handed her the *Mail*. Two smartly dressed girls in black trouser suits got out of the car, flexed their shoulders and shook out their smooth auburn tresses. Laura watched as one of them started issuing orders to the team of men that emerged from the lorry. 'You didn't say they were identical twins.'

Sir Repton followed her gaze. 'Tam and Pom? Impossible to tell them apart. Delightful pair. Sometimes a little brusque perhaps,' he continued. 'But always having new ideas; keeping ahead of the market, they say.' He sat down on the chair beside her.

'Is it a partnership you've got going with them and your friend Robert Hanley Jones or do they pay you rent for Mount Cod?' she asked.

'To a degree a partnership I believe. It was Matilda's idea originally – she loved a wedding and she understood the business far better than I do. The girls, or one of them anyway, are very clever at handling the books, I leave it all to them. They have created a separate company for me personally. It's called, "Part of the Union". Now I think you will have to agree that's witty,' Sir Repton chortled weakly.

'Very droll,' Laura smiled.

'It's only our second season but they tell me that soon the money should start rolling in,' he continued, as the two girls disappeared around the side of the house, followed by four men carrying long rolls of plain white fabric and a lot of camera equipment.

'Whatever are they up to now, I wonder?' Sir Repton said. 'And where are they going?'

'To the new entrance I was telling you about.'

'All that work on the house must have been expensive.'

'I leave that side of things to Robert.' He put on his glasses and turned to the obituary column of the paper. 'Oh no, not dear Hermione. She once played Blanche DuBois to my Stanley at the Chichester Festival.' He pulled out a handkerchief and blew his nose before returning to the article.

Laura wondered if Venetia was up yet. She was getting bored and the morning was going nowhere fast. 'Have you ever thought about remarrying?' It was not quite appropriate but Laura dangled the bait anyway.

Sir Repton folded the paper with a sudden crackle. 'My dear Laura, I'm sure if the right opportunity were to arise, Matilda would not hold it against me.' He slid from the chair onto one knee. 'Will you...?'

'Please don't start getting amorous. I'm not in the market for it.' She felt foolish; it was an impetuous thing to have asked.

'I didn't think you were.' He returned to his chair and resumed the article. 'No, no, Hermione never got a Bafta, I'm sure of that.'

As Laura flicked through the *Mail* she heard the sound of banging coming from the direction of the ballroom.

'They must be making ready for some sort of themed reception party,' Sir Repton said. 'It was all dolled out like a Hawaiian Island the other week. I had sand in my shoes for days.'

The noise from the ballroom and the paucity of the journalistic content of the paper was making Laura irritable. 'Shall we take the dogs out?' she suggested.

They wandered through the park – Parker and Sybil Thorndike making good their rapprochement as they stopped to compare notes on particular scents – and had stopped to admire a particularly fine horse-chestnut tree, when a lorry carrying a mini-digger came up the drive.

'Must be something to do with the gardeners,' Sir Repton said. 'I never seem to know what's going on these days.'

'You should make an effort to find out,' Laura said.

'Tam and Pom have everything under control and I have my own little projects to look after; something always needs mending, but my main achievement was having the chapel re-consecrated. I told you didn't I?'

Laura nodded.

'When Matilda and I bought Mount Cod, it hadn't been used in years. We rather forgot about it and Matilda's faith was of an eclectic nature. She didn't find the need for sacred space to convene with her particular deity. In the past I was never drawn to the church but recently I have taken to using it myself. I feel the power of prayer may be the way forward with Rosalind.'

'The elusive ghost.' Laura heaved a sigh of exasperation. 'Shall we take a look at it?'

They skirted a mass of thick laurel bushes to the side of the main house and came upon the little building. The architecture was a mish mash of Arts and Crafts meets cottage style. A squat circular brick tower jutted out of the middle of the thatched roof as if added as an afterthought to give the structure a more ecclesiastic ambience but it reminded Laura of something from Grimm's fairy tales.

'The girls have made this pathway from the ballroom,' Sir Repton said, as they scrunched over some newly scattered gravel through which the earth underneath could clearly be seen. He lifted the latch of the oak door and pushed it open.

'This is new,' he said, as they stared at a length of pink and green polka dot carpet running down the aisle.

They walked past the pews covered in brightly covered scatter cushions up to the altar. On top of the yellow and purple tartan cloth stood a large, clear Perspex cross and on either side, a pair of golden candlesticks in the shape of minarets.

'Very interdenominational,' Laura remarked.

'Tam and Pom are all for that sort of thing and now every occasion has to be more exotic than the last. Still as long as the money starts coming in I can't complain. I'll be able to re-roof the stable block by the end of this season they tell me.'

By the time they had returned to the house, there were more cars parked in the driveway. As they entered the hall, they heard a commotion coming from the direction of the ballroom.

'Get the old bat out of here,' a male voice shouted out. 'She's totally ruined the shot.'

'Calm down Danny,' a girl's voice answered back. 'I'm on it.'

One of the double doors swung open revealing Tam – or Pom – with one arm around Venetia's neck. 'Come on Granny, let's get you back where you belong,' she said, kicking the door shut behind her. 'Honestly, who let you out in the first place?' She looked up and saw Sir Repton and Laura. 'Really Repton,' she said. 'You've got to keep control of your guests.' Her eyes blazed. 'We're doing a virtual honeymoon at the Niagara Falls in there and the cameraman charges six grand a day.'

'Oh Laura,' Venetia cried. 'I've been looking everywhere for you.' She struggled free. 'I heard noises and thought it might be you. And then I got disorientated.'

'The back projection's been specially filmed for this couple.' The girl thrust Venetia forward.

'Profuse apologies, ' Sir Repton said, taking Venetia by the arm. 'What now dear coz? Let me assist you.'

Venetia's lip twitched. 'Better late than never.'

'Hopefully they'll be able to airbrush her out,' the girl was saying. 'But it all costs money and the bridegroom wants it on Facebook by tonight. Just keep her under control in future.'

'My dear, profuse apologies again.'

'And Repton...'

'Yes?'

'How many times do I have to tell you, the ballroom door must be kept locked. You forgot again when you went away. Last week I found a load of guests using the bathrooms upstairs. It took me hours to round them up.'

'But I thought you had a set of keys?'

'I do, but I shouldn't have to check each time and it would be good if either you or Cheryl could remember. That woman does precious little as it is and you all know the ballroom's out of bounds.' The girl disappeared, shutting the door behind her.

Sir Repton turned the key. 'I'm sure I did lock it,' he said.

'She's rather officious isn't she?' Laura took Venetia by the other arm and together they guided her into the sitting room. But the shock of it all was too much for her and she said she'd like to go back to bed again. Laura took her back upstairs. Venetia sat down and picked up a chocolate biscuit from the bedside table. 'I think I'd like to go back to Wellworth Lawns.' She let out a little hiccup of distress. 'Would tomorrow be too soon?'

'Of course not, dear.' It was too bad that poor Venetia was so upset. 'Repton's simply out of control and this whole ghost thing of his has inflamed your imagination again. It's only natural for you to be discombobulated.' Laura puffed up the pillows. 'Now you stay here and I'll bring you up something on a tray.'

Cheryl had left them a note saying there was bread and a jar of fish paste in the fridge and could they make themselves sandwiches. As Laura spread the butter, she asked Sir Repton if this was his normal lunchtime fare. He said he found he didn't need a great deal to eat at his age.

'You're right of course,' Laura said. 'We have quite unnecessary amounts of food at Wellworth Lawns.' She took off the crusts, cut the sandwiches into neat little triangles and took some up to Venetia.

'Do try one,' she said.

Venetia sniffed them and said she wasn't hungry, so she took them away with the empty biscuit wrapper. Walking back downstairs Laura felt in agreement with Venetia. What was the point of staying on? The only hints that something untoward had happened – the key to the bathroom door and a note about a P45 – were hardly evidence that the weak-minded Repton or anyone else had anything to do with his wife's demise.

Laura tried to imagine Sir Repton committing an act of domestic violence, as she and he spent the afternoon out of harm's way looking round the bog garden that lay beyond the formal gardens. They reached it by means of a winding path lined with Acers and a series of stone statues of dancing nymphs.

'Matilda said it was her homage to *A Midsummer Night's Dream*,' Sir Repton explained, patting a nubile cherub on the rear. 'She created it the year I played Puck at the RSC.'

Two men were working near some bushes on a bank above a small pond. One was manoeuvring the small digger they had seen arriving earlier, the other was standing with a shovel on top of a large mound of earth.

'Ah, now here is young Kevin.' Sir Repton waved to the man with the shovel and called out 'Good morning Kevin.'

The man's chin jutted forward momentarily before he turned his back to them. 'He can be a little on the moody side.' Sir Repton tore at an overhanging leaf to disguise the failed attempt at familiarity. 'But he has been doing sterling work here for some time now. Matilda had to admonish him on one or two occasions but the great outdoors has transformed his character.'

'From what?' Laura asked, disentangling the sleeve of her jumper from a low-hanging branch.

'Robert took him on after he was released from prison. He's awfully good that way.'

'What had he done wrong?'

'A spot of brawling I believe. They'll be creating another photo opportunity I'll be bound. Funny though, I seem to remember a stone bench stood there. They've probably had it moved, like the pagoda. I wonder where they've put that?'

'Don't remind me of benches, Wellworth Lawns is stacked with them. But talking of Wellworth Lawns,' Laura took the chance to explain her predicament with Venetia. 'She gets confused if her routine is altered. I'm afraid I must take her back in the morning.'

'So soon? Alas...'

Laura waited for a quote, but it was not forthcoming and as Sir Repton stared down at his black patent galoshes, she saw a drip land on one of them. She couldn't be sure if it had come from his eyes or his nose.

They arrived back at the house as the wedding planners and their entourage were leaving and watched as the vehicles snaked their way down the drive and then onto the grass as Lance's Land Rover, coming in the opposite direction, refused to pull over. Instead of turning into the stable yard, the Land Rover continued up to the front of the house and stopped beside them.

Cheryl was at the wheel and she wound down the window. 'Sorry,' she said, handing Sir Repton a Tesco plastic bag. 'I didn't have much time as I had to go to the hairdresser in Woldham this morning. Had a bit of a problem with the Sun-in last night.' She patted her now ash blonde hair. 'You'll be all right with baked beans won't you? You can't go wrong with 'em really. I've got you some nice white sliced. Can't stop I'm afraid, Lance says he's not going anywhere so I've got the car.' She waved as she drove back down the drive.

Chapter seven

Laura put Venetia's disturbed night down to her high intake of pulses, but Venetia was convinced it wasn't wind.

'I'd taken my Gavescon,' she protested. 'It was footsteps and then an awful clanking noise coming from this direction that woke me.'

They were standing in a small, dilapidated bathroom on the opposite side of the landing to Venetia's bedroom. It had obviously been omitted from the 70s facelift. Both the cast iron bath and basin had rusty orange marks formed by the long forgotten but persistent dripping of taps. In one corner, above a huge square wooden toilet seat, the arm connecting the chain to the ancient overhead cistern hung down.

'Then you must have pulled the chain too hard or something. These old mechanisms are very delicate you know.' Laura could smell a damp musty aroma coming up from the sodden floorboards.

'But I didn't go to the bathroom. I was too frightened to move,' Venetia said.

They went back downstairs to the pantry next to the kitchen. A pile of ceiling plasterwork lay in the middle of the room. Beside it stood Lance Wilkes leaning on a shovel, the wheelbarrow by his side.

'Right mess this and now Repton's disappeared,' he said. 'Lucky I knew where the stopcock was. Still, not much else I can do I'm afraid.' He leant the shovel against one of the many empty shelves and walked out.

Laura and Venetia went to find Sir Repton. He was in his

office on the telephone to the plumbers so they returned to the pantry and Laura began clearing up the debris.

'It must have been the Cointreau. That's what made you forget you'd been to the bathroom.' Laura scooped up a load of plaster. 'Put the barrow a bit closer, dear. Funny I didn't hear anything and I was right next door,' she continued.

'I'd say that was pot calling kettle black. I didn't have any Cointreau if you recall.'

'Here, you hold the shovel and hand me the broom.' As Laura began sweeping, she remembered that Venetia was right. 'Perhaps it happened earlier, before you went to bed.' She brushed the remaining plaster into the shovel. 'You flushed and that's what started it off. Then perhaps you heard me getting ready for bed.' Laura looked round as Sir Repton came panting in.

'No. I've said it before,' Venetia was saying. 'It was all that clanking. As if someone was hitting the pipes. Why won't you believe me Laura?' Venetia dropped the shovel. 'I'm going to go and sit down,' she said and headed down the passage.

'You know, of course,' Sir Repton said, 'that it was Rosalind. I also awoke and heard. I was too petrified to move.' He held the back of one hand to his forehead. 'I lay in bed paralysed with a feeling that my intestines were at any moment about to bubble out of a hole in my stomach, and what's more, she left the back door open.'

'We probably forgot to lock it last night. Or perhaps Cheryl came in early for something. Now let's go and make a cup of coffee.'

As they walked through to the kitchen, Sir Repton remained agitated. 'It's another of her signs. I know it. The door... It can only mean one thing, a stranger is approaching and that stranger is death. I feel the net around me drawing closer.'

'How would an eighteenth-century serving wench know how to use the bathroom?' Laura removed a large spanner that had been left beside the Aga before putting the kettle on. 'Back in the days before Wellworth Lawns was converted, we had countless plumbing incidents of this sort. What you want to do is forget about restoring the stable block and get some modern pipework installed. That's the way forward.'

Sir Repton slumped into a chair. 'That may be true but this was Rosalind's work. I am beginning to understand her now. Her message is clear.'

'Meaning what?'

'Water! I don't know why I didn't see it before. It's proof that Rosalind was responsible for Matilda's death.' Sir Repton was wide-eyed with anxiety.

It was par for the course, but still Laura admired his acting skills.

'I remember having a hunch, a presentiment, that affected the inner recesses of my colon that very morning,' he continued. 'But I put it down to the artichoke soup we'd had for supper, because Matilda was also suffering from flatulence when I took breakfast with her in her room.'

'I was only saying to Venetia, wind is the bane of all our lives.'

'Ah yes, but Matilda was so hale; granted a little irked that Lance's chickens were still off lay, but the porridge sufficed.' Sir Repton shook his head. 'We had had such a happy evening the night before. There was a winter wedding and I took her out in the wheelchair to listen to Jez Abelson playing. It was only unfortunate that while I had parked her outside the ballroom windows and gone to fetch a shooting stick to sit on, that Tam came across her. Matilda had joined in the chorus to Jez's rendition of Frank Sinatra's "Silent Night" – her voice always did have a resonant timbre.'

'How do you know it was Tam?'

'Matilda knew; she could tell them apart. She was not overly fond of Tam.' He sighed. 'I had promised her singing lessons...' He put his elbows on the table and covered his eyes with his hands.

'So what happened?'

'I gave her her pills and she had recovered her temper by the next morning and was busy reading the *Daily Mail* at her writing desk when I left her after breakfast to let Canon Frank in. That's why it was such a terrible shock.

When Canon Frank discovered her naked body, he rushed to find me. He was only minutes too late and was inconsolable – Matilda gave most generously to his cause.'

'Canon Frank Holliday was in her bathroom?'

'He often called upon Matilda to give spiritual guidance if she was particularly vexed. He thought perhaps she had fallen when he found her bedroom empty.'

'Vexed?' Laura frowned.

'Matilda found the situation of her diabetes frustrating after her big toe was amputated. Her balance was never the same again. I'm sure Cheryl tried her best with her but often it was only Canon Frank who could calm her shattered nerves.' Sir Repton lowered his head and covered his eyes again. 'And now Rosalind is warning me. She drowned my wife and I am next.' He let out a sob and jumped up from his chair. 'I must call the Canon now. He'll know what to do. Please forgive me.' He hurried from the room.

Another spectacular display of dramatic skills Laura thought, as she went to find Venetia in the sitting room. She told her to wait while she went upstairs to collect their belongings.

Looking in her purse, she toyed with a ten pound note then begrudgingly changed her mind and left a twenty on top of the desk in Grimsby for Cheryl. She went into the bathroom one last time to check she hadn't forgotten anything. Looking at the empty bathtub, she thought again about Matilda. Was she wrong to dismiss the idea of foul play? The diabetes had obviously been taking hold judging by Repton's description but had it got to a stage that could lead to such drastic and sudden consequences? It was hardly a normal medical progression that one amputated big toe should lead to a fatal coma. The fact that Repton was insistent the ghost had something to do with it was manifestly an idiotic idea, but if not him, then who could have been instrumental in Matilda's death? What of this elusive clergyman? He was obviously a key player, but Laura could not stay on to meet him now, she had to get Venetia back to Wellworth Lawns.

Chapter eight

'Thank God we're off. The man's an absolute headcase.' Laura put the key in the ignition. She watched Sir Repton in the rear view mirror as he doddered back towards the house, Sybil Thorndike under one arm.

'Do up your seatbelt, dear,' she said to Venetia beside her, as she saw a battered white van careering up the drive. 'That doesn't look like the wedding planners.'

The van drew up beside them scattering gravel and a middle-aged woman dressed as a punk got out.

'It's not, it's my daughter Angel,' Venetia said.

'Goodness, she must be the bishop of a very progressive ecclesiastical see.' Laura wound her window down.

'What are you talking about?' Venetia said.

'Her attire, I thought you said she was a bishop.' Laura watched as Angel waved her arms and shouted to Sir Repton, who was making his way up the steps to the front door, 'Wait, Uncle Repton.'

'A bishop, heavens no,' Venetia said. 'She left the church ages ago, didn't I tell you about it? Perhaps I didn't – best forgotten anyway. She's working for a donkey sanctuary now.'

Angel was running after her uncle.

He quickened his pace. 'I'm no good for anything today. Goodbye,' he called out, before shutting the door behind him.

Angel cursed loudly. She turned and for the first time, noticed Laura and Venetia sitting in their car. She came towards them, her Doc Martens pulverising the gravel beneath her feet.

'Mummy, what are you doing here?' she said, her hennaed Mohican catching in the window frame as she leant in the driver's window next to Laura.

'I might ask the same of you.' Venetia cowered in the corner, gripping Parker to her chest. The pug growled at the black clothed apparition.

'I often visit Uncle Repton. The old boy rattles around here with enough space to house London's entire population of homeless cats.'

Laura saw a glint of metal as she watched a gobbet of spittle arc from Angel's mouth and land on her lap and realised that a tongue piercing was the cause of Angel's slight lisp.

'But I've had a feeling for some time that his spiritual needs are not being met,' Angel continued. 'He may have got away with it but he needs to address his guilt. I've been trying to extract a written confession from him.'

'You should leave him alone. He's done nothing wrong.'

'Mummy, you know nothing and that sidekick of his, Canon Frank Holliday is evil. His religious intentions are way out of line, and he and Repton are thick as thieves. Made Aunt Matilda mad with all their talk of transubstantiation.' Angel wiped her mouth. 'What with him and all the other detritus Uncle Repton has around him, he's being positively encouraged to live the lie. Nothing good has happened here since he and Aunt Matilda started surrounding themselves with all these lovers of mammon. In fact she'd turn in her grave if she saw the amount of meat that gets chucked in the bin after those wedding bashes.'

'How do you know?' Venetia asked.

'Recycling is an important part of my business. You never know where you might find a discarded bale of hay.' Angel turned and gave an expansive wave of one arm in the general direction of the house, her many brass bangles jangling noisily like a drawer full of cutlery thrown on the floor. 'Who knows, those two girls might even be hiding a donkey right here at Mount Cod. Right under his very nose. Lungworm's gone crazy this year.' Her arm came back to rest on the open car window. 'And I like to check he's looking after that dog of his. He can be very careless. Look what happened to Yorick.' There was yet more jangling as she wagged a finger at her mother. 'That pug looks overweight.'

'I beg your pardon?' Laura patted Parker as he sat beside her on Venetia's lap.

Angel extricated herself from the window but then her head burst in again, a nose stud inches from Laura's face. 'What are you doing here anyway? Have you been putting him against me, Mummy?'

'We've been visiting, if it's any of your business and of course I haven't. I had no idea you even saw him.'

'Well I haven't seen him have I? I'll have to try again another time. Meanwhile I've had a potential sighting in a field by the Hare and Hounds in Chipping Codswold.'

'Sighting?' Laura said. Was this yet another mad person seeing apparitions?

'Woman thinks it may be a mule. But it's lame. Donkey, mule, either way it needs investigating. Cheerio.' Angel stamped back to her van, her short black skirt straining around her sizeable thighs.

'Was your late husband a big man?' Laura asked.

Venetia relaxed her grip on Parker and sighed. 'Angel has always suffered from what she calls, "weight issues". I wonder if she watches *Cash in the Attic*?'

'What?'

'Well, if I know anything about my daughter, she'll have an ulterior motive for seeing her uncle. I don't for a minute believe in all that spiritual nonsense she was talking about.'

'She was pretty convinced of his guilt.'

'I don't know where she got that idea from but knowing my daughter she'll be trying to use it to her advantage.'

'Well, I think she has a right to look out for herself. It's she who stands to inherit after all.'

'Talking of inheritance.' Venetia's eyes lit up. 'Do you think we'll be back in time for *Heir Hunters*? Come on Laura, let's get away from this fearful place.'

Chapter nine

Laura realised that her friends, Strudel Black and Jervis Willingdale, were in danger of information overload as she recounted the tale of her stay at Mount Cod to them, so she tried to slow her pace. 'Venetia's daughter Angel thinks Sir Repton is the culprit, but I'm not so sure. At least not acting alone. There could be a man called Canon Frank Holliday involved and then again, it could just as well be the housekeeper Cheryl Varley who murdered Matilda Willowby in her bath.' She gave a curt nod of her head for emphasis.

As she and Parker had taken the short walk over to their bungalow in Mulberry Close, she had felt, for the first time since the death of the Brigadier, a certain exhilaration brought about by the potential of solving the crime.

Jervis adjusted his Woldham Bowls Club tie and took a swig of banana daiquiri. 'Does it really matter if someone bumped off the old girl? Life's short enough without having to worry about other people's dead wives and anyway, what makes you so sure she was murdered?'

Laura reached for her glass – it was the slippery slope when Jervis announced that the bar opened at three-thirty but they had agreed that a spot of alcohol mid-afternoon sharpened the mind.

'Something's not right about her death,' she said. 'It was altogether too unexpected, also I've discovered a couple of things that make me suspicious. Firstly, the positioning of the keys in the bathroom door, and then a scrap of paper

Venetia found, that leads me to believe that the house-keeper, Cheryl, was about to be sacked.'

'There, you see Jervis, you are too harsh.' Strudel said. 'This is just the kind of project to which Laura excels and she has already found a motive.'

'Fair play, my love.' Sitting on the sofa next to Strudel, Jervis patted her knee.

'Thank you Strudel,' Laura said. 'But it's more than just a project; Angel's inheritance may be at stake.' A picture of the overweight punk crossed Laura's mind but she carried on. 'Finding out the truth is important. It's a matter of justice.'

'In my home country of Bavaria the police are taking much interest in such things. Should you not be talking with Woldham CID in this instance, Laura?'

'Not Phil Sandfield, please.' Laura had a long established mistrust of the local Woldham Inspector that, amongst other things, involved his allowing her late husband, Tony to fall asleep on the green of the eighteenth hole of Woldham golf course while under the influence of narcotics – it was a long story, best forgotten. 'Anyway I've nothing concrete I can tell him. That's the problem; I must find real evidence.'

'So this Mrs Varley worked for Sir Repton's wife?' Jervis said.

'Yes and a handyman called Lance Wilkes. And then there's the wedding business. I don't know what the financial arrangements were with them when Matilda was alive but they seem to be taking over the place, despite what Repton says. The identical twin girls boss him around – well they all boss him around.' As Laura took another sip of her drink, the striking colour of Strudel's cerise silk dress seemed to soften. 'I met the man who heads the business too,' she continued. 'Robert Hanley Jones; bit of a slippery sort of chap if you asked me and Repton doesn't seem to have a clue what kind of profit, if any, they make.' She put her glass back down on the table beside her.

'So you are unclear as to Sir Repton's financial situation regarding this wedding business, but what has that to do with the housekeeper?' Jervis said.

'I don't know. All I can do at the moment is try and build up a picture of the circumstances leading up to her death.'

'So why pick on the housekeeper?' Jervis asked.

'Call it a gut feeling. From what I gather, Matilda didn't suffer fools, although, as I've said I don't much care for any of the people at Mount Cod, they're all manipulative in one way or another. One of the twin girls even manhandled Venetia and, what's more, she has all the keys to the house.'

'I'd bump them up to the top of the list of suspects, if I were you.' Jervis laughed then held his stomach. 'Christ, Strudel where are the Rennies?'

Strudel picked up a packet on the table beside her and handed it to him. Jervis ripped open the box, popped out a couple of pills from their foil containers and lobbed them into his mouth.

'You're right,' Laura said. 'I should leave no stone unturned. I don't suppose any of your successful Ancient Eros couples have had to plan a wedding?'

Jervis chewed and swallowed. He got up and paced about before sitting down at the swivel chair in front of his desk, the expression of acute agony beginning to fade. 'What's the name of the wedding company?' he asked, fingering his computer mouse.

'State of the Union.'

'This is something we will be finding out for you. Jervis can be Facebooking shortly all our clients who have happily yoked. And talking of yolks Laura, I must show you my latest creation. We are having the anniversary of one year of ballroom dancing classes at Wellworth Lawns next week. Come upstairs and see the celebratory gown I have created.'

Once Strudel had slipped off the pink silk and clambered into the yellow dress that was lying on her bed, Laura almost wished she had brought her sunglasses. The froth-ing mass of lace bubbled up around Strudel as if she had emerged from a vat of canary cappuccino froth.

'I have only just completed the neckline,' Strudel explained as she fingered the matching netting bows. 'We must show it to Jervis.'

Strudel squeezed down the staircase and back into the sitting room.

'I say my love, a bombe surprise,' Jervis said. 'But isn't it a little short? What will our delightful new manager, Mr. Parrott say if he sees you in it?'

Strudel looked down at her exposed knees. 'He can go to hell, the sanctimonious prig.' As she sat down crossly on the sofa, Parker jumped up and nestled in the dandelion duvet of her lap.

'Edward Parrott? What's brought this on?' Laura asked.

'We've got serious concerns about him.' Jervis wiped a lump of banana from his chin with a doily. 'He seems to be taking a rather pious attitude.'

'You are not believing what he is saying to Jervis.' Strudel began fanning herself. 'He is saying we are not setting a good example.'

'Bounder told me to do the decent thing and tie the knot with Strudel. Said living in sin was not the sort of thing the residents of Wellworth Lawns expected. I couldn't possibly tell him Strudel is already married to a gangster living on the Costa Brava.'

'I have given up all hope of my Ronny,' Strudel said. 'But there is worse, Laura; Mr. Parrott is saying we are too noisy with our dancing in the Recreation Room and he is ban-ning the rumba. He is saying it is the vertical expression of an horizontal desire.'

'He said it could lead to an outbreak of sexually transmit-ted diseases. Can you credit it? For Christ sake the rumba is the nearest thing most of the old dears are going to get to sex at their time of life, so why not!'

'Naughty boy!' Strudel took a sip from her glass. 'This drink is too thick, Jervis. It is of a vichyssoise soup consistency and I am needing a spoon.'

'Easily remedied.' Jervis reached for the drinks trolley at his side and poured more rum into the cocktail shaker.

'Perhaps a little more ice?' Laura said. 'I'll have a word with my granddaughter about Edward Parrott. It turns out that Repton knows him from when he was a stage manager. I'm sure Vince never said anything about Edward Parrott being an ex-stage manager when he took him on. I'm sure he said he used to work at Claridges.' Laura thought of her granddaughter Victoria's husband Vince Outhwaite, the Leeds underwear magnate. It was the money from his company "Foundation Rocks" that had saved Chipping Wellworth Manor from the grips of the bank when the family finances had gone so disastrously wrong.

'Curious.' Jervis picked up the tongs and opened the ice bucket. 'Either way, I'm absolutely positive Victoria and Vince would want the residents here to have as much fun as possible.' He plopped some cubes into the cocktail shaker, rattled it around and filled up their glasses. 'I got the distinct impression Vince was a bit of a party animal himself when we met him at the Horticultural Club Fete last year.' Jervis gave an extravagant wink.

'He was most impressed by the dancing display you put on. In fact he now has a private tutor who comes to his office in Leeds and gives him lessons in Scottish reeling. Victoria, of course knows all the dances from her youth.'

'Strip the Willow and all that. Top hole. But we're digressing. Dancing is not the reason why Laura came to see us.'

'How silly we have become,' Strudel said, looking suddenly embarrassed by her appearance in the middle of the afternoon. 'Let me think seriously of what you have said.' She rested her head on the back of the sofa and closed her eyes. 'I am thinking that your Sir Repton may not be of a murdersome nature from what you are telling us,' she said. 'But this woman looking after him, we must return to her.'

'Joking aside, I'd say she's got good motive.' Jervis eyed his glass. 'About to be sent packing by Matilda; decides to get rid of the tiresome old bag and live the life of Riley at the expense of the old boy. I can feel crime in my bones.'

'I'm pleased you think my theory's got legs,' Laura said.

'It's Strudel that's got the legs.' Jervis laughed. 'Come here you saucy buttercup.' He attempted to rise from his chair but fell back as his indigestion returned. 'Christ that's painful,' he said, crossing his arms over his chest.

Laura picked up her handbag 'I'll get onto the case of the housekeeper right away.'

'And I'll...' Jervis gasped. '... check out our married couples and this wedding brigade of Sir Repton's.' He turned to Strudel. 'Have we more bananas my love? I'm feeling a tad tipsy.'

As Laura walked back over to the main house she recalled Cheryl's comment about going over Matilda's room with a fine toothcomb... Not fine enough to find the note in the lift, but had Laura be thorough enough?

'Why didn't I check in the drawers of the writing desk?' she said to Parker, as he sniffed the leaves of a topiary box bush, obstinately refusing to budge. 'I'll have to go back but first I think a little background checking is in order.' Something Cheryl had said during Laura's stay had alerted her to a possible way of finding out about the housekeeper. She had been to the hairdressers in Woldham and there was only one hairdresser in Woldham. It was Laura's old friend, Dudley of "Dudley's Hair Designs" and she had her weekly appointment booked for the next morning.

Chapter ten

As Laura walked down Woldham High Street, it began to rain and she had to run the last few yards to the salon, pulling Parker behind her.

'Lawks, Lady B,' Dudley said. 'It may be June, but this is England. Fancy coming out without a brolly.' The tall gangly hairdresser picked up Parker, sat him on his lap and waved the hairdryer over the pug.

'I've forgotten it somewhere,' Laura said, remembering as her own hair dripped down the collar of her coat, that she had left it in the hall at Mount Cod.

Dudley's assistant, Kelsey got up from behind the reception desk. 'Let me take that for you, Lady B. I'll put it on a radiator.' She took the coat and returned with a gown.

Dudley finished drying Parker and put him in the basket he shared with Dudley's aged rescue greyhound on the occasions Laura brought him with her. The greyhound stared complacently as Parker shoved and snuffled until he had manoeuvred the docile creature into the position he wanted, and then went to sleep.

'Let's get you shampooed,' Dudley said. 'I've got a new product for you to try. Organic oatmeal with sage.'

'Chicken stuffing?' Laura leaned back over the basin.

'Don't be cheeky now. Mind you it does say it gives great body.' Dudley stroked his own mop of transplanted hair that he had told her proudly, many times, was from Scotland – the only place for really top quality blonde hues.

She closed her eyes as he ran warm water over her head and then she heard a glugging sound as he squeezed the bottle.

'Are you sure you're not meant to thin it with a drop of milk?' she asked.

'Trust me.' Dudley smeared the glutinous mass onto her head and began massaging.

Once back in her chair in front of the mirror, Dudley unwrapped her head from the towel turban and combed it through.

There was only one other person in the salon and she was under an old-fashioned dryer, its ancient hum filling the salon, so Laura took the opportunity to quiz Dudley.

'Have you come across someone called Cheryl Varley?' she asked. 'I think she may have damaged her hair.'

'What a woman, I ask you. These people who think they can do it all themselves, then they go and make a cock up of it – excuse my French, – and expect us to step in and save the day. It's not the first time either. I refused to touch it. Kelsey did her.' Dudley shouted across the salon, 'Kel, Lady B wants to know about that woman with the "Sun-in".'

'What a nutter,' Kelsey shrieked from behind the reception desk.

'I'm getting very hot here. Am I nearly ready?' called the woman from under the dryer.

Kelsey ran over and flicked the switch. 'I've turned you down. Not long now,' she shouted at the woman.

Dudley beckoned Kelsey over. 'So what's with this Cheryl Varley?' he said.

Kelsey sat down beside Laura. 'Between you and me, there's something odd about her. She acts as if she's got no money. Complains that her employer doesn't pay her, hence the 'Sun-in'.'

'I'm getting very cold now,' came the voice from under the dryer.

'Turn the old moo up again Kel – actually you can turn her off.' Dudley turned on his hand held dryer. 'She won't be able to hear from over there with this on.'

Kelsey returned.

'Let's hear it Kel.' Dudley curled Laura's hair with the brush and waved the dryer over her head.

'Well, when I was doing her hair, Billy came into the salon, he's my boyfriend.'

'We know that.'

'Lady B might not.'

'Go on.' Laura was beginning to feel as if she was morphing into Mary Berry – Dudley always tried to make her hair look too neat for her liking.

'Well, Billy's a waiter at The Lamb. And that night he saw her again. She was there having dinner. Eighties night it was. They're into themed evenings at The Lamb.'

'Get on with it,' Dudley said.

'OK, OK. Well, according to Billy, she and the man she was with ordered the most expensive things on the menu. He told me 'cos the chef was furious 'cos Billy took the order late and then they wanted those flaming pancakes with that Grand Marnier liqueur. Billy's told me about it before. So she can't be short of money can she?'

'Perhaps the man was paying. Who was he anyhow?' Dudley said.

'Billy didn't know him and it was her Billy remembered 'cos she paid with cash.'

'What did the man look like?' Laura asked.

Kelsey said she hadn't asked. 'But they were all lovey-dovey Billy said and she was showing him her hand and she'd a diamond as big as a sugar lump on her finger. Billy said, "Who needs a ring that size?" But then I don't suppose he wanted me getting any big ideas.'

'Did Billy notice which finger?'

'Sorry Lady B, that's not the kind of thing my Billy would take much notice of.'

'If it isn't too much to ask...' shouted the woman under the dryer. 'Or shall I take the rollers out myself?'

Kelsey jumped up. 'Just coming.'

'Got everything you wanted Lady B? We'll do your cut and colour next time.' Dudley reached for the hairspray.

'Please not,' Laura begged but Dudley was insistent.

There was an "Out of Order" notice on the lift door when Laura returned to Wellworth Lawns. Underneath, it said "Exercise Improves Circulation".

She took the stairs to her room, Parker snuffling crossly behind her. Having damped down Dudley's bouffant creation she went to find Venetia. Knocking on her door, she let herself in.

Venetia put the paintbrush she was holding down onto some newspaper on her dressing table. 'I thought you said you were going to the hairdressers?'

'I did, now have you rung Repton?' Laura asked.

'I've been too busy.' Venetia stood back to admire her handiwork. 'It's called shabby chic. Anyway why do I have to ring him?'

'Shabby I can understand. That was a perfectly good ladder-back chair. Because you were the one who was so worried about him.'

'But it was brown. Brown furniture is so last century. Kirsty Allsop says this is the very thing to brighten up one's life. What time is it? I'm not missing *Escape to the Country* am I?' As Venetia fumbled under the newspaper for the TV remote control, the paintbrush slipped to the floor.

'Well I'll ring him then. I've found out something about that housekeeper of his.'

'I didn't care for her. When I got lost that day, I came across her in Repton's office. Sitting at his desk. She got up in an awful hurry.'

'I knew it was a mistake Repton keeping the safe combination for all to see. Did Matilda have much jewellery? '

'Lovely things; Laverack heirlooms mostly I should think. I wonder what Repton's done with them? Mind you I can't imagine Angel would have much time for diamonds. I suppose when the time comes she'll check them out on *Antiques Roadshow* then sell the lot and put the money into more food for her donkeys.'

Laura picked up the paintbrush and balanced it on top of the tin. 'On second thoughts, I think I'll take a drive over there and collect my umbrella. I don't suppose I can interest you in joining me?'

'Go back to Mount Cod? Not on your life and anyway I want to get another coat on.'

'Don't!' Laura cried out, but it was too late. Venetia sat down on the chair and pointed the remote at the TV, jabbing at it impatiently. 'Why ever not? It's Robson Green.'

'No I mean you've sat on the wet paint.'

'What?' Venetia jumped up and attempted to view her rear.

'You'd better ask Mimi if she can wash your skirt. It is water based isn't it?'

'I think so.' Venetia undid the skirt. It dropped to the floor leaving her standing in her thick brown tights. She bent down and picked up the paintbrush. 'Anyhow, I'll get about much easier without it.'

'Well, just remember to put something on before you go down for lunch.'

As Laura passed the Land Rover parked outside the lodge, the sky darkened and she heard a low rumble of thunder. She wasn't sure how she was going to get upstairs to search Matilda's writing desk. Neither could she realistically confront Cheryl on the state of her finances and demand to see her jewellery, if the housekeeper was even there, and after all Cheryl hadn't actually done anything except appear insubordinate which was hardly a crime. But perhaps a chance encounter might throw up something more concrete, Laura could only hope.

She drew up beside a dark blue Ford Mondeo parked outside the house. It didn't look like something the wedding planners would drive. Relieved that there was obviously no wedding in progress, she got out and peered in the driver's window as Parker dashed up the steps and began scratching at the front door. A copy of the Bible lay on the passenger seat, next to it, a packet of opened jelly babies. She felt a drop of rain land on her head and made a dash for the house.

'Hello dear friend.' Sir Repton stood at the open front door; Parker and Sybil Thorndike frolicking together at his feet like long lost friends. 'How utterly charming to see you again, I saw your car arriving from the window. Come in before you get a soaking.'

'Too stupid, I left my umbrella here and as I was just passing, I thought I'd collect it. It's not inconvenient is it?'

'Not at all, I have Canon Frank Holliday here with me.' Sir Repton looked up as a flash of lightening split a pendulous black cloud. 'Oh, when shall we three meet again?'

'Meet again?' Laura had to raise her voice as the rain splashed down onto the gravel. The quote must signify something, but it made no sense. She hurried up the steps. 'I haven't ever met him.'

'I beg your pardon, just a small Scottish moment, often happens in a storm.'

She followed him into the hall. She must have been wrong about the quotes; they were meaningless.

'But it's strange that your paths have not crossed. Have you time to spare?' he said, opening the sitting room door. 'You see Canon Frank and I have been discussing the possibility of a séance, but with just the two of us it was looking unhopeful.'

'A séance?'

'There has been a delivery of Norfolk mead to the house. Tam and Pom say it's nothing to do with them. The time has come to pin Rosalind down.'

Chapter eleven

Laura was somewhat taken aback by Canon Frank Holliday's appearance as he held out his hand to her; he must have been at least six foot four. She smiled up at the startling blue eyes that fixed on her from below raven coloured crags of jutting eyebrow. Above these outcrops, thick white hair swept back from his forehead like a small avalanche reaching down his neck to where it met his dog collar.

'Sir Repton has been telling me all about you,' he said.

'All good I hope?' Her gaze travelled down. He wore a black serge suit. The jacket fitted perfectly across his shoulders and the trousers held an immaculate crease. Laura was thinking, these ecclesiastic tailors aren't half bad, when Parker, breaking off from his game with Sybil Thorndike at the Canon's feet, growled at the cleric's shiny black-tasselled loafers. She did wonder if he hadn't directed a small kick in the direction of the pug.

Next to the Canon, Sir Repton appeared more enfeebled than ever. 'My dear Laura,' he said. 'How could Frank think anything but the best when I have been extolling your virtues.'

'How embarrassing,' Laura said.

'Not at all Lady Boxford, Sir Repton is ever the faithful purveyor of fact.'

Laura was momentarily pondering this twofold gush of compliments when Sir Repton excused himself. 'I'll go and make us a fresh pot of tea,' he said.

'No Cheryl?' Laura's heart sank, this was going to be a fruitless mission.

'She had to drive Lance to the doctor. I shan't be long.' As Sir Repton hurried out, Laura excused herself to the Canon and took the opportunity of going upstairs to check the writing desk. It too was a wasted journey and revealed nothing. She returned downstairs to the sitting room where Canon Frank was languishing, like a Roman general on one of the sofas. Laura sat down in the velvet tub chair and put her handbag on the floor beside her. 'Repton shouldn't have to be making the tea at his age,' she said.

'I agree. But he is buoyed by the idea of the séance.' The Canon's eyebrows rose at an angle. 'Getting to the bottom of his wife's death will be a weight off his shoulders. He feels that if he can understand why it happened and specifically what the serving wench is now foretelling, he will be able to take control of the situation. Forearm himself; I'm all for it.'

'It's this sort of thing not against church teaching?'

'I take a nondenominational approach; we must not abandon the Wiccas after all. And when it comes to helping such a tortured soul, God does his work in mysterious ways.'

They heard the door handle rattle and Sir Repton veered in at the helm of the wooden tea trolley. His progress was not made any easier by the immense Egyptian headdress he had donned, on top of which a golden cobra swayed. Beneath this he wore a floor length purple robe tied at the waist with a yellow dressing gown cord.

'Heavens Repton. What's all this about?' Laura asked.

'Thought I'd better do the thing properly. I've been researching the readings of Aleister Crowley.' He parked the trolley next to the sofa opposite Canon Frank. 'Earl Grey?'

'Whatever next?' Laura laughed. 'Ectoplasm? Levitation?'

'Sir Repton is deadly serious, Lady Boxford. Two sugars please. It's all hands to the bridge.'

'Bridge, that's it. Now where did I put the bridge table? Frank, could you pour?' Sir Repton hurried off again.

Laura and Canon Frank were finishing their tea when Sir Repton returned with a collapsible card table covered in green baize that he erected in front of the window seat. Around it he placed two more chairs that were standing either side of the tallboy.

'Are we ready?' he asked, opening one of the drawers of the tallboy. He brought out a small Duralex glass tumbler and an envelope. He placed the glass upside down on the table and opened the envelope, out of which he took bits of paper. These he placed randomly in a circle around the table.

Laura walked over and inspected the letters of the alphabet that he had written in unsteady black ink on each of them.

'You have been busy,' she said, sitting down on the window seat.

'Curtains please, Laura, behind you. Canon Frank, will you join us?'

Laura looked out of the rain-lashed window. The sky was leaden, a deep bruise blue. At her feet, Parker began to whine. 'Don't you think it's dark enough already?' She picked him up and sat him beside her.

'I don't believe Rosalind will communicate in anything other than candlelight,' Sir Repton said, producing a single white china candlestick that he placed in the middle of the table. The cobra wobbled like a pecking hen as he searched the pocket of his robe and brought out a box of matches. As Laura pulled the thick brocade curtains closed behind her, Sir Repton lit the wick. A tiny flame spluttered in the darkness. Now Sybil Thorndike began to whine. Laura picked up the dachshund and placed her next to Parker.

'But this won't work,' Canon Frank said.

'Why not?' Sir Repton asked.

'Well if the glass starts moving, it's going to knock over the candle.'

'I see. Yes. That would be unfortunate.' Sir Repton disappeared into the shadows. They heard a thud and he returned with the tripod table on which the Buddha tea caddy had sat. 'This will do the trick,' he said putting it beside his chair, and placing the candle on it.

'Now, I think we are ready.' He rubbed his hands together and sat down at the table.

Laura felt her arm tiring and she was feeling increasingly chilly as the minutes ticked by. Her little finger, resting on the upturned glass in the middle of the table, was developing cramp as Sir Repton, for the umpteenth time called out, imploring Rosalind to make contact. But just as she was thinking, this is going nowhere; she felt a slight pressure on her finger… as if it was being pushed.

Slowly the glass moved towards her. Laura's finger was so numb it was hard to tell from which direction the pressure was being exerted. Her finger fell away from the glass as it came to a halt in front of her.

'Holy Father! What's it stopped at? This candlelight's not strong enough to see,' Canon Frank said.

Which of them had done it? Was the Canon trying to placate Sir Repton? Or was it Sir Repton, playing out his fantasy? 'Wait, I've got a torch somewhere.' Laura fumbled in her bag and located it. She pressed the switch and directed the beam at the little piece of paper in front of her.

'Y,' Canon Frank said. ' Couldn't be clearer. We'll take that as a yes.'

It must be him.

'A definite invocation.' Sir Repton raised his head to the ornate plasterwork ceiling. 'At last, she is with us,' he gasped, clutching his headdress.

No, it must be him, Laura thought, as they resumed their positions.

'What shall I ask her now?' Sir Repton's voice was high with anticipation.

'We could ask her how she managed to hold Lady Willowby under.' There was a certain hint of relish in the Canon's voice.

'How very tasteless,' Laura said.

'Forgive my forthrightness but we must strike while the iron is hot.'

'Oh my, I feel my innards all atremble. Are you sure about that Frank?'

'Don't be silly, both of you,' Laura found herself saying. 'Do you want to frighten her away the minute we have her attention?'

'You are so right Laura,' Sir Repton said. 'Thank goodness we have you here.'

'Point taken.' The candle flickered as Canon Frank rubbed his chin. 'Ask her...Ask her if she had the delivery of mead sent to the house.'

'Yes, that's it. Rosalind... Fair Rosalind... Would you join us in a wassail? Are you pining for a haunch of venison? Or is it a tankard of mead you're after?'

'For goodness sake Repton,' Laura said. 'Your riddles will be quite beyond her. Ask a straightforward question.'

'I agree, keep it simple,' the Canon said. 'Don't ask her to make choices or the list may be endless. You know what women can be like.'

'I take that as a sexist remark, Canon,' Laura said. Keep it simple, so the only letter you need push us towards is the "Y". It's you all right.

'My sincere apologies, Lady Boxford.'

Sir Repton cleared his throat. 'Rosalind, my dear, did you order a certain beverage from Norfolk?' His voice quivered in the gloom. 'Tell me or I shall have to take you over my knee and give you a good...'

Canon Frank coughed. 'That's enough Repton, now it's you trying to frighten her off. Just ask her if she ordered the mead.'

Sir Repton rephrased the question and for a few minutes all Laura could hear was the steady breathing of the Canon, as if a doctor was checking his lungs with a stethoscope. But then... Again Laura felt a pressure on her finger. But was it coming from a different angle? The glass lurched towards her and came to a halt. She shone the torch. The battery was fading.

'Y again. I'd say she definitely ordered the mead,' she said. This was absurd. She was now convinced that it was Sir Repton who was pushing the glass. Still, if that was the game he wanted to play…

Laura was thinking fast now, she had to take control. 'Ask her if she ordered the mead as a clue.'

'What?' Sir Repton said.

'Well, that's what we're here to find out isn't it? Why she's doing it.'

'Good thinking, Lady Boxford,' the Canon said.

'All right then.' Sir Repton resumed his communications. 'Rosalind my dear, now clear your head and tighten your corsets, was the mead intended as a hint?'

Again they waited. Again the glass moved and again with the aid of the now dimming torch they saw that it had come to a halt at the Y.

'Emphatically a "yes".' Sir Repton was overcome with joy. 'The mead has meaning. Do you believe me now?'

Laura scanned the table to ascertain the whereabouts of the N. It was placed directly between the Canon and Sir Repton. Neither of them, singly, would manage to push the glass there without her aid. Her mind raced as she replaced the glass in the middle of the table. What could they ask, that the so-called "ghost" would answer in the negative? Had she killed Matilda was the obvious question but Laura had already scotched that idea.

'We know Rosalind's character is malevolent but she also has a mischievous side to her and I don't believe killing a pet in the eighteenth century would carry nearly the same weight as nowadays, so I think we could ask her if she killed Yorick.' It was a tenuous argument. Laura attempted to back it up. 'I think we have her confidence now.'

'But we know she killed Yorick,' Sir Repton said. 'Why would we ask her that?'

'She may not want to admit to it. It will be a way of seeing if she is reliable.' Laura was not entirely sure of her own logic. 'Fingers on the glass, gentlemen.' She tapped the table to hurry them along.

'I see.' Sir Repton sounded equally unconvinced, but he joined Laura and the Canon, replacing his finger on the glass. 'Rosalind, my dear,' he whispered. 'Did you by chance do away with my saluki?

The glass remained motionless.

Whoever it was, this has foxed them, Laura thought but then she felt a sideways pressure. She put all the force left in her little finger against it. Canon Frank grunted. It had to be him. She felt renewed pressure and again resisted. Sir Repton had begun panting. Finally, with one short push against her, the glass slid away to the left. She flashed the torch down to where it had stopped.

'It's on the R,' she said, as the torch died.

'Blast!'

She distinctly heard the Canon say it under his breath.

'Oh woe,' Sir Repton cried out. 'The R must indicate my name. It is a portent. It must indicate she thinks it's me, that I am somehow responsible for Yorick's death.' He let out a moan. 'I can feel a terrible strangulation descending upon my nether regions,' he bewailed and rose from the table. He swung round and knocked over the candle. The already dim interior was plunged into darkness.

Laura heard a crash and at her side, Sybil Thorndike began to howl. 'Unsex me here,' Sir Repton mewled from the direction of the floor.

Another crash ensued. Laura fumbled behind her to find the edge of the curtains. Sybil Thorndike howled louder and Parker began to bark. A long low metallic bong struck up and then she heard the Canon invoke the name of the Lord. 'Jesus Christ,' he called out. 'I think I've broken my ankle.'

Laura pulled one curtain open, but at that moment the lights came on. She looked down at the table and realised that the glass was not actually at the R at all but at the H. Still it mattered little as the whole thing had been such a farce.

'What on earth are you lot up to?' Cheryl said, standing in the open doorway.

'You may well ask.' Laura got up and surveyed the scene.

Sir Repton was lying beside the fireplace. Next to him an ornamental brass gong was swaying, its rhythm gently decreasing by the moment as if trying to conceal its own complicity in the drama.

Sir Repton sat up and rubbed his head. 'Where's my turban?'

'In the grate,' Laura said.

He picked it up and dusted the ash from it. 'Are you all right Canon?' he asked weakly, as he sat down in a daze on the club fender.

Canon Frank was lying in a position not dissimilar to a prone Michelangelo's *David* beside a sofa, one foot stuck under the low table covered in magazines and books.

Cheryl walked over to it with the purpose of a district nurse. 'You lift this end, Mrs Boxford,' she said.

'It's Lady...' Sir Repton's voice faded and he began to cough.

'You stay where you are, Repton.' Cheryl wagged a finger at him. 'I'll deal with you in a minute.'

As Laura lifted the table – magazines and books tipping onto the floor – Cheryl grabbed the Canon's trouser turn-up and pulled his leg clear.

He cried out in pain then sat up to inspect his ankle. 'Great Scott, it's the size of a tree trunk. Call an ambulance.' He toppled sideways, his head taking a glancing blow on a leather bound volume of *Debrett's Peerage*, as he fainted clean away.

'Frank, you're a bloody nuisance,' Cheryl said, as she picked up the phone and dialled 999.

Chapter twelve

'I don't know what the Canon thought he was up to, but really Repton, you must stop all this hysterical nonsense.' Laura paced up and down as Sir Repton sat on the sofa nursing his turban. They had seen Frank Holliday safely escorted to the ambulance and he was now on his way to Woldham Hospital.

'As I said before,' Laura continued. 'I understand the grieving process but this ghost business is making you paranoid and you are reading things into normal everyday occurrences.'

'But the mead...' Sir Repton hitched up the purple robe as he crossed his legs.

'I'm sure you'll find it was an innocent mistake; the wrong delivery address or something. Have you asked Cheryl about it? Perhaps she ordered it for herself?'

'Cheryl drinking mead?'

'It's not impossible but either way, I think we can say with some certainty that for whatever reason, Canon Frank was manipulating the séance. Unless of course he killed Yorick; you know the glass didn't stop at the R as you thought but actually the H. H for Holliday.'

Sir Repton's jaw dropped. 'No no, that couldn't be.'

'I'll take your word for it but there's probably a perfectly rational reason why the dog died. Did Cheryl and Lance, for example, get on with him?'

'Yorrick was inclined to leaving little messages about the place that a person, if they were not aware, may have found they trod in. Both Lance and Cheryl did on occasion find this something of a nuisance.'

Nuisance? The word rang in Laura's ears. 'So one of them trod in dogs mess perhaps while undertaking household chores and decided to shut him in the billiard room.' Or more than likely having a game themselves to while away their idle hours. Who knows even a party? 'Then they simply forgot about him.'

'But I know it was Rosalind.'

'How?'

'I had smelled tobacco in the billiard room shortly after. I knew it to be Rosalind, and Cheryl reminded me of the eighteenth-century habit of ladies smoking pipes.'

Laura was about to point out that Lance smoked but foresaw a lengthy discussion on the difference in the aroma of ancient and modern Mellow Virginia. 'Well lets go back to the real reason we are here, namely Matilda. Have you ever stopped to consider where Cheryl was on the morning of your wife's death?'

Laura left Sir Repton to ponder this as she pieced the facts together in her head. 'Frank, you're a bloody nuisance.' That's what Cheryl had said. She must have known the Canon; he had been a regular visitor at the house and was the one who found Matilda's body after all, but Cheryl's words showed a degree of confidentiality that was unexpected.

Laura was reminded of Dudley's assistant Kelsey's story when she was having her hair done. The diamond ring Cheryl was flashing in the pub.

'Where did Matilda keep her jewellery?' she asked.

Sir Repton clutched the turban to his chest. 'I beg your pardon?'

'I'm sorry,' Laura said. 'I'm not meaning to pry and it may be idle gossip but Cheryl was seen out wearing an unusually large diamond ring.'

'Are you suggesting Cheryl may have stolen my late wife's jewels? She maybe insolent but I'm sure she's not a thief.'

'I'm only saying it would be prudent to check. Did Matilda have a diamond solitaire?'

'She had her emerald engagement ring and one with sapphires and diamonds that I gave her on the occasion of my knighthood. But there may have been others. Laverack heirlooms... I never looked.'

'Well, I think we should do so now.'

Sir Repton stared up at Laura with misty eyes. 'If you insist.' He paused. Two small spots of colour rose on his pallid cheekbones. 'There is a small safe in my... our bedroom.' He put the turban to one side and tightened the dressing gown cord around his waist.

'Don't tell me, you keep the combination on a piece of paper in your desk with the other one?'

'It's a key actually.' Sir Repton prickled. 'But Cheryl never goes into my office.'

'I'm afraid she does. Venetia saw her. Come on.' Laura set off in the direction of the office.

As Sir Repton riffled through the drawer, Laura glanced at the pile of correspondence on his desk. He obviously had not replied to the man Ned Stocking as his letter was still on top. But then she saw the date and skimmed through the typewritten words and realised that this was a second request asking for a meeting. Sir Repton had plainly not replied to the first.

'Here we are.' He held up a key with an old brown label on a piece of string attached to it.

They went upstairs. To Laura's surprise, they did not turn right at the top of the stairs. She had supposed the master bedroom to be situated at the end of the landing beyond Grimsby and Bridlington, but instead they turned left. They followed the corridor and at the end went up three steps – one reason for Matilda's move from the matrimonial bedroom, Laura supposed.

Sir Repton opened the door ahead of them. Laura could

not make out much of the interior of the room as the windows were shuttered. In the gloom she could see the bed. Above it, a vast canopy of dark orange material swagged like the sails of an Essex barque from the ceiling. Sir Repton hurried to the bedside table and turned on a lamp shaped like a miniature yacht. Above it, another stormy seascape hung. Sir Repton lifted it off the wall exposing the safe.

He stood the painting up against the bedside table, inserted the key and turned the lock. He took out a leather box and put it on the bed. Then he got down on his knees and opened it, staring at the contents.

'There is her engagement ring,' he said. 'And here's the sapphire one. But look.' He held up a gold and enamel brooch. It was a modernist creation of stupendous ugliness, possibly from the 1960s, in the shape of a fish.

'Her mother gave her this,' he said. 'We called it, "The Cod Piece". How Matilda cherished it.'

'But are there any empty spaces?'

Sir Repton shuffled sideways as Laura nudged him out of the way.

There was no way of telling, for Matilda had not kept her rings neatly in the chamois-padded recesses of the case. Strings of pearls jostled with earrings, paste or otherwise. Laura was reminded of her own untidy jumble of jewels as she spotted an expensive looking evening watch next to a pink stoned ring that might have come out of a cracker.

'This is hopeless,' she said, shutting the lid. 'But I am sure Cheryl has some questions to answer. We must find out what she is up to.' She handed the box back to Sir Repton.

'What Cheryl is up to?'

'I'm sorry, but I believe that she may have something to do with this serving wench you are so convinced is behind the demise of your late wife?'

'What can you mean?'

Laura had a moment of panic that she might not know where she was going with all this but she took the bull by the horns and hoped for the best. 'You must know Venetia's daughter Angel is under the impression that you yourself had a hand in it.'

'Angela was very fond of her aunt. I have been forgiving her for her sinful accusations and putting them down to misguided grief.'

He sounded convincing. 'But have you ever thought that while she may be mistaken about your involvement, there may be some truth in what she says but that she's got the wrong person?'

'Oh my, I am left speechless.' Sir Repton slumped further onto the floor.

'Try to think back Repton.' Laura pulled him up and sat him on the bed. 'Was there anything that gave you cause for suspicion?' She sat down beside him and waited as his brows knitted in concentration.

'There was one thing that did puzzle me.' He turned to her. 'You see Matilda had her makeup on.'

'In the bath?'

Sir Repton nodded. 'It was something of a mess by the time Canon Frank and I pulled her out, but the mascara was waterproof.'

'Could she have forgotten to take it off the night before?'

'Not that much lipstick and I feel I would have noticed the false eyelashes at breakfast. Although come to think of it she only briefly turned to me from her writing desk when she told me off for finishing all the prunes.'

'Did she often wear false eyelashes?'

'Not since the sixties but Cheryl admitted she had found some and given them to her. She said my wife was suffering from low self-esteem.'

Had Cheryl played some kind of cruel joke on her? Laura felt suddenly sorry for Matilda.

'It was an act of kindness,' Sir Repton continued. 'Yes, that's all it was.' He stopped and thought for a moment. 'But through this small act, did Cheryl inadvertently become the catalyst that motivated Rosalind to implicate Cheryl in the heinous act of fatally submerging Matilda?' He put his hands to his head. 'Was it jealousy of Cheryl, my wife's bountiful purveyor of female accoutrements? Oh, irony of ironies... just like Millais' poor tragic Ophelia!'

Wrinkled senior citizen, caked in makeup... toeless... dispatched in bath by female apparition? And the comparison to the Pre-Raphaelite portrait of the young Danish noblewoman was laughable, but had the great actor won the day again? Laura kept her thoughts to herself. She refrained from positing the theory that had sprung to mind, that in fact, it was Cheryl who was the ghost.

Chapter thirteen

Laura returned to Wellworth Lawns in time to join Venetia for dinner. Her friend's concentration was sporadic, but Laura persisted with the story as they waited for Mimi to bring the starter.

'Matilda was plainly in the process of getting up. She had had her bath but the water was still in the tub. Cheryl pushed her in after she had applied her makeup for the day.'

'But wouldn't she be dressed? I thought you said she was naked.'

'This sounding most interesting,' Mimi said, as she placed bowls of soup down in front of them before carrying on to the next table.

'Perhaps she was in a dressing gown,' Laura said. 'Why didn't I ask about a dressing gown? It could be a vital clue.' This toing and froing of ideas in her head was like windscreen wipers going full tilt in a snow storm. 'Oh, I don't know, perhaps the person removed the dressing gown after they had drowned her.' she said. 'It's not impossible is it?'

'Of course not, in fact I remember a case on *CSI* once. The man abducted the girl outside a nightclub. Then they went back to her flat and he raped and killed her.'

'Good grief Venetia.'

'Then early the next day before any one was up, he got her dressed and left her sitting at a bus stop.' Venetia held a spoonful of the thin consommé in her shaky hand. 'She could have been there for hours what with rigor mortis but the fact was it was a very windy day and she fell off the bench.' Venetia slurped her soup. 'They're awfully badly designed those bus stop benches. I don't know why they haven't asked Wayne Hemmingway to come up with some better ones.'

Laura waited while Mimi came and took the bowls away and replaced them with the main course before continuing the conversation.

'Really Venetia, the stuff you watch – but now I think about it, Matilda could easily have still been in her towel. But then again when did Canon Frank Holliday appear in the bathroom? I must talk to him.'

'This is all too much for me, Laura,' Venetia said.

'He positively encourages Repton's hysteria. But why? And where was Sir Repton all this time?' Laura felt the windscreen wipers going again. 'And what was most pertinent was that Cheryl and the Canon appeared to know each other,' she continued. 'They were having some sort of private conversation while we waited for the ambulance.' She paused and stared at the chicken slice on her plate. 'Too much for you?' She looked at Venetia, then back to her plate. 'But there's hardly anything of it; is Alfredo putting us on reduced rations for some reason?'

'I meant all this information and all these people,' Venetia said.

Mimi came round with roast potatoes. 'You wanting?' she asked, dishing one out onto Laura's plate before turning to Venetia.

'What's going on, Mimi?' Laura said. 'I normally have at least three.'

'I so sorry Ladyship, I hearing Mr. Parrott, he say Alfredo, them old things eating way too much. You got to cut it down or they getting obesity.'

'Mr. Parrott said that?'

'He say obesity very dangerous. Leading many times to serious infections. Here you going.' Mimi put another potato on each of their plates.

'As I was saying,' Laura sliced into a potato.

'About obesity?'

'No. About Cheryl and the Canon. I think I will pay him a visit.'

Laura rang the hospital the next morning and was told the Canon had not yet been discharged, so she set out for Woldham General. She left Parker in the car and paid for a ticket before tramping down the endless corridors in search of the correct ward.

Finally she found him. He was lying on the bed, one trouser leg still neatly pressed to the ankle. The other had been cut off Laura noticed, ruing the waste of good cloth, exposing a pink kneecap and blue plastic splint out of which his toenails poked, like miniature dinosaur teeth.

'Most kind of you to visit,' he said, resting his tattered copy of the Bible on his chest. 'Have a seat.'

Laura didn't have time to see what particular text he was reading but judging by the way the book was opened, she guessed it was Old Testament. 'Reacquainting yourself with the miracles?' she asked.

He snapped the volume shut, and put it next to the water jug on the table beside him before easing himself up into a sitting position. 'I expect you've come about the séance,' he said, pulling out the pillow behind him and repositioning it.

Laura felt the proximity of the chair beside the bed was too close for comfort. She pushed it further away with the back of her legs as she sat down. 'Sir Repton needs to shake off these delusions of his, not have them compounded.'

'I was only trying to help.'

'Well, I'm afraid I don't believe you did.' Laura watched as the Canon's eyebrows sank like two synchronised burrowing moles into the bridge of his nose.

'Has he been to visit you?' she asked.

'Not yet, but as it happens I've been discharged. I shall be returning home this afternoon.'

'Will you be able to look after yourself?'

The eyebrows resurrected themselves. 'Since my dear lady wife passed away – some years ago now – I have learned to fend for myself. Anyway it's only a fracture. I'm only still here because the doctor wanted to check my pacemaker and I shall be able to get around with this.' He waved a crutch propped up beside the bed.

'Have you booked a taxi? I could drop you off myself, if you like. Where is it exactly that you live?' Who knew what clues his domestic arrangements might throw up. Cramped accommodation that could be alleviated by a move to more commodious and genteel surroundings; Laura imagined the Canon continuously hunched in a Victorian Almshouse.

'Most thoughtful of you. I'm only on Campden Road, but as a matter of fact Ch... Mrs Varley is coming to collect me.'

'Cheryl?' Laura hoped her voice contained the right level of mild disinterest.

'Yes, I've known Cheryl for some years. Before she took up her position at Mount Cod, she used to do the odd job around the place for me, darning, that sort of thing. It was she who introduced me to Sir Repton and Lady Matilda. Dear Lady Matilda, such a tragic end.'

'It was you that found her was it not?'

'I found her room empty. The bathroom door was open... I thought... sadly I was too late.'

'But why were you in her room? And why was she alone?'

'She would often call upon me to give spiritual guidance during her illness. Often was the time I managed to pull her from the abyss of agnosticism. Take the risk in God, for to be sure, He took the ultimate risk in delivering mankind, I extolled her. And I'm sure Cheryl would have been about. But Lady Matilda was in many ways capable of looking after herself. Talking of which I'd better have a practice at getting up. I don't want to keep Cheryl waiting.'

Canon Frank swung his trousered leg over the side of the bed. Then, cradling the other above the knee with two hands, he gave a grunt and eased it down so that his foot reached the floor. 'Between you and I,' he said, looking round to check the other patients were not listening. 'Cheryl is most concerned about Sir Repton.' His penetrating gaze disconcerted Laura.

'Sir Repton, Why?'

'Those twins girls. She says they are taking over the place behind Sir Repton's back. Things are going missing.'

'What things?'

'Well all the old gilt ballroom chairs for example were replaced with plastic ones. But where are the originals? And more disturbingly, one of them was upstairs with Lady Willowby, and later Cheryl overheard them talking about euthanasia. She didn't like to mention it, but...'

'What?' From the corner of her eye, Laura could see a figure approaching pushing an empty wheelchair.

'She believes they killed their own grandmother...'

'Wotcha Frank. You ready?' Cheryl called out, and, as she neared, 'Oh, it's you Mrs Boxford.'

The Canon did not attempt to correct Cheryl.

'Well, come on then, I've only got parking for half an hour.'

Canon Frank stood up. He picked up his Bible in one hand and sat down in the wheelchair.

'I'm sorry our meeting was so brief,' he said to Laura. 'Do give me a call sometime. Now I think we should find a nurse. I wouldn't want them to think I'd been abducted.' He winked at Cheryl.

'You are a one, Frank,' Cheryl said, dumping the Canon's overnight bag and the crutch onto his lap.

She must have brought his things in for him last night, Laura thought, as she left them at the nurses' station and walked out of the hospital to the car park. As she reached her car she could see Parker standing up at the passenger window barking at a woman getting out of a car in the next bay. He didn't hear her open the driver's door.

'Do be quiet,' she said and he slunk back down onto the seat and stared at her contritely.

'What d'you think?' she asked, switching on the engine and edging out of the space. 'Canon Frank changed the subject pretty fast from being in Matilda's bathroom to laying blame of some sort on those girls. Do you think the wedding planners are ripping off old Repton?' She tapped the steering wheel as they waited for the car park barrier. 'Perhaps Matilda knew?' She put the car in gear, her foot pressing down on the clutch. 'Or are Cheryl and the Canon in it together; covering their backs by laying a trail of blame elsewhere? She gripped the handbrake. 'And what on earth was his comment about Tam and Pom killing their grandmother all about?' Laura watched as the barrier rose and juddered to a vertical halt. It reminded her of an old-fashioned level crossing. The ideas in her head were like the train shooting past. She could only hope she knew where the next station was. 'Parker,' she said. 'I think it's time we called on our friends Strudel and Jervis again.'

Chapter fourteen

Laura was still thinking about her encounter with the Canon as she turned into the driveway at Wellworth Lawns and then took the turning that led to Mulberry Close. She parked outside Strudel's bungalow, walked up the path and pressed the bell. Bing bong it chimed and a few seconds later, Strudel held open the door. 'Come in, come in,' she called out, as Parker jumped up at her legs.

'Oh, you naughty young man,' she said, brushing down the calves of her green, leotard-enveloped body. 'Lucky I am leggings in. But this is most fortuitous timing. Jervis and I were just thinking of you. We have a little problem with Gladys Freemantle.'

'What kind of problem?' Laura followed Strudel into the sitting room where Jervis was sitting in front of the computer. 'Councillor Gilman's received negative feedback again. He's too forward by half,' he said, scrolling down the screen. 'We'll have to cancel his date with Gladys.'

'I'm not so sure.' Strudel polished her nails on her chest. 'It might be just the thing – a taste of her own medicine.'

'Has Gladys joined Ancient Eros? I thought she was wedded to widowhood,' Laura said.

'She's changed her tune all right.' Jervis turned to face Laura, his highly polished dancing shoes making little pas de deux on the carpet as he swivelled the chair. 'Dramatically.' His eyes widened as he nodded in confirmation.

'What has she done?' Laura asked.

'We are sending her on a date with the old bank manager

in Woldham; a gentle soul and keen arborealist. But she is terrifying him with her cleavage.'

'Oh dear, Gladys is normally so modest But now I think about it, she was rather forward with Sir Repton.'

'She told me she is taking pine bark extract for her libido,' Strudel said.

'That's a new one on me. I thought a bar or two of dark chocolate did the trick.'

'She's plainly got the dosage wrong. Came at him like a...'

'This is enough Jervis.' Strudel wagged a finger at him and turned back to Laura. 'I am thinking a little word from you would not go amiss?'

Laura said she'd talk to Gladys. It was a situation she felt she could handle well and she was reminded of when she was a prefect at her convent school and one of the junior girls in her dorm had got a crush on the chaplain. The girl had started to cry of course but Laura had told her to buck up and get a guinea pig like the rest of them.

'But tell us,' Strudel continued. 'How is the case of the late Lady Willowby progressing?'

'I was hoping you'd ask. How do you fancy a trip to Mount Cod?'

Laura gave them a brief outline of the séance, her hospital visit to see Canon Frank and what Cheryl had told him about Tam and Pom.

'So the housekeeper's out of the frame?' Jervis said.

'Not necessarily. This is just a new avenue that needs exploring and I need your help.'

'So you think the two girls might be involved? Fair play.' Jervis swivelled back to face the computer. 'I haven't found out much about State of the Union I'm afraid. Only one of our couples who have subsequently married had heard of them.'

'What did they say?' Laura asked.

'They were told that they would have to take out an extra

life insurance policy on account of being over ninety. They emailed me a copy of the confirmation letter. The cheque had to be written out to Robert Hanley Jones personally. I need to do a bit of digging on him; Companies House should shed some light. Should have done it earlier really.'

'That certainly doesn't sound right... Positive ageism, I don't think that's legal,' Laura said.

'True, but there were various issues. Potential dangers relating to bridal trains for wheelchair users in public spaces; proximity of bridesmaids and pageboys to ECG machines; visually impaired cutting of the cake; not to mention the throwing of the bouquet – a bride in Belgium managed to give some chap on crutches behind her conjunctivitis. The subsequent enquiry identified genetically modified gladioli.'

'Gladioli in a bouquet?' Strudel huffed.

'Absurd I know. But our couple were up against a whole raft of EU health and safety directives. In the end it was all too expensive so they decided on a family skiing trip to Aspen, Colorado.'

'Too silly at their age,' Strudel said. 'Frostbite is a big problem if you are with low blood pressure and it must be treacherous keeping to the piste with macular degeneration.'

'Well, I've had a different idea about checking out the State of the Union set up,' Laura said. 'How about Ancient Eros offering them a business proposition? You suggest your oldies don't want a dinner dance when they get married. Breakfast is the way forward; so much easier on the digestion. The potential couple do the registry office in the afternoon, have dinner in a pub, then go on to stay the night at Mount Cod. The next morning, their friends join them for a jolly good fry up by way of a celebration.'

'Sounds like an absolute winner,' Jervis said.

Strudel agreed. 'I am seeing the invitations now. Eros in his spectacles in front of a plate of eggs sunny side up.'

'I thought I'd arrange for you to meet Tam and Pom,'

Laura continued. 'You could sell it as "Full English Union". Put like that they couldn't fail to see the significance. In fact they'll probably offer to buy you out.'

'This we will not be allowing,' Strudel protested.

'Steady my love, this is all a pretence isn't it Laura?'

'Oh yes, all you are going to do is meet the girls and give me your opinion on them. I'll square the rest of it with Repton. We'll tell them he's agreed for you to test drive the sleeping arrangements. That way you can tell me what you think about him and the housekeeper too. Who knows what we might dig up if we are all there together.'

'Staying the night at Mount Cod, but what about the ghost?' Strudel gave a little shudder. 'I am not so much liking this plan Laura.'

'The serving wench is pure fiction, a figment of Repton's febrile imagination, or it's Cheryl in disguise.'

'If you are sure, I suppose it will do no harm,' Jervis conceded. 'But don't arrange it for midweek. Strudel and I are on a new regime; Detox Wednesday's and I'd prefer to have a hip flask with me all the same.'

As Laura walked back to the main house in search of Gladys she found herself vaguely disturbed by the concept of an alcohol free day of the week and wondered sadly if she should take a leaf out of their book. Luckily she didn't have much time to dwell on it as she saw her friend sitting in the lounge.

Gladys was poring over a large glossy book.

'Come and look. It's trees of the world,' she said. 'I'm thinking of a horse chestnut.'

'What for?' Laura asked.

'My memorial. I'll have to get permission of course. D'you think your grand-daughter would ask her husband if it would be possible to plant a tree?'

'Victoria ask Vince?'

'Yes, I thought somewhere in the parkland behind the

bungalows would be good. It's a substantial beast, the horse chestnut.'

'It sounds a lovely idea Gladys, but what's brought this on? You're not thinking of leaving us are you?'

'It comes to us all in the end. I had a conversation with Mr. Parrott that convinced me that there is no such thing as an afterlife. "Believe me Mrs Freemantle", he said. "When the lights go out, there's no big man with a beard up there flicking the switch of a supernatural generator ready to hot wire you to the pearly gates." It's not an image one forgets easily.'

'Harsh, I'd say.'

'I'd rather the truth.'

'You mean you've lost your faith? Why don't you have a word with Reverend Mulcaster?'

'I haven't time for all of that. I've got too much to do while I'm still here. You know what John Betjeman said was the thing he most regretted?'

'What?'

'That he hadn't had enough sex in his life. Well I for one am not going to fall into that trap. I've got these marvellous pills…'

'Don't tell me… Pine bark?'

'How did you know?'

'How did you?'

'I was researching the French pine tree on the computer in Woldham library and then it linked up to a site selling the pills. As it happened the French pine would have been most unsuitable. The horse chestnut is truly a more memorable specimen.'

'So you've had positive results from the pills?' Laura asked.

'I'm on the verge of a breakthrough with a retired bank manager. He's hot to trot. I believe I'll have him in the sack any day now.'

Laura was wondering how to counter this information when they heard a loud clanging noise. 'Whatever was that?'

'No idea,' Gladys said picking up her book. She began turning the pages. 'Fastigiate oak... Now there's a possibility.'

Laura walked out into the hall and watched as Reggie Hawkesmore slid down the stairs on his bottom.

'Lift's still out of order,' he said. 'Had to throw my Zimmer frame down.'

'Excellent idea.' Laura passed him and continued on up to her room. What was the manager up to? He should have had the lift fixed by now. She apologised to Parker for the lateness of the hour as she made his dinner then watched as he chased the last few bobbles round the dish and licked his lips before going to his water bowl. Then she went to call Sir Repton.

She told him about the wedding breakfast plan and the added benefit of enlisting Strudel and Jervis to give their opinion on the wedding planners – she'd have to park the idea of Cheryl and Canon Frank's involvement for the meantime.

'Tam and Pom, surely not?' There was a momentary silence. 'But then again, why not? You are so astute Laura. Why, they could just as easily have been the impetus for Rosalind's actions.'

There was nothing else to do but ignore this. 'What did Matilda think of them?' Laura asked.

'On the whole...' There was another pause.

'Exactly,' Laura said briskly. 'She would doubtless have agreed that the balance of power was getting out of hand. We must address the problem. I've a feeling there's more to them than meets the eye.'

'Are your friends detectives?'

'Strudel and Jervis? Of course not. Don't you remember you met them at Wellworth Lawns. They run Ancient Eros, the dating agency and I have a ruse that they have agreed to be party to.' Laura explained further about the wedding breakfast package. 'All you have to do is pretend you've seen a business opportunity for Ancient Eros to team up with State of the Union. Ancient Eros is high profile in the dating game. I suppose it's no surprise that all these lonely old people want to find a mate.' She was thinking not so much of Repton, as of her own heady romance with the Brigadier. 'Many of their clients end up getting married.' She remembered wistfully the moment he had got down on one knee and held open the box containing the heartfelt ring for her.

'Perhaps I should join. Are you a member?' Sir Repton said, bringing her back to reality.

'Of course not.' He was definitely looking for a replacement. 'Now let's get back to the bed and breakfast plan.'

'Eight wild boars roasted whole…'

Laura couldn't be certain it was a quote but she could ascertain no significance to the mention of such a surfeit of pork. 'I don't think we need go that far, and I'd like Strudel and Jervis to stay the night,' she said.

'At Mount Cod?'

'I think Bridlington, the room Venetia was in, could be made perfectly acceptable and the lift is handy. Then it's straight through Grimsby – which could act as a dressing room – to the bathroom – a veritable master suite in fact. The bedsprings on Venetia's bed seemed in good order and I don't suppose many of Ancient Eros' clients go in for much frisky behaviour. They're none of them particularly agile. Who is at our age, apart from the Dalai Lama?' Laura laughed. 'If Cheryl could be persuaded to do the sheets,' she continued. 'I think it might be a nice little bonus for the Mount Cod kitty. You could even side line those two girls, so the money for the accommodation went directly to Part of the Union. They could just provide the morning entertainment.'

'You mean it might really happen?'

'Who knows?'

'This sounds promising. I've just had the bill for the repair to the ceiling… But what if Rosalind didn't like it?'

The irritant had returned. 'Repton, let's try and put this ghost business to rest, literally. I mean the séance really proved nothing, as I explained after Canon Frank's accident. You must try to move on. That's why I'm suggesting Ancient Eros. I will arrange a meeting for Strudel and Jervis with Tam and Pom. We must flush them out. I bet you Matilda knew the ballroom chairs were missing.'

Chapter fifteen

As Jervis drove them to Mount Cod one afternoon some days later – Strudel in the back and Laura with Parker on her lap in the front – they discussed Gladys Freemantle's sexual awakening.

'The bank manager won't go near her again, I'll tell you that much for free,' Jervis said, swinging the old Mercedes Estate out onto the main road. Behind them a car hooted its horn and overtook. 'That was a damn fool thing to do,' Jervis huffed.

'Please my love, you must be stopping at a T-junction. But of Gladys, I am thinking of that man we were having very bad feedback of the wandering hands; much worse than Councillor Gilman. This might put her off.'

Laura turned to Strudel. 'Wandering hands?'

'Harvey Elgood, she means.' Jervis tapped the automatic gear stick and inadvertently sent it into manual. 'Sells the poppies outside Tesco for Remembrance Day.' As their speed dropped, he realised and pushed it back.

'You can't possibly send Gladys out with him,' Laura said. 'He used to come round to the house rattling his tin. The old letch terrified Nanny.' Laura was reminded of the dear little Tiggy-winklesque figure who had run the house with a rod of iron for so many years.

'But it's the only way of stopping Gladys making a complete fool of herself.' Jervis mounted the verge as a lorry passed them in the opposite direction. 'Now remind me again, what's the procedure if Sir Repton's serving wench comes corridor creeping in the middle of the night?'

'You are keeping your hands to yourself,' Strudel screeched.

'Christ Strudel, only joking.' Jervis righted the car as it veered over the double white lines and headed up the hill. 'You nearly gave me a heart attack.'

'Slow down Jervis. We've plenty of time before the meeting.' Laura clutched Parker to her chest. 'Remember, you have to be my eyes and ears with the wedding planners. I need your judgement.'

'Don't you worry Laura. I intend to take a direct approach. Ask them if they think a post-breakfast assisted suicide package might be a goer for clients who are terminally ill.'

'Jervis, you are being ridiculous.'

'I only said it because of what Laura told us about them euthanising their grandmother, but perhaps it is a step too far.'

Laura watched the cyclist ahead of them crouch lower over the handlebars as the incline steepened. 'But we should try and eliminate them from the picture as soon as possible if there's no truth in that part of Cheryl Varley's allegation.' She glanced in the wing mirror. The Lycra-clad figure appeared to be unharmed as he clambered out of the ditch.

'Leave it to me,' Jervis said.

While Strudel and Jervis had their meeting, Laura and Sir Repton waited in the sitting room. 'I've had a new idea about the accommodation,' Sir Repton said. 'Bridlington's no good; it doesn't have a bell. It was fine for Matilda; you could hear her shouting all over the house if she wanted something'.

Before Laura had a chance to ask where he meant, there was a knock on the door and a man in dirty white dungarees came in. 'Can you come and inspect the new cistern, your lordship,' he said.

As Repton followed the plumber out, Laura picked up an old copy of *The Thespian Times*. Matilda shouting? She was flicking through the pages musing on this snippet of information when Jervis poked his head round the door.

'There you are,' he said.

Strudel pushed past him into the room waving a brochure. 'I am writing down some prices as they are talking.' She handed Laura a glossy brochure with a photograph of a young couple in all their wedding finery. They were embracing on the edge of the parapet roof of Mount Cod.

'How did they get up there?' Laura asked. 'It looks dangerous to me.'

'Photoshopped I'd say. Those girls are pretty hot on safety. Said they'd been thinking about embracing an older clientele since they'd had some enquiries recently.' Jervis nodded confidentially. 'We didn't get to the insurance I'm afraid. The one called Tam led the meeting. She wants to talk to someone called Robbie about the possibility of active marketing. Said this chap has a company that specialises in that sort of thing.'

'Repton hasn't mentioned anyone called Robbie.'

'Well I've got the name of the company.' Jervis took a scrap of paper out of his pocket. 'It's called "Promoco". I'll do a bit of digging when we get back home.'

'I am asking them about Sir Repton's dearly departed wife,' Strudel said. 'They are most fond of her it seems, but…'

'But what?' Laura asked.

'Yes, that was a tad disturbing.' Jervis turned back to the open doorway. 'But shhh, here comes Sir Repton.'

'All well with the new loo?' Laura asked, as he tottered in.

'It's a splendid gadget. You merely wave your hand over the button and, whoosh. Pity about the other fitments in that room… But how was your tour, young man?' he said, turning to Jervis.

'Top rate facility you've got here. Those girls know what they're doing.' Jervis patted Sir Repton on the back.

'Jervis,' Strudel gasped, as Sir Repton lurched forward and grabbed the back of a chair with one hand.

'You young'uns don't know your own strength,' he puffed. 'I'll just catch my breath and then we'll go and inspect Flamborough Head. I think it will be most suitable for Ancient Eros guests and I'm excited to see your reaction.'

They set off into the hall and up the stairs.

'The guests can still use the lift in here if necessary.' Sir Repton gestured into the open door of Bridlington, as Parker and Sybil Thorndike bounded along playfully growling at each other. They walked on past Grimsby down the corridor to a set of double doors at the end – the ones that Laura had assumed led to Sir Repton's private quarters.

He pushed the doors open to reveal a chintz suite. The shades in the floral motif were of muted browns and orange.

'Most sumptuous,' Strudel said.

'Top hole,' Jervis agreed.

Laura was not so sure. The room had a similarity to the master bedroom on the royal yacht *Britannia*; slightly more comfortable, but only just. As she swung her gaze over the furnishings she pinpointed the problem. The valance on the bed was marginally too short and there had been a certain skimping on the box pleats. The headboard lacked the depth of padding that would have brought it up to scratch.

'This is looking most inviting,' Strudel said, sitting down on the low-slung bed.

Laura continued assessing the room. Three fabric drops and interlining would have made the curtains so much better. She walked over to the window. Still, the carpet was Wilton and the view over the formal garden would divert the eye from the faded blue striped wallpaper. But weren't there two statues either side of the yew hedge before?

'It's two singles put together,' Sir Repton pointed out. 'A double can be inconvenient after a certain age, but I can always get one in, if you prefer?'

'Twin beds is the way forward for our clients. Would you not agree, my love?' Jervis said.

'They can still have hanky-panky if they so desire.' Strudel patted the bedding and winked at Jervis.

'Let me show you the sanitary arrangements.'

They followed Sir Repton into the bathroom. The solid chrome fittings of the 1950s eau de nil suite glistened in the vast space. A huge mirror in an ebony frame hung above the basin, beside which a heated rail was stocked with well-plumped towels. Laura was impressed until she noticed a rickety looking wheelchair that had been placed beside the bidet. It had obviously taken a few knocks and some of the spokes of one wheel were bent out of shape.

'That will have to go,' she said, pointing at it.

'I am finding the bidet a most indispensable object for the washing of the small things.'

'Strudel my love, I don't think Sir Repton needs to know about your laundry habits.'

'I didn't mean the bidet. I meant the wheelchair,' Laura said.

'I thought it might give the impression of thoughtfulness,' Sir Repton said.

'Perhaps you could put some cushions on it,' Jervis suggested.

'I wouldn't want to be reminded of my age or impending infirmities on my wedding night,' Laura said. 'Fold it up, or better, put it out of sight in a cupboard.'

As Sir Repton wheeled it out of the room, Strudel whispered to Laura, 'you are being something of unkindness, he is only trying to help. And anyway it is not really mattering is it?'

'No, I'm with Laura,' Jervis said. 'We need to get the thing right.'

'What?' Strudel asked. 'Are we really going to be bringing clients here?'

'Why not?' Laura said.

'I agree. Bit of promotion on the Ancient Eros website and I'd say they'll be flocking in. Now I'm getting pretty hungry, I don't know about anyone else. Laura, d'you think we should find out about the catering?'

Strudel patted her washboard stomach. 'Oh yes, I too am starving.' She turned to Laura. 'Are you not also?'

'But you didn't finish what you were saying downstairs; what did Tam and Pom say about Matilda?' Laura whispered.

But before Strudel had time to answer, they heard the creak of floorboards and Sir Repton shuffled back in. 'I've parked it in the airing cupboard,' he said.

Chapter sixteen

Sir Repton confirmed that there was nothing to eat at Mount Cod.

'I'm afraid Cheryl has, unexpectedly had to drive Lance to see a chiropractor in London,' he explained.

'Couldn't he have taken the train?' Laura asked.

'He said it would be quicker in the Land Rover and they could be back in time for him to put the chickens away. Matilda was always most insistent he follow a strict code of avian husbandry. There's nothing a chicken likes less than a lack of routine.'

'I tell you what,' Jervis said. 'I'll drive us to the Hare and Hounds in Chipping Codswold for dinner.'

They arrived and found a table beside the inglenook fireplace in the restaurant area. The waitress brought them menus and while they waited for the wine they decided unanimously to have the lamb shanks.

'I could probably have found some leftover canapés from the wedding last weekend. Quite often the girls leave a plate or two of smoked salmon in the kitchen,' Sir Repton said, as they waited for the food to arrive. 'But then again I'm never sure about seafood if it's been left out overnight. It must have something to do with my late father-in-law, Sidney Laverack.' Sir Repton twisted the stem of his wine glass. 'Many was the flounder brought home unsold from market and turned into fishcakes by his wife that I had to endure during my courting days. Sidney didn't care for wastage. '

'I tend to agree. I'm not one for leftovers,' Jervis said. 'Mind you Strudel's rollmops last forever. But I gathered from Tam and Pom, that they are thinking of expanding their catering operation.'

Sir Repton looked up. 'Are they?'

'A new kitchen is what they are saying.' Strudel adjusted the diaphanous turquoise scarf she was wearing round her neck.

'They said it was absurd the caterers took half the profit,' Jervis continued. 'Sound business sense I'd say.'

Sir Repton took a sip of wine. 'Did they say where this new kitchen was to be situated?'

'Really Repton,' Laura said. 'You mean you don't know? We'll talk to them tomorrow, together. You must have these things set out clearly.'

'Good idea,' Sir Repton said. 'That's enough talking shop for one evening. Now tell me more about Ancient Eros. Is there a joining fee?'

The lamb arrived and the conversation turned to the topic of food in general. They discussed Mr. Parrott's cutbacks at Wellworth Lawns.

'Eddie hasn't always been so frugal,' Sir Repton said. 'I remember Matilda had to admonish him for pandering to the cast who wanted bacon butties in the interval during a run of *Les Misérables*. Mind you it was an interminable production.'

'Well, we're making up for it now,' Laura said.

'It is indeed most delicious'. Strudel looked at the substantial bare bone on her plate.

'Helluva beast.' Jervis stifled a burp.

Laura was trying to remember what exactly the shank was when she heard the click of the front door latch. She turned to see who had arrived and to her amazement she saw that it was Angel Hobbs. She appeared to be on some sort of a mission, her Mohican hair brushing the low beams as she strode across the flagstones towards the bar, but then she noticed them.

'Uncle Repton,' she said. 'What are you doing here?'

Sir Repton gripped the arms of his chair.

'I should have warned you about this place,' she continued. 'I've had them in my sights for some time now.'

'Whatever for?' Laura asked.

'Passing meat products off. Hand reared on our own farm, my foot. I mean did they tell you what that actually was?' Angel pointed at the bone on Strudel's plate.

'Lamb shank?' Sir Repton offered meekly.

'Lamb shank?' Angel said. 'That's no more lamb shank than I'm a flying buttress.'

'All done?' said the waitress, who had appeared to collect the empty plates.

"I'll have that.' Angel picked up the bone from Strudel's plate and brandishing it, she marched towards the kitchen, pushing through the swing door.

'You've cooked the mule, you bastard,' she bellowed.

The door swung shut.

The waitress carrying the plates pushed the door open with her foot.

'The mule's in it's stable if you'd bothered to look,' they heard a man shout.

As the door swung open again they heard the man call out, 'One of you, come here and give us a hand with this fat dyke.'

'Would you like to see the sweets?' the waitress asked, handing out menus and ignoring the clatter of pans followed by a screech and, 'Oww, my hair,' that came from the kitchen.

Then they heard another door slam.

'We've got a nice sticky toffee pudding on,' the waitress said.

Laura turned to her fellow guests who shook their heads. 'I think we've probably had enough, thank you,' she said.

The kitchen door swung open again and the manager hurried behind the bar. 'Sorry about that,' he said. 'Wouldn't be surprised if she'd escaped from Woldham psychiatric unit. Anyone for an Irish coffee on the house?'

Sir Repton said he'd take him up on the offer but without the coffee or the cream. They all agreed and ordered whiskies.

'My niece can be something of an embarrassment at times,' Sir Repton admitted, finally relaxing his grip on the arms of his chair.

'Bit of a firebrand you've got there to be sure,' Jervis said, looking at the bill. 'Shall we go Dutch?'

It was after midnight by the time they left the pub but Jervis' driving was distinctly improved by his alcoholic intake and he drove with considerable caution back to Mount Cod. He parked the car in the driveway and they walked up to the front door.

From within the house Laura could hear Parker howling. She had left him there contentedly curled up in a basket with Sybil Thorndike, but now he sounded most distressed. As Sir Repton opened the front door Parker bolted out. He must have eaten something, Laura thought, as he bounded down the steps past her and disappeared into the moonless night. She dropped her bag in the hall and ran after him.

Stopping where the gravel met the grass at the edge of the driveway she called him. A wind had got up and her words were carried away. She began to walk around the side of the house until she reached the covered walkway that led to the wedding guest's entrance.

It was now pitch black and she decided to go back and get the torch from her bag. She felt her way, one hand on the brickwork, her hair blowing into her face, until she reached the thick round column on one side of the porch. She edged her way up the steps. The front door was wide open but for some reason there were no lights on inside. As she walked in, she could hear a sort of choking sound. She fumbled around for the light switch and eventually found it.

The hall was of a sudden illuminated.

Laura's gaze was immediately drawn to the sight of Strudel on her knees. She had somehow managed to get her scarf wrapped round a wooden ball on the bannister rail of the staircase.

'Help me,' Strudel croaked. 'I am strangulating.' She pulled desperately at the scarf.

Laura rushed round Sir Repton who was lying face down on the marble floor and past Jervis who was sitting next to him, his legs splayed; eyes wide open; short greying hair standing up at an angle like and elderly Tintin.

'What on earth were you doing?' Laura said, disentangling Strudel. 'Why didn't you turn on the lights?'

'The darkness was part of the evil happening,' Strudel cried. 'A whirlwind of the Devil swept me off my feet. It was terrible.'

'The wind must have caused a temporary power cut,' Laura said.

'Paranormal Twister, more like. Damned unnerving. I've never known such blackness.' Jervis' normally steady voice was tinged with what Laura realised was something akin to fear.

Sir Repton lifted his head. 'You cataracts and hurricanes, spout. My god, she nearly did for us.' He sank back to the floor.

Laura looked around for damage but everything appeared to be in order bar a few leaves that had eddied into one corner. 'The wind must have gusted in through the open front door,' she said. 'I could feel it gathering strength when I was searching for Parker. It must have taken you all by surprise.'

At that moment Parker trotted in, sniffed the air and took himself off into the sitting room.

'I am assuring you Laura,' Strudel said, rubbing her neck. 'This was not a mere blowing of the wind.'

Jervis ran his fingers through his hair. 'Never in my life...'

Sir Repton lifted his head again. 'The wench has brought this upon us,' he said, before his head sank to the floor again.

Laura went to him, rolled him over and tapped him smartly on the cheek. His eyes flickered open. 'Jervis come and help,' she said.

Jervis managed to get him to his feet, and with Sir Repton leaning heavily on his shoulder, took him up to bed.

Laura, likewise, hauled Strudel into the sitting room, where the dogs lay fast asleep curled up on a sofa together. She laid Strudel down on its pair and sat down beside her.

'It must have been the doubles you ended up drinking,' Laura said. 'Whisky after wine's asking for trouble at our age.' As Strudel sobbed, Laura recalled a monumental hangover she had incurred on a skiing trip in Switzerland. She and her first husband Tony had been caught in a blizzard in Gstaad with a charming young commercials director named Hugo. My what a night that was. The three of them, high as kites under the soft feathery duvet in his chalet. It was the first time Laura had encountered the Swiss style of bedding. She could feel her cheeks glow as she wondered what the Brigadier would have thought.

Beside her, Strudel gave another little sob. 'This was not of alcoholic effect, it was a supernatural occurrence of that I am sure. I was in fear for my life... Oh where is Jervis?'

'Calm yourself Strudel, you'll only make matters worse if you become hysterical. I'm sure Jervis won't be many minutes. Then he can take you up and you'll be right as rain in the morning.' Laura patted Strudel's wrist. 'But while you are here, you still haven't told me what it was Tam and Pom said about Matilda?'

'I am feeling faint...' Strudel put one arm over her eyes.

'Strudel, wake up. What did they say?'

'They are saying...'

Laura moved Strudel's arm and leaned in close to her. 'What did they say?'

Strudel sighed. 'One of them is saying, they are finding Matilda is in her wheelchair, after her operation…' Strudel's eyes flickered.

'Where?' Laura demanded.

'At the top of the stairs with Sir Repton.' It was Jervis. 'They gave us the distinct impression it was after a particularly gruesome row between Sir Repton and his wife and if they had not been passing, there could have been a nasty accident.'

Chapter seventeen

Laura's thoughts were in turmoil again. It was like someone was pulling the lever of a one-armed bandit and every
time the windows juddered to a halt, her suspects faces
appeared. She had decided that she would try out the bed in
Bridlington, as it was meant to be more comfortable. It was,
but still she was unable to sleep.

She stroked Parker under the covers. 'Have I made
another error of judgment? Bing; up came Repton's face.
Could it be him after all, or has Strudel got the wrong end
of the stick?' Both Strudel and Jervis had acted in a wildly
histrionic fashion to what can only have been, at most, she
thought, a freak of nature.

She closed her eyes again. The house was quiet, but, bing;
up came Tam and Pom. Were they telling the truth in their
implication against Sir Repton? She rolled onto her side.
Bing; or was Cheryl nearer the mark? She turned again.
Perhaps it was just wishful thinking on the twins' behalf
that Matilda should be in her wheelchair at the top of the
stairs, precariously close to a successful mercy killing?

Hearing the soft rustle of the old satin eiderdown as it
slipped onto the floor, she sat up, reached for the bedside
light and leaned over the side of the bed to retrieve it. She
was now wide-awake. Perhaps the Brigadier's diary would
act as a soporific? She had brought 1959 with her – the
Brigadier must have been 30. She picked a random page in
January. 'Malaria better. Arrived in Nairobi. No Mao Mao
action to report. Pleasant accommodation. Met Thesiger in

the bar and decided to accompany him up country. Cleaned service revolver after dinner.'

Laura followed his progress as she turned the pages, weeks of nothing more than game figures as he shot his way down to the border of Tanzania. Fancy killing all those creatures, but then that's what they did back then, she thought before finally falling asleep somewhere between the fourth rhinoceros and the thirty-third impala.

Parker woke her the next morning as he burrowed up the bed, his warm wet nose snuffling into her elbow. She lifted the bedclothes slightly. An endearing smell of rotten dog breath greeted her. He crawled up and licked her on the chin.

'No breakfast in bed here, I'm afraid,' she said.

She got dressed and took him downstairs. Sybil Thorndike came trotting out of the sitting room to join them. Unlocking the back door, she took them for a short walk.

When she returned to the kitchen Jervis and Strudel were sitting at the table, drinking tea.

'I am no longer staying here more than one minute,' Strudel said. 'Jervis will pack the car and we will be making the scarper as my Ronny would have said.' She took a tissue from her pocket and blew her nose. 'My nerves are in tatters. There is no way we can bring our clients here.'

'Out of the question,' Jervis agreed. 'Shall I bring your bag down for you, Laura?'

Laura thought for a moment. 'Actually, I might stay on a day or two.' She watched as Strudel raised her eyebrows in astonishment.

Sir Repton was overcome with emotion that Laura had decided not to abandon ship.

'I completely understand your friends wanting to leave this godless place,' he said, as they stood in the drive and waved Strudel and Jervis goodbye. 'But you are like a mighty oak, supporting me in my hour of need.'

'No need to be overdramatic, let's take a stroll shall we? Was Matilda fond of gardening?'

'Oh yes. Voracious. That is, before her toe incapacitated her. But even then I would wheel her round the garden if the weather was clement and she took great pleasure in seeing that Lance or Kevin did things to her satisfaction.'

They walked around the side of the house and took the path leading down towards the bog garden.

'Matilda was a stickler for double digging,' Sir Repton continued. 'Just a pity Lance's spade should have slipped that morning planting leeks down by the lodge.'

Laura turned to him. 'What happened?'

'Unavoidable, even Matilda had to agree that the ground was far too wet. Lance had his weight on the spade but he lost his balance as the sod broke loose and fell, inadvertently knocking Matilda into the mire.' Sir Repton sighed. 'She was not best pleased when I referred to the old thespian adage "break a leg" when I visited her in hospital.'

He bent down to pick up a bit of branch that had fallen on the path. 'Poor Lance...' He swung his arm and bowled the stick overarm frowning in dissatisfaction as it landed at his feet. 'Still he got over it and it's probably fortuitous in the long run that Kevin and Robert's other men run the show now.'

As they walked on, Laura wondered what it was that Lance had "got over"; an earful from Matilda, no doubt. Her thoughts were interrupted as they passed a large newly dug hole where she remembered from her last visit, a rather fine specimen shrub had stood. Why would it have been moved? She racked her brains trying to think what the Brigadier might have said. "The cloven hoof of the wildebeest marks the way," was one of his favourite idioms, but what use was bush talk now? – Except for not beating about it.

'Are you short of money, Repton?' she asked.

He was taken aback. 'Whatever makes you say that?'

'Well, it looks to me like you are selling things off.'

'What do you mean?'

'The Cornus Kousa that was planted here, for example; you can get good money for a plant that size.' Laura pointed at the hole in the ground. 'Don't tell me Tam and Pom have had it moved, I mean it's hardly creating a vista for another photo opportunity.'

Sir Repton stared at the hole. 'This is a tragedy,' he said. 'Matilda and I planted it on the occasion of my nomination for the award for best actor in 1982. But why would Tam and Pom want to move it?'

'You must ask them. Right now. It's not just the plant; remember the bench and the pagoda?' He hadn't denied being short of money but then his genuine grief at the missing shrub was evident. Laura was concentrating hard as she accompanied him back to the house. It must be those two girls, and whatever they were up to Matilda must have found out. That's why they had tried to lay the blame at Repton's door by suggesting to Strudel and Jervis – two perfect strangers – that there were safety issues with Matilda.

They reached the stable yard and Laura left him outside the State of the Union office.

'Don't mince your words, Repton,' she said taking the dogs and heading for the back door.

'Lance, come here right now!' Cheryl shouted from the kitchen.

'It's me actually,' Laura said.

'Mrs Boxford, what are you doing here? I thought you'd all gone.'

'Apparently not, I do hope it is not an inconvenience to you.'

'Not really, I'm off out but Repton didn't tell me, so you'll have to look after yourselves. There's bread and cheese and, hold on...' She reached into a cupboard above the toaster and pulled out a can of pilchards. 'You can heat these up. Full of omega 3; just what you need at your age. Put them on toast for your tea, if you're staying.' She glanced up at the kitchen clock. 'Would you look at that; I must run.' She handed Laura the can and walked out.

Sir Repton reappeared as Laura was inspecting the cupboard. It was stuffed full of cans, all pilchards; there must have been at least twenty.

'Kevin the gardener told Robert the plant was diseased,' Sir Repton said. 'He spotted a canker on the bark that he believes to be caused by the deadly Belgian Cornus beetle. The girls organised for it to be taken to the Ministry of Horticulture's special quarantine facility for further investigation.'

'But what about the bench and the pagoda?'

'I forgot to ask about the other things, but really they are unimportant. I'm afraid the matter of the shrub took up my thoughts; Matilda was most indignant when I didn't get the best actor award. I simply can't get it out of my head.'

They spent much of the afternoon attempting an inventory of the garden statuary and other ornaments. The two statues in the formal garden that Laura had noticed from the Flamborough bedroom window were indeed missing.

'Perhaps they were a safety hazard.' Repton studied the bare patches in the yew hedge where they had stood. 'They've probably been moved somewhere out of harm's way.'

'So why don't Robert or the girls keep you informed of these things?' As Laura rounded the pond, she peered into the depths. Water boatmen hovered over the lilies and a dragonfly swooped down. 'Are there carp in here?' She bent down and scooped aside a lump of weed.

'I expect the heron got them,' Sir Repton said.

They walked on through an avenue of wisteria. It had finished flowering and the long tendrils waved about in the breeze.

'Shouldn't there be something at the end?' Laura asked. 'Something to draw the eye.'

Sir Repton plodded on.

'Think Repton.'

'I can't remember. We once had a bronze of Falstaff... But actually I'm feeling rather parched. Do you care for sparkling elderflower? I know we've got some because I ordered it myself. We could take it and sit in the summerhouse. Perhaps we'll find him there.'

They walked back round to the front of the house and collected a bottle from a larder opposite the kitchen that Laura had not noticed before. Taking it and some glasses they went out of the back door into the stable yard and from there, through a small wooden door next to the State of the Union office – again it was something Laura had missed on first inspection. The summerhouse was attached to the back of the wall like an elaborate lean-to with French windows. Inside and array of rattan chairs with faded striped cushions gave it a dilapidated air. Falstaff was not in residence and there was no sign of two more urns that Sir Repton admitted had stood on the now empty plinths either side of the glass doors.

He dusted off some dead flies from a low table, put down the glasses and opened the bottle. 'Perhaps Matilda sold him,' he suggested.

Laura watched the bubbles that popped to the surface as he filled her glass. 'Was she likely to do that without telling you?' she asked.

'Matilda could be fickle in her taste... Capricious you could say. I wonder if the notices for *Henry IV* were not to her liking when I played him last. 1984 in Regent's Park, I believe.'

It was obvious Laura had reached a dead end. The ever-increasing list of Matilda's character defects were not helping and Laura wondered if they were even living at Mount Cod in 1984?

She changed the subject and they discussing the vagaries of dog psychology as Parker and Sybil Thorndike dug up a molehill in the grass outside.

Laura felt more positive after they had eaten. 'While a pilchard on toast is a perfectly respectable supper dish,' she said, putting the plates in the dishwasher. 'It is still a fact that Cheryl is not fulfilling her job description.'

'I felt the claret complemented them well,' Sir Repton offered. 'Let's open another bottle and sit in front of the fire. Even in midsummer, this house has always been cold. Do you play cribbage?'

'No, and don't try avoiding the issue Repton. This may seem harsh but I get the feeling all these people you are surrounded by are taking advantage of you. Are you sure you are being straight with me?'

'I am afraid it is the inherent weakness of my character, but at least my wine merchant is reliable.'

Back to square one. His self-depreciation only added to Laura's lack of direction as she tried to make head or tail of him. She sighed. 'Come on then, I don't suppose it will do us much harm to have another glass.'

Sir Repton turned out to be a ferocious cribbage player and combined with her own competitive streak, it was nearly midnight before Laura got to bed. She lay back on the pillows, again reviewing the situation. She was no nearer solving the mystery of Matilda's death. The wheelchair at the top of the stairs really amounted to nothing. It was all hearsay. The Ancient Eros plan had been a complete waste of time and Strudel and Jervis had been sucked into Repton's neurotic delusions. Cheryl had done a bunk again but that did not imply anything more than her normal unreliable nature. Laura sighed and picked up the Brigadier's diary. He was on the shores of Lake Tanganyika and had fallen in with a group of village elders, when she fell asleep.

Some time later, she opened her eyes and realised she had left the bedside light on. But it was not this that had awoken her. She had heard a thud. She waited. All was quiet. She turned off the light and closed her eyes, thinking of the Brigadier making camp on the shores of the lake. She dozed. But there it was again. A thud. She listened. Footsteps on the landing. One heavier than the other – a sort of clump, thud, clump, thud went right past her door. Her heart started pumping. 'Don't be silly,' she whispered to herself. 'It must be Repton... but what was he doing at this time of night? She prayed it wasn't a misguided attempt at corridor creeping, but no, it couldn't be, he hadn't got a club foot.' She waited and then she heard the turning of the door handle to Grimsby.

Right next door.

She pulled the bedclothes up around her chin. Silence. And then the click of the door closing and the clump, thud, but this time followed by a sort of gentle rustling sound.

Laura lay wide-eyed. Had Repton mentioned the serving wench having some sort of limb deformity? I must be going mad, she thought, putting her hand down the bed and grabbing Parker by the collar. She pulled him up and held him tight to her chest. It calmed her. But who was it? She thought of Repton, paralysed with fright in his own bed. 'Well Parker, I think I'd better find out.'

She clambered out of bed, put on the old pink kimono she used as a dressing gown and her sheepskin slippers then picked up the torch she had taken out of her bag in case there was another power cut. Looking quickly round the room for a likely blunt instrument, her eyes alighted upon a tortoiseshell hand mirror on the top of the dressing table. 'That's no use,' she said, rueing not packing the Brigadier's truncheon as she threw the bedclothes over Parker. She badly wanted his company, but, in her furtiveness, he would be sure to start whining and give her away. She shut the door behind her and shone the torch up and down the passage.

Nothing. All was quiet.

She tiptoed to the head of the stairs and as she did so she heard the soft swoosh of the green baize door leading off the hall. Gripping the bannister rail tight, she descended and crept across the hall. She pushed open the door and held onto the handle on the other side so that it closed silently behind her. She stood still and turned off the torch. Her heart was thumping loudly in her ears, but above it she could detect – very faint – the sound of voices.

She inched forward down the servant's corridor. The voices grew louder. She stopped outside one of the closed doors next to the kitchen. It was coming from inside. She put one ear to the door. She knew that voice... Forces, Cromarty... This was no malformed wanton strumpet plotting a manifestation... Dogger Bank... It was the shipping forecast on Radio Four.

She turned the handle, flung open the door and flashed the torch. On the floor in the middle of the room a mass of eiderdown and bedspread wobbled.

'Lady Boxford,' Canon Frank Holliday sat up with a start from the camp bed.

He attempted to get up but fell back.

'Excuse me one moment. I've overinflated it.' He attempted to rise again but lost his balance as the air filled mattress bounced him sideways and he was left grappling on the floor in his striped flannel pyjamas.

'Won't be a tick.' He managed to get himself on all fours. Laura could see the sole of one bare foot and the blue plastic splint on the other. 'I can explain,' he said, pulling himself up with the aid of an old leather armchair. He turned to face her. 'There we are.'

He brushed back his white hair with his hands and then with a deft stroke of his index finger, attended to his eyebrows that were attempting take-off.

'Does Repton know you are here?' Laura asked.

'I have not acquainted him with the fact, no. You see...

Well this is embarrassing. I tripped over a step yesterday. I had to call Cheryl for assistance.'

'So why are you here?'

'She thought I needed looking after, silly really, but there is only one bedroom in her apartment and she said it was more convenient for me to stay here and then ask Lance to drive me home on the morrow. I really didn't want to bother Sir Repton with the minutiae of it all.'

'So what were you doing upstairs?'

'I found that I was short of bedding. For some reason Cheryl had forgotten my duvet you see. I had no idea that you were staying… Cheryl must have omitted to mention the fact. Did I disturb you?'

'Of course you did. And you didn't seem to have much of a problem climbing the stairs. I'm surprised you didn't take the lift to Bridlington. That really would have given me a fright.'

'But I've never taken the lift. It was in Cheryl's bedroom.'

'Cheryl slept in Bridlington next to Matilda?'

'Lady Willowby slept badly. She would often call for Cheryl in the early hours.'

'Talking of the early hours, what time is it?'

Canon Frank looked at his watch and gasped. 'It's nearly three, you must go back to bed.' He took her arm and escorted her, limping, to the door.

'I certainly must. And we will see about all this in the morning.'

'You'll find the way alright won't you?' Canon Frank continued, ushering her out.

'Of course I will. I found my way here didn't I?'

'May I say how fetching you look in that dressing gown, Lady Boxford,' he said, as Laura set off down the passage, torch in hand.

She made her way back upstairs trying to work out what she had just witnessed. Had he been flirting with her too? But more to the point was Cheryl really his guardian angel and why had he not gone into what had been her room, Bridlington but had taken the eiderdown and bedspread from Matilda's bed in Grimsby, the room beyond?'

Chapter eighteen

There was no sign of Canon Frank or Cheryl the next morning. The inflatable bed was nowhere to be seen but the bedding from Grimsby was neatly folded on the leather chair.

'How very sad, and to be so cold at two in the morning.' Sir Repton said, as they made their way to the kitchen.

'How do you know it was two o'clock?'

'My bedside clock. I heard noises. I thought…'

'You thought it was the ghost didn't you?'

'My nerves were frayed. I took a pill. But I had no idea the Canon was in such dire circumstances,' Sir Repton continued hastily. 'I shall have to extend a formal invitation to him. We can't have him hiding down here in the servants quarters when there are perfectly good bedrooms upstairs.'

While he made them a cup of tea and some toast, Laura laid the table.

'I think you should have words with Cheryl. I mean what did she think she was doing?' Laura took the lid off a pot of honey she had found in a cupboard.

'Her kindness was possibly misplaced…' Sir Repton sat down with the tea.

'Kindness? No, I'm sure she will have had some ulterior motive.' Laura heard the back door slam and moments later Cheryl appeared in the doorway holding a bag of shopping.

'I hope you're here for lunch,' she said to Laura. 'I've been and got a nice quiche from the Co-op. The chickens are still on strike or I might have made one myself.'

'A treat.' Sir Repton clapped his hands together.

Laura looked at him, then to Cheryl, then back to Sir Repton. 'Well, if you are not going to say anything, Repton, I am.' She turned back to Cheryl. 'Are you going to tell us what's going on?'

'I've been to the shops that's what's going on.'

'And what about Canon Frank?'

'Canon Frank?'

Sir Repton intervened. 'Lady Boxford only means it was too kind of you to bring the Canon here to stay on account of his ankle.'

'Frank, here?'

'Lady Boxford found him last night. You had forgotten to bring his duvet and he had to go all the way upstairs to borrow an eiderdown, poor man. Has Lance taken him back home in the Land Rover?'

'Yes. No, what am I talking about, Lance took me to the shops and we dropped him home at the same time.' Cheryl dumped the bag on the table. 'Well, I must get on. The quiche should take about twenty minutes. I might do a spot of dusting later if I've time.'

Laura sighed in frustration. Repton had singlehandedly wrecked any chance of finding out what was going on. She noticed a filmy skin on her now cold tea and took it to the sink.

As she was standing by the Aga waiting for the kettle to re-boil, Tam and Pom came in, one marching ahead of the other. If it weren't for their loose auburn tresses, they could have been a couple of traffic wardens in their crisp white shirts and black suits.

'Morning all,' said the first one, leading the way. 'Just to say, don't worry if you see some diggers arriving; we're going to temporarily flood the bog garden for a couple who want a Venetian style wedding.'

'A boating theme?' Sir Repton rubbed his chin. 'But I am uncertain as to the quality of clay in the bog garden.'

Laura stirred in some milk to the new cup of tea. 'Isn't lack of clay a prerequisite to the successful bog garden?'

The first girl flashed her a momentary glower. 'I said temporarily flood it.'

'We thought when they said gondolas, they meant a fairground attraction.' The second girl giggled. 'We've had to totally cancel the amusement ride we'd booked.'

'The diggers aren't much more expensive, the water's free and we've managed to borrow some rowing boats from Woldham Fishing Club,' the first girl continued in a curt vein.

'Jez Abelson's doing a *Showboat* tribute act,' said her sister. 'It's a bit random but the bride really went for the idea. It'll be so cool, you're going to love it, Repton.'

The first girl frowned. 'From a distance obviously, anyhow the bride's family are loaded so that's all that really matters.'

The two girls returned to their office.

'Jerome Kern – how I love all those old Broadway musicals but now I think about it Laura, I believe you are right. I don't think there is any clay content in the soil of the bog garden.' Sir Repton took the quiche out of the shopping bag and opened up the packaging.

They stared at the jaundiced tart. The egg mix was wrinkling away from the sides of the pastry and a few small lumps of bacon protruded like rocks in a barren desert.

'I think I must get back to Wellworth Lawns. I'll call a taxi, if you don't mind,' Laura said. The quiche aside, she felt momentarily guilty at abandoning Sir Repton, but Canon Frank and Cheryl's behaviour was too suspicious to be ignored. Had Canon Frank some sort of hold over Cheryl and not the other way round? Was the séance all part of a bigger scheme to derail the already weakened Repton. She must find out if there was something in the Canon's past that could provide a clue.

Chapter nineteen

As the front door to Wellworth Lawns swung open, Laura pulled Parker to her side, snapping the lock on his extendible lead to avoid bumping into Gladys Freemantle who came striding out. She was wearing a tight black minidress. The magenta paper peony crushed in the V of the low neckline was doing little to conceal her ample bosom. As if this was not bad enough, she had on her feet a pair of trainers.

'Gladys. Wherever are you off to dressed like that?'

'Morning Laura. No time to stop and chat I'm afraid. I'm going to be late meeting my new friend Harvey for lunch. I have high hopes of a bonk later this afternoon. Wish me luck.' She adjusted one bra strap. 'Oh, and by the way, don't let Mr. Parrott catch you. He's very busy trying to bump up numbers for his lecture this evening on the benefits of suttee.'

'Suttee?'

'Yes, you know, Hindu women were big on throwing themselves on their husband's funeral pyre. One way of getting rid of a surfeit of widows, I suppose. See you soon.' Gladys waved and bounded down the steps.

Laura walked on into the hall and was about to go upstairs when the manager's office door opened and Edward Parrott scuttled out.

'I'm glad I've caught you, Lady Boxford.'

'I don't believe in self-immolation, if you were about to ask me to your seminar.' Laura noticed with alarm that he was wearing socks and sandals with his suit.

'The point I am trying to get across is one of financial impact.' The manager straightened his worn silk tie. 'In this day and age when all you, "skiers" have spent your kid's inheritance it is important to think of the cost of a full on funeral service. The hygienic aspect of a pyre is also worthy of consideration. The elimination of miasma is key. We must at all costs avoid...' His red nose quivered. 'Innn... fection' He sneezed into a handkerchief and then inspected the contents. 'Christ.'

'How very thoughtful of you and talking of the Lord,' Laura said, sidestepping the issue. 'Is Reverend Mulcaster about? He's often here in the mornings.'

'As a matter of fact he's administering extreme unction to Mrs Reynolds.'

'Again?'

'She was most insistent.'

'I'm sure she won't mind my joining in. Hope the lecture goes well.' Laura continued up the stairs. She left Parker in her room and went down the passage to Topsy Reynolds' room.

Topsy had been at Wellworth Lawns ever since it had opened and Laura knew her well. She had turned to the Catholic Church some months ago, having decided erroneously, that she was close to death. But she couldn't quite break her ties with Reverend Mulcaster.

Keen to keep his flock in the fold, and of an ecumenical nature, he was happy to oblige.

Laura knocked and opened the door.

Reverend Mulcaster looked up from the game of racing demon he was playing with Topsy on a tray on her bed. 'Hello Lady Boxford,' he said, with a jovial smile.

'Darling how lovely to see you.' Topsy lowered her cards unaware that Reverend Mulcaster was taking a sidelong peek at her hand. 'As you can see a miracle has occurred and I am once more back from the brink.'

There was a knock on the door and Mimi came in

carrying another tray. 'I bringing lunchtime special,' she said.

'Reverend Mulcaster, if you would be so good...' Topsy indicated to their makeshift card table. 'I've suddenly regained my appetite. What have you brought me Mimi?'

'Alfredo making you eggs white omelette. Mr. Parrott he now saying yellow eggs is bad for bedridden.'

'Well pass it here – I may just have to get up for tea.'

'I'll leave you to it,' Reverend Mulcaster said, placing the card-strewn tray on top of Topsy's chest of drawers. 'Pity, I felt a bit of a winning streak coming on.'

As Mimi placed the tray of food on Topsy's lap, Laura and Reverend Mulcaster took their leave.

'Could I have a word with you in private?' Laura said and suggested he join her for a drink. 'Glass of sherry sound in order?'

'One for the road sounds a splendid idea.' Reverend Mulcaster followed her back down the passage.

'I'll come straight to the point,' Laura said, as they sat in her sitting room, schooners in hand. 'What d'you know of Canon Frank Holliday?'

'Frank?' Reverend Mulcaster tossed a handful of peanuts into his mouth then wiped his hand on the sleeve of his old anorak. 'He used to be bloody useful at Christmas – Midnight Mass and all that,' he swallowed. 'Helped with the communion. But I haven't seen much of him since I axed the service – I saw no reason why I should stay up in the middle of the night to fulfil the expectations of a lot of drunken heathens...' Reverend Mulcaster took a healthy slug of sherry. '... waiting for Father Christmas to arrive with mountains of unnecessary computer games.'

'He's not originally from round here though, is he?'

'I believe he was head of St Botolph's College in Hammersmith for some years. He and his late wife moved here when he retired.'

'St Botolph's?' The name had a familiar ring to it.

Reverend Mulcaster looked at his watch.

'I mustn't keep you,' Laura said. 'But one more thing before you go…'

'Anything to assist.'

'Gladys Freemantle; if you had a moment. Edward Parrott has filled her head with "doubts". He really is most unhelpful at times.'

'We mustn't let that fester. Fester… the very word would sent poor Edward into a spin, he's becoming a touch obsessive I've noticed. But back to Gladys, I'll make a point of seeing her next time I'm over. Tomorrow probably, Mrs Reynolds is bound to have a relapse.'

Laura let the Reverend out. 'St Botolph's in Hammersmith,' she said, patting Parker. 'Now I remember.'

She could hear the sound of the TV blaring before she had even opened Venetia's door.

Her friend was glued to *Homes Under the Hammer*.

'I like to imagine how the previous owner was murdered,' she said, not shifting her gaze. 'After all, what other reason would a house be put up for auction. I expect that's how Mount Cod will end up. Hard to shift the smell of homicide.'

'This would make a very nice child's bedroom,' the presenter was saying.

'It's a coalhole you fool,' Venetia huffed.

'I thought you'd changed your mind about Matilda?' Laura said.

'Well it's you that's been confusing me. I'll bet you anything that coalhole's where they found the body. Poor child, that's all I can say.'

'So you've given up on the painted furniture?' Laura had to shout.

'What?'

'Turn it down.'

'Hold on it's just getting to the exciting part.'

Laura sat and waited while a property developer bought the damp basement.

'I think he did it don't you? I expect we'll find him in prison next week.' As the news came on, Venetia poked the remote at the TV. The volume decreased. 'So where have you been?' she asked.

Laura could see Venetia's eyes glaze over as she related the story of her stay at Mount Cod. 'I couldn't believe both Jervis and Strudel could be taken in by a mere gust of wind,' she concluded.

Venetia gave her a beady look. 'Jervis is no fool,' she said. 'Mind you, did you know there was a twister in Wolverhampton recently? It was on the news and that reminds me, Mimi should be hear any time now with my sandwich. I simply can't miss *Countdown*.' She began to flick through the channels.

'I won't keep you then,' Laura said. 'Just one question though, I wonder if you remember where Angel did her training for the priesthood.'

'St Botolph's, you mean?'

'I thought as much.'

'I remember visiting her there before she had some exam or other. I bought her a very nice little china owl from a charity shop in Hammersmith for good luck. She was most ungrateful.'

'Where did you say Angel was living now?'

'In Woldham above The Old Bakehouse in Sheep Street. Talking of baking…' Venetia flicked channels.

Laura felt a frisson of excitement at this new information, but for now Angel Hobbs would have to wait. She needed to make peace with Strudel. She went to fetch Parker and they walked over to the bungalows and knocked on Strudel and Jervis' door.

Strudel opened it an inch. 'We are in the middle of our

lunch,' she said, and was about to close it when Jervis called out behind her.

'Is that Laura? Strudel, let her in for goodness sake.'

Strudel opened the door and stood like a ramrod to one side.

'I'm so sorry,' Laura said. 'I'd completely lost track of time.'

'Come in,' Jervis said. 'You must join us in our humble repast.'

Laura followed Jervis into the kitchen as he pulled out a chair for her and laid an extra place. They chatted as they ate the meal and Laura noticed with relief that Strudel was beginning to defrost.

Jervis folded a piece of white sliced bread and butter in his fingers. 'I'm afraid I've been a bit tied up and I haven't had a chance to look into the marketing company and the man Robbie the twins were talking about.'

'Jervis and I have been most preoccupied with important matters pertaining to Ancient Eros,' Strudel said.

'It must be so much work for you both.' Perhaps not entirely at room temperature, Laura thought.

'We've been making some small but significant changes to the website,' Jervis said. 'You've no idea how a gender tick box can simplify registration. No more Jo and Andy cock-ups.'

'Sam's and Jesse's a thing of the past.' Strudel conceded.

'Oh yes, gender's not something you can take lightly these days; according to Google there are fifty-four different ways of being a man or woman. Have another herring.' Jervis passed Laura the plate.

'Mind-boggling.' This was a heavy price to pay for reconciliation, Laura thought as, out of politeness she put another fish on her plate. She patted her chest to quell the air playing like a tuba half way up her throat. 'But to change the subject, I've been thinking,' she swallowed hard. 'About the evening at Mount Cod.'

'Do not be reminding me.' Strudel turned her face away from Laura.

'I'm afraid Strudel's sleep pattern has been fractured as a consequence,' Jervis said.

'I have been entirely winkless.'

'I think,' Laura said. 'That what happened was a minor tornado. They're not uncommon in this area, Venetia reminded me of it.'

'I can assure you that it was nothing so simple as a freak weather occurrence,' Jervis said. 'And what's more, while it's impossible to prove, the body of evidence is stacked in favour of a supernatural occurrence. There are pages and pages of it on the internet.'

'But...' So that's what he'd been spending his time on.

'No Laura, it's well documented. The wronged wife – well maybe not wronged wife but wronged one way or another. This is what I believe has caused the serving wench to come back with such a vengeance.'

'But I've got a new lead that I'm going to see Angel Hobbs about.'

'Well, report back by all means,' Jervis said. 'But I think Rosalind is the supernatural mouthpiece of Matilda and it is to this end that you should be directing your energy.'

Chapter twenty

'Who'd have thought Jervis could be so misguided?' Laura said to Parker as she turned into Sheep Street. This dissention in the ranks made her nervous. 'Still, onwards and upwards,' she continued, 'Let's see what Angel can bring to the party.' She drew up on the opposite side of the road to The Old Bakehouse. It was a building she remembered well from years gone by when, as a special treat after taking her son Henry to the dentist further down the street, she had brought him here for an iced bun. Invariably he was still suffering from the effects of the anaesthetic – he always seemed to need a filling – and the dear boy was inclined to dribble.

Now she could see it had been turned into a charity shop, and a rather fine tweed suit was on display in the window. With a pang, she thought of the Brigadier. When she had asked Edward Parrott if he could dispose of her late fiancé's clothes, she had not stopped to ask him where he might take them. She sighed and got out of the car leaving Parker standing up at the steering wheel yapping.

As she crossed the road, she assessed the rest of the building. A buddleia was sprouting from the roof gutter and the tiles clung on under a thick layer of moss. At the shabby windows, tatty half-opened curtains hung limply. She walked to the side of the shop and pressed the single doorbell to the flat above.

She heard the sash of a window open above her and took a couple of steps back. She looked up as Angel stuck her head out.

'What d'you want?'

'Angel, it's me, Laura Boxford.'

'It's not about the pub is it? I may have been misinformed about that mule.'

'No.'

Laura watched as Angel hit her head on the window frame and tiny pieces of paint fell like dandruff onto the pavement.

'Fuck... Hang on I'll have to let you in.'

Laura went back to the door and waited. She heard Angel's thundering footsteps and then the door opened.

'Mind the cats,' Angel said, as Laura followed her up the rickety stairs and into the dim living area.

The room was filled with felines of all shapes and sizes – Laura counted eight but they were coming and going between the jumble of furniture. A huge mangy white one jumped onto the table, hissed at a doddering Siamese that fell silently to the floor and began licking a dirty plate.

'Who's this then?'

Laura turned to see where the voice had come from. In one corner, on a dirty beige velour chair, lolled a man whose elongated angular proportions reminded Laura of a Giacometti sculpture. He appeared dangerously underfed.

'This is Mum's mate Lady Boxford,' Angel said, picking up the white cat and kissing it.

'Please to meet you Lady Boxford.' The man rose and held out one heavily tattooed hand. 'Rich.'

'I wouldn't say that,' Laura said.

'That's his name. Rich, short for Richard,' Angel said. 'So what was it you were wanting?'

'I was wondering...' Laura looked from Angel to Rich and back again.

'Don't mind him. He's just come in from a night patrol in Basingstoke. Found a shocking case of neglect.'

'Chronic laminitis, I've never seen a donkey hobble like it.' Rich shook his head and slumped back down in the chair.

'Such a pity when people don't know how to look after animals,' Laura said.

'Shocking.' Angel and Rich said in unison.

'I'm sorry there's not more that can be done,' Laura ventured.

'Cash donation?' Rich said. 'Then I should get going. Had a call from a mate in Adlestrop. Some banker's wife's got one as a companion for a kid's pony. He says he's pretty sure its depressed.'

'Adlestrop?' Laura got out her purse and handed Rich ten pounds.

'Cruelty crosses the rich-poor divide Lady Boxford.' Rich headed for the door. 'Cheers.'

They heard him going down the stairs and the front door slammed.

'Now that we are alone, Angel,' Laura said. 'I'd like to talk to you about Canon Frank Holliday, I'm aware of your feelings towards him but did you ever come across him when you were at St Botolph's in Hammersmith? I'm keen to find out something of his past.'

'Sure I came up against him there. The problem was he just didn't get transgendering.'

Transgendering was not a subject that could be glossed over in a sentence or two and Laura was glad Jervis had briefed her so recently.

Angel made them a cup of tea.

'I've plateaued at the moment,' she said. 'I'm about 80% female today. But back then I was at least 60% male and it got in the way of the Canon's gospel teachings. The whole Judas Iscariot thing turned into a major issue. I told him it wasn't a betrayal of my sex, I was just gender queer.' Angel took a gulp from her mug. 'But why d'you want to know about him?'

'I met him at Mount Cod and I remember you saying you were worried about your uncle.'

'Who wouldn't be, but old Frank does a pretty good job at

covering up Repton's guilty secret. I mean whatever you say about Aunt Matilda being so ill and all that, Repton deliberately shortened her time on planet earth.' Angel gave a little shudder. 'Chilly for the time of year.' She picked up a handy tabby and shoved it up her voluminous black jumper. 'Mind you it suits Frank to have Repton in his pocket. The pity of it is that he doesn't use his influence over Repton to get rid of Cheryl, and Lance; that man gives me the creeps.'

'Lance?'

'Slimy so and so's knocking off Cheryl on the side if I'm not much mistaken. Body language; noticed it when I was last there.'

'You think they are having an affair?'

'Deffo and I reckon they've got their own agenda; Repton's cash. Mind you, every time I've tried to sting him for a quid or two for the animals, he claims he's skint.'

Laura noticed with distaste the heavy staining in the bottom of her mug. 'What about when your aunt was alive?'

'Aunt Matilda was ever so generous. Never saw a shortage then.'

'Really?'

'Oh yes, and she always made sure I was welcome. Before she got ill, I used to stay with them a lot. Then that Cheryl moved in and after her the wedding crowd...'

The conversation was halted as the cat popped its head out of the top of Angel's jumper and crawled onto the top of her head, its tail swaying down the side of her face. Angel's Mohican flattened to one side so that she looked like Davey Crockett in a stirring north-westerly. It must have dug its claws in. 'Ouch,' Angel cried. She flicked it off and got up from her chair.

'You've been a great help, thank you Angel,' Laura said. 'If there is anything I can do for you?'

'Now I think about it...' The chair creaked as Angel sat back down.

Laura was about to get out her purse again.

'You know about killing foxes don't you?' Angel said.

'Are you referring to fox-hunting?'

'Rich wants to set up a fund to re-home the old dogs that are past their sell by date.'

'Foxhounds?'

'Thinks they'd make great pets. He'd like to find a few to try out his realignment techniques on.'

'He might find that a tall order where cats are involved but I'm sure I could ask the old kennel huntsman, if he's still there.'

Angel leaned forward, her forehead visibly pulsating as three scratch marks oozed blood. 'Cool,' she said. 'Could you maybe arrange a visit?'

'I'll see what I can do. But talking of pets, do you happen to know what the Canon's pet cause was?'

'Canon Frank's not big on animals, you're right there. He fell out with Aunt Matilda about pets once or twice; Church dogma – or dog-less-ma. Eschatological sentimentality he called it. But she was hot on the final destination of the soul and according to her Yorick, well maybe not him, but that dachshund deffo would be sitting up there with her in heaven having a good old time barking its head off.' Angel picked up another passing cat and rocked it like a baby in her arms. 'Quite convinced she was and she sure could put the Canon in his place if she felt like it.'

This was a lot to take in but if pets did not feature in Canon Frank's creed, they cannot have been the 'cause' Repton had mentioned to which Matilda gave so generously. She rephrased her question. 'Were there any other areas of charity the Canon felt strongly about?'

'He had a thing with some kind of orphanage when he was at St Botolph's, I seem to remember,' Angel said. 'But I don't think Aunt Matilda would have gone for that. She always said she preferred dogs to humans. That was enough to drive old Frank nuts.'

Laura left Angel and returned to Mulberry Close; this new motive for the murder of Matilda was too compelling not to impart immediately to her friends. Laura felt confident as she waited for Strudel to finish making what she called her Bavarian-style egg mayonnaise. Strudel tipped half a dozen hard-boiled eggs from a bowl onto a wooden board on the kitchen work surface and took out a knife from the rack.

'I fully appreciate you and Jervis' belief about a ghost being Matilda's representative from beyond,' Laura said, pacing up and down beside her.

Strudel began chopping the eggs with swift staccato swishes, her little finger raised at an angle as the rest of her hand gripped the handle of the blade.

'But what if it was Canon Frank Holliday all along,' Laura continued as Strudel raised the knife and brought it down with a thud onto the board.

'Of course the ghost might still be part of it.' Laura watched as the tension in Strudel's fist relaxed.

'And what motive are you giving to this new gentleman suspect?' Strudel reverted to her dainty method of slicing.

Laura stopped her pacing. 'Religious differences.' She sat down and put her elbows on the kitchen table cupping her chin in her hands. 'It's a well-known fact that doctrinal argument can lead to violence. From what Angel said this looks increasingly probable, but I'm not sure how best to tackle him.' The smell of the eggs was getting irksome. 'Where's Jervis? Laura asked. He'll know what to do.'

'We will disturb him in a minute when he has finished responding on Facebook.' Strudel dolloped mayonnaise into a bowl and mixed in the eggs then added the already chopped raw onion and frankfurters to the dish. 'Harvey Elwood has posted something most unsettling. He says he did not sign up for sexual deviancy when agreeing to go out with Gladys.'

'Gladys in trouble again?' Laura was thinking Jervis might also be in trouble again. Indigestion looked inevitable.

'I'm afraid so.' Strudel put the egg mixture in the fridge.

'Oh dear, and I did hope Reverend Mulcaster would have a word with her,' Laura said. 'I'll have to go and see her myself.'

'Please do. We must be scotching this in its prime. Jervis is saying we will have to unsubscribe Gladys if she can't be controlled.'

'Come and see what I've found,' Jervis shouted from the sitting room. 'Robbie and Robert Hanley Jones are the same person.'

They hurried in as Jervis sat jiggling the computer mouse, his miniature glitter ball cuff link sparkling. 'And he's got quite a little empire of companies to his various names. Robbie Hanley, Bob Jones. '

'Not very inventive,' Laura said.

Jervis started typing with two fingers. 'Look here's his CV on LinkedIn. Harrow, then a disappointing third in politics from Leicester. It doesn't seem to have held him back though; a stint at acting school was obviously all he needed to get him going.'

'Well actually…' Laura told them what Repton had said about his acting career being cut short by Matilda.

'He's got a lot to thank her for by the looks of things,' Jervis said. 'At present, along with State of the Union and the marketing company Promoco, he and his aliases run some sort of import export business in the Ukraine that I can't make head or tail of but more importantly, a property investment company called "RHJ Associates", that runs a subsidiary called "RHJ Care Homes". Something doesn't smell right to me.'

'What is this Jervis?' Strudel said.

'There seems to be a connection between the wedding venues and the care homes.' Jervis tapped the side of his nose with one finger and Strudel sniffed her armpit.

'Care homes?' Laura paused.

Jervis typed in a different web address and scrolled

down. 'From the records it seems that State of the Union is by no means his biggest player. In fact it looks more like a recreational toy. The profits for State of the Union are small compared to the property company, and the care homes are catching up.'

'Jervis is the maestro of cross-checking, are you not my love?'

Jervis winked at Strudel then turned his attention back to Laura.

'But here's the thing. There's a property on the State of the Union books from a couple of years ago that now turns up in the RHJ property portfolio under the heading "pending planning". It's going to be turned into a care home.'

Laura's eyes widened as she took in the implications of Jervis' revelation.

'Mount Cod?'

'Just what I was thinking. They'd have to get Repton to sell up first,' Jervis said.

'They could frighten him into it.' With the aid of a fake ghost? Laura kept the idea to herself. 'And what about the planned kitchen extension?' she continued. 'Saying it was for the weddings but actually it would be perfect for a care home. All costing Repton money that would eventually benefit RHJ.'

'Run the place down. Keep profits to a minimum. Pile on the pressure. Yes, I see what you mean.' Jervis got up from his desk and stretched. 'I think this might be one for Vince Outhwaite's legal chappies to look into. They'll know all about their rivals in the care home sector. I need to do a bit more digging. Find out the circumstances of the sales. See if there are more places that might have been sold privately that had been used as wedding venues.'

'This is excellent, Jervis,' Laura said. For now, Canon Frank would have to wait. 'I think we're in business.'

Chapter twenty-one

Impatient though she was, Laura felt that she must wait for Jervis to get back to her with further information before she contacted her granddaughter. Victoria's husband Vince was not a man to trifle with. There was no point wasting his time until Jervis was sure of his facts. So in the meantime she kept her word and arranged for Angel to see the foxhounds.

The hunt kennels were situated just off the end of Woldham High Street down a short lane and, incongruously, next to a butcher's shop. It was about the only part of the town that had not been prey to developers and still backed onto open countryside. Laura waited in the sunshine at the appointed hour outside the gate to the kennel complex. She could see a pack of hounds standing up at the bars of their enclosure, tails wagging, tongues hanging out. As a man carrying a bucket of food arrived, they began to bark wildly. Parker, who had been standing quietly at Laura's feet, attempted to bolt back to the car. As there was no sign of Angel, Laura walked him back and deposited him on the front seat.

On her return, she could see two figures waiting.

'Wotcha, Lady Boxford.' Angel called out. She had made a great effort with her appearance and had put a flat cap over her Mohican. A waxed jacket and gumboots finished the look. Beside her stood Rich. To Laura's consternation, she saw that he was wearing the tweed suit from the charity shop window, a pair of white sock clearly visible above his trainers.

Laura greeted them and they went to find the kennel huntsman.

'Re-homing retired hounds?' he said, scratching his head with blood spattered hands. 'You wasn't thinking of having 'em indoors were you?'

Rich folded his arms and surveyed the baying dogs. 'We're still at the planning stage at the moment.'

'We've got some fundraising to do,' Angel said. 'What do you feed them?'

'Tripe mostly. Horsemeat if they're lucky.'

Angel fiddled with the zip of her jacket. 'Donkey?'

The kennel huntsman considered this.'D'you know, in all my years, I can't remember a single incident of a dead donkey being fed to hounds.'

Angel sighed with relief at the passing of a potential conflict of interest.

'Mind you we was once donated a llama.'

Angel winced.

'And I've heard tell of other exotic creatures. Old Lord Ramsbury used to keep a herd of zebra once upon a time.'

'We mustn't keep you on this lovely morning,' Laura said.

'If that's all you're wanting, I'd better get back to work. I haven't hosed down the bitches' yard yet. Smells pretty bad once the sun gets on it.'

Laura, Angel and Rich walked back to the High Street.

Angel was in high spirits. 'I see absolutely no reason why you can't housetrain a foxhound.'

'But which one? There are so many.' Laura wished she'd kept her mouth shut.

It was plainly a quandary that was vexing Rich. 'How many do you think were in that pen?'

'Twenty?' Angel offered.

'They were just the dogs.' Laura pointed out. 'And how many other hunts are there?'

'In England?' Angel asked.

'You mean Wales and Scotland too.' Rich rubbed his stubbled chin.

'I think you might find you've got quite a lot of funds to raise to realise your project, but I hope I've been of some help. My car is parked over there.' Laura pointed across the road.

'Thanks Lady B.' Angel held out her hand for a high-five.

Rich took the cue. 'Yeah, sure. Plenty to think about. Milton Keynes wasn't built in a day.'

Laura crossed the street and looked back as the pair walked on, apparently deep in conversation.

Driving back to Wellworth Lawns, she engaged with Parker about the plight of elderly foxhounds. 'I suppose it must be someone's job to shoot them...' Parker curled up tight on the seat beside her. 'Don't take it personally,' she said as she pulled up at the lights on the pedestrian crossing. 'But talking of shooting, we must drag Venetia away from the latest instalment of *CSI* and tell her about Angel's plans.

Venetia was not impressed by her daughter's charitable efforts.

'She is a very stupid girl and I really don't have time for her infantile behaviour. It's *Pointless*.'

'I don't know, animal welfare is important.'

'I mean it's *Pointless* on now.'

Laura said she'd come back later and take Venetia down to supper where she had arranged to meet Gladys.

As they rounded the corner into the dining room they heard a familiar yapping and from underneath a table Sybil Thorndike appeared. Parker rushed forward to greet his friend.

Sir Repton turned from where he was sitting with his back to them, opposite Gladys Freemantle. He gave a feeble wave as Laura and Venetia walked over to join them.

'Repton,' Venetia said. 'Whatever are you doing back here?'

'Oh woe is me, dear coz. The world is grown so bad...'

'Please try not to take it to heart.' Gladys reached across the table to stroke his hand. 'You see someone has stolen the eagles from the roof of Sir Repton's house.' There was a hint of hysteria in her voice.

'What are you talking about?' Venetia asked.

'Tam and Pom did say that they had certain reservations about the booking. We'd never had a big fat gypsy wedding before. They wanted photos from the parapet to post on Facebook.'

'Like in the brochure?' Laura asked.

'Yes, that's why the crane was ordered. The bride was too fat to get up the ladder to the roof.'

'Jervis said that sort of thing was photoshopped,' Laura said.

'The bride wanted photos of herself and the groom in the foreground with the caravans and horses that were gathered in the park below. It was as they were being hoisted up after the actual ceremony that someone noticed the eagles had gone. But as it stands we will never know if it was them; they were a charming family.' Sir Repton shook his head. 'Then the whole night was such a commotion – even with my earplugs and a substantial sleeping draught, I could hear it going on. It was past three in the morning when I last checked my alarm clock.'

'But surely someone would have seen four giant stone eagles being carted off?' Laura said.

'They took a Henry Moore from the Yorkshire Sculpture Park. I heard about it on *Antiques Roadshow*,' Venetia said.

'Inspector Sandfield admitted that he was stunned by the audacity.'

'Phil Sandfield?' Laura said. 'Stunned about sums him up. I wouldn't hold out much hope of finding the eagles with him in charge.'

Gladys stretched her arm across the table again. She clasped Sir Repton's hand in hers, squashing the white roll that he had just picked up. 'You must go higher up the chain of command.'

She let go and turned to Laura. 'If only the Brigadier was here, he'd have known someone in the SAS who could have helped.'

Sir Repton shook the bun from his palm and wiped his hand on a napkin. 'A forensic team has cordoned off the entire place. Today's wedding has been transferred to a barn near Northleach. The bride is distraught. Tam, or Pom say it's my responsibility and suggested I retire here to Wellworth Lawns for a spot of peace and quiet while they sort out the insurance.'

'It's the best thing that could have happened.' A look of unadulterated joy illuminated Gladys' craggy features.

Laura rang Strudel and Jervis.

'Most suspicious I'd say, Jervis said. 'You mentioned that other statuary had gone missing.'

'Yes.'

'Leave it with me. I must get to the bottom of Robert Hanley Jones's import–export company. He may be shipping antiquities via the Ukraine. Meanwhile I think it's time you called Victoria.'

Laura agreed and spoke to her granddaughter. Victoria said she would get Vince's trusty accountant, Bernard to look into RHJ Care Homes.

Over the next few days Laura waited and watched. She watched from Venetia's bedroom window; from the car park; from the lounge; from, well, almost every corner she watched as Gladys mounted her campaign to win Sir Repton's affections. Laura's theory that it was Sir Repton who was hellbent on a rich widow was scattered to the four winds; there could be no doubt that it was Gladys who was on the offensive.

Feeling out of sorts one morning, she ordered breakfast in bed. It was not that she was actually ill but staying in bed was the only way she could think of quelling her impatience.

Mimi waited as Laura closed the volume of the Brigadier's dairy she was reading and put it on her bedside table. 'You down dumps morning time Ladyship?' She placed the tray on Laura's lap. 'Not thinking poor old Brig again?'

Laura glanced back at the diary. He had been stuck in the village on the shores of Lake Tanganyika for a very long time. Almost two years in fact. Laura had always thought of him as such an active sort of person but his scant diary entries made little sense and spoke mostly of ceremonies that had taken place within the village. He was obviously highly revered as he made reference to feasts that were put on and the celebratory outfits that he wore. But she felt that there was something he was not telling. And then his handwriting became so poor... Perhaps he had contracted malaria?

'I have been thinking of him actually,' she said, as Mimi handed her the morning paper.

'Good thing Brig not here now for sure he losing temper time.'

'Why's that?'

'Mr. Parrott not allowing mobility scooters. '

'Why?' Laura pulled at a piece of croissant and Parker surfaced, pushing back the bedclothes beside her.

'Parkee!' Mimi stroked his head. 'He say them old things lazy. He is making my Tom put them all away in garage. Tom saying Mr. Parrott gone fitness bloody mad.'

Mimi said she'd come and collect the tray later and left Laura to her breakfast.

Laura gave Parker a piece of croissant. 'I shall have to call Victoria again. Edward Parrott is getting way above his station.'

She heard a knocking and Venetia popped her head

around the door. 'Oh dear,' she said 'I'm quite out of breath but I had to come and tell you.' She collapsed on the end of Laura's bed. 'I've just heard something most intriguing.' She fanned her face with her hands. 'I thought I'd just go and see if I had any letters at reception – I've written to the *Jeremy Kyle Show* to ask if I can participate. I thought they might have responded and as it was I had a few minutes to spare after *Homes Down Under*.'

'Get on with it,' Laura said, getting out of bed and putting on her kimono.

'I am, I am. You see Mimi was at the desk talking with a young man. Terribly good looking. Rather like Jeremy Kyle actually, only younger, and taller and… not so weasily. Not very like him now I think about it…'

Laura sighed. 'And?'

'He was asking for Repton.'

'So?'

'He said his name was Ned something… Oh dear, I did think it was important at the time…'

'Do try to remember.'

'Underwear, his name had something to do with underwear… Ned Smalls?' 'It can't have been.'

'Gusset?'

Laura opened the top drawer of her chest of drawers and pulled out a pair of tights.

'That's it,' Venetia said. 'He said his name was Ned Stocking.'

Laura wrapped the tights into a ball and replaced them in the drawer; so Repton had finally answered the letter. 'Unusual name,' she said.

'There was that MP.'

'Oh yes, Humphrey Stocking. Made a frightful hash up over something or other.'

'And of course there was the actress, Jezebel.' Venetia's eyes widened. 'Now I remember it; they were in *Macbeth* together.'

'Jezebel Stocking. Goodness I'd forgotten her.'

'Yes,' Venetia smiled. 'Now it all makes sense…'

'What does?'

'And the timing is about right – it must have been about thirty years ago.'

'What are you talking about?'

'He says he's Repton's son.'

Angel's inheritance was in the forefront of Laura's mind as she and Venetia hurried downstairs. If he turned out to be Repton's son, Repton was far more likely to embrace him with Matilda out of the way and that left Angel in an even more precarious situation. Having said that, Laura had been having doubts about the wisdom of Angel inheriting Mount Cod, but who was she to say? Heaven knows, the value of the estate would be enough to give an awful lot of foxhounds a very happy retirement.

They spotted Sir Repton sitting at a table in the lounge staring out of the window.

'Is he alone?' Laura whispered to Mimi, who was coming out from behind the bar.

'Yes, him son gone, I thinking very dishy.'

They went over to join him and attempted to exchange pleasantries. He sat in morose silence studying his shoes.

Laura whispered to Venetia, 'You ask him.'

Venetia quivered a little and then cleared her throat. 'So where's this chappie who says he's your son?'

'Ned Stocking,' Laura interjected in case there was any doubt.

Sir Repton looked up. 'He's Jez Abelson. Ned Stocking is Jez Abelson.'

'Oh my goodness,' Laura said. 'The tribute act?' She rubbed her chin. *'Jez abel… son.'*

'How clever.' Venetia smiled. 'Jezabel Stocking's son.' She turned to Laura and whispered, 'It's just as I said.'

'She once played opposite me in The Scottish Play.'

'*Mac...*'

'Go no further cousin. Don't speak the word.'

Laura reminded Venetia of the omen then turned to Sir Repton. 'So you had an affair with her?'

'I simply don't remember.' Sir Repton slumped back, letting one arm dangle over the arm of the chair.

'You mean you had that many affairs?' Venetia huffed. 'It's you that should be on *Jeremy Kyle*.'

'I don't know how it could be possible in any event. Matilda and I were unable to reproduce. She always said it was to be expected that I should fire blanks. I had assumed that my tubes had been rent asunder by some childhood complaint...' Sir Repton wiped his eyes.

'He's probably an heir hunter,' Venetia said. 'There's a lot of it about. He'll have been watching the programme and filled his head with grand designs. Grand designs... now that's very witty.'

'How did he know you were here at Wellworth Lawns?' Laura asked.

'He was at Mount Cod for the wedding but then it was cancelled. The idea of being married in a barn in Northleach was too much for the bride-to-be and she broke off her engagement. Someone told him I was here and he decided to use the opportunity to confront me. He's coming back tomorrow afternoon with evidence.'

'What time?' Laura asked.

'Three-thirty.'

'I think Venetia and I had better accompany you. This is not the kind of meeting you should have alone. I shall ask Mr. Parrott if we may use the small sitting room that he conducts interviews in. There's a "Do Not Disturb" sign he puts up in cases of bereavement.' Laura fingered her bracelet. 'But why has it taken Ned or Jez until now to come out with it?' she asked. 'I mean he's been at Mount Cod playing his tribute act for some time hasn't he?'

'He did write to me. Somehow I failed to answer his

letters. He says he's been wanting to come forward since his mother passed away six months ago.'

Laura looked down at the three turquoise stones set in the Navajo silver. 'About the same time as Matilda died; quite a coincidence.'

Chapter twenty-two

Laura eyed the young pretender with calculated curiosity, as Ned Stocking crossed his long lean legs and ran his fingers through his wavy slicked back hair. Buff. That's how Dudley would have described his sort of physique. The very antithesis of his frail, supposed, father. Laura noted his attire; the neatly pressed wool checked shirt; heavy brown boots unlaced to a fashionable degree; jeans, apparently ripped randomly about the knees. What had she read about such young men in the paper recently? She racked her brain. There was so much new jargon to keep up with. Euro Dandy, was that it?

'This really is a charming spot.' Ned Stocking smoothed his reddish beard with one hand. A full and immaculately shaped set of whiskers. 'The hotel I'm staying at has a four poster that James the Second slept in on his way to the Battle of the Boyne.'

It came back to Laura what the paper had said. Haute Lumbersexual, but Ned Stocking had plainly never been near an axe let alone in conjunction with a tree.

Sir Repton sat in silence opposite the young man, stroking Sybil Thorndike as she lay curled up on his lap.

Laura decided it was time to cut to the chase. 'So tell us Ned, what is this evidence that you have regarding your parentage?'

Sir Repton jolted as Ned Stocking reached down to the leather satchel at his feet and drew out a faded copy of *Life* magazine.

'This is dated November 1985,' he said, holding it up so that they could all see the cover. The title read, "Jezebel Stocking– The New Ellen Terry." Below was a picture of Sir Repton clasping the actress as he gazed dramatically at her upturned face. Both heavily made-up actors were sporting cumbersome iron crowns; it looked an uncomfortable embrace. Ned handed the magazine to Sir Repton who gave it straight to Venetia.

'Oh Repton, how young you look,' she said, before handing it back to Ned.

'He was sixty and my mother was forty-seven. It was her finest hour.' Ned wiped a tear from his eye. 'But after that my poor dear mother never worked in the West End again.'

Laura watched Sir Repton wince. 'I don't remember.'

Had he really forgotten such a conquest?

'She became pretty much of a recluse.' Ned Stocking kept up his gaze on Sir Repton. 'And then of course I was born almost exactly nine months after the curtain came down for the last time. She was no spring chicken and bringing me up alone… In penury… Well it ruined what remained of her health. She kept the secret to her dying day.'

'When exactly did your mother pass away?' Laura asked.

'Quite suddenly in January. Not long after your own wife Matilda actually Repton…'

So he wasn't trying to cover that up.

'It was a double tragedy,' Ned continued. 'Luckily there were no weddings at the time or I should have found it very hard to keep the tribute act going.' He shook his head and sighed. 'It was when I began to go through my mother's private papers, that I had my first inklings as to my true ancestry.'

'How was that?' Laura asked

Ned crossed and re-crossed his legs. 'These things are really not important, it's all in the picture you see.' He handed the magazine to Laura. 'Look, it's plain as the nose on my face.'

Laura studied the picture. 'What is?'

Ned Stocking stroked one side of his fine aquiline nose with a well-manicured finger.

Laura looked at the picture and then back at the young man. 'Do you mean to tell me that you are basing your claim of heredity on a single similarity between yours and Sir Repton's nasal protuberance?'

'Let's face it Lady Boxford, without my muzzle lashings, he and I could be brothers. Actually it was Pom who confirmed the similarity when I showed her the magazine.'

'Pom?'

'I've known the twins since RADA. We kept up after they left. That's how I got the Mount Cod gig. ' He sighed. 'Dear Pom!'

'They were at RADA?' Laura said. Had he found the perfect way to infiltrate the Willowby's through Tam and Pom?

Sir Repton gave a bemused giggle. 'How do you tell them apart?'

'As a connoisseur of faces, it's a no-brainer. Pom has such a delicious little mole on her neck, just above the clavicle, more of a freckle really, but that aside, she is the more simpatico of the two. Tam has a hardness about her and that, almost indistinct, hint of a moustache that does not bode well for the future.'

Sir Repton's brow furrowed as he took this in.

'So what happened to their acting ambitions?' Laura said.

'They had to have a career rethink after the first seminar on tragedy. Tam's not good with what she perceives as sentimentality. Heartless it might be said, whereas Pom is quite the opposite. Anyhow she convinced Pom that acting was not for them. Probably the right decision – Pom took things too much to heart and Tam's much better suited to the world of commerce.'

'But in the wedding business she must have to deal with sentimentality all the time,' Laura said.

'Pom is the perfect partner in that respect. She deals with

the brides. She was the one who encouraged me to come forward. You see… ' Ned let the words hang for a second before turning his attention to Sir Repton with an adoring smile. 'That while this must come as something of a revelation to my father,' he leaned over and patted Sir Repton on the knee. 'I would hope that this meeting would give him time to stop and think about the situation and having seen the joy it would bring, to accept it. I believe it is still not too late to make amends for the distance that has passed between us in all these years. It make take time I know… But I wish him to embrace me,' he ended with a flourish.

Laura noted that there was a certain similarity in his dramatic speech pattern to that of Sir Repton, but then he too, was an actor. 'How long will you be here?' she asked. 'I'm sure Sir Repton will, as you say, need time to assimilate this news.'

'My agent wants me to be at a casting in Bermondsey tomorrow morning at eight.'

'How thrilling,' Venetia piped up. 'What is it?'

'A biopic of Jim Morrison.'

'*Animal Magic*, I used to love his show.'

'That was Johnny Morris, Aunt Venetia, may I call you Aunt Venetia?'

'Aunt?' Venetia asked.

Ned left her pondering this. 'I should make a move,' he said. 'I need to get in the zone. The Lizard King was a complex persona and I must be well prepared for the audition. I'll come again soon, once you've had time to digest my proposition.' He rose from his chair, walked over to Sir Repton and kissed him on both cheeks before bidding them all farewell.

As the door closed Sir Repton lurched from his chair dislodging Sybil Thorndike. 'I can see it all clearly now,' he said. 'This is what Rosalind has been trying to tell me all along.' He hurried to the window and peered from side to side in an agitated fashion. Then he went to the door, opened it, looked out and closed it. 'This young man...' He opened the door again, glanced out again and shut it before picking up Sybil Thorndike and returning to his chair. 'This young man,' he repeated. 'Is the threat Rosalind has been trying to warn me of. He has plainly entered my life with evil intent.'

'You could be right; he may be an impostor.' Laura couldn't believe she was condoning the ghost. 'But I don't think we should jump to conclusions. We must wait and see what his next move is.' He'd plainly had access to Mount Cod but he didn't look like the sort of person who would have killed Matilda to gain his inheritance. 'On the other hand,' she continued. 'He was most illuminating on the characteristics of the twins; Tam in particular.' She turned her bracelet. 'I think it's time to show our faces at Mount Cod.' She was contemplating this when there was a knock on the door. Parker growled and Sir Repton floundered forward from his chair, once again dislodging Sybil Thorndike onto the carpet as Edward Parrott put his head round the door.

'Have you nearly finished?' he said. 'I have a meeting with a nutritionist from the Institute of Age Related Inconvenience.'

'But it's too unfair!' Gladys stamped her feet. 'Repton said he was going to show me round the park. He said he has a fastigiate oak at Mount Cod. And now you are going there without me.'

Laura had foreseen trouble and had taken the precaution of inviting Gladys to her room in order to break the news to her. 'There will be plenty of other opportunities to visit Mount Cod, I'm sure but on this occasion it would be better if I went alone with Repton. There are certain matters that I must have his undivided attention over.' She handed Gladys a box of tissues.

Gladys blew her nose. In the background the local news had just come on the TV.

'Police are asking people to be aware of the theft of statuary and garden ornaments in the locality,' the newsreader was saying.

'If I could just get in there,' Gladys said. 'I know he fancies me. My body clock's only got so much battery life left and I must take my chance soon...' She let out a little sob. 'I'm a ticking time bomb.'

The newsreader was on the next item, 'Break out at Woldham Kennels...' Laura watched old footage of a hunt galloping over green pasture.

'I've got a pencil skirt I know would do the trick,' Gladys continued.

'... a cat was tragically killed...'

'Hang on a minute, Gladys.' Laura turned the remote volume up.

'... it is not clear how the hounds escaped. DCI Phil Sandfield is leading enquiries and would like to hear from anyone who may have information.' There flashed a local telephone number across the bottom of the screen.

'Phil Sandfield. He's about as much chance of running the culprits to ground as...'

'I could have the hem lifted if you thought it would help?' Gladys said. 'Venetia would help I know, she's good with a needle.'

'Exactly, as finding a needle in a haystack,' Laura said. 'But I on the other hand, have a pretty good idea who is responsible.'

Chapter twenty-three

Laura and Sir Repton arrived at Mount Cod to find that there had been an incident involving the creation of the boating lake. The contractors had gone for lunch leaving the pump from the river unattended. The hose had sprung a leak where it rounded the corner of the laurel bushes and the short incline of the path was enough to channel the flow. The chapel had been deluged with water.

'Oh woe is me, what can Rosalind mean by this latest aquatic misadventure? It can only be related to Ned Stocking,' Sir Repton moaned, as they went to meet Tam and Pom to inspect the damage.

As they joined them on the lawn, one of the girls said, 'I hope you've got insurance for this Repton?'

More insurance? Laura scrutinised her.

'Part of the Union is going to have to cop for it I'm afraid.' The girl thought for a moment. 'But talking of cops, you could try contacting the police and say the contractors acted with malicious intent.'

A ray of sunlight illuminated her face and Laura saw a line of downy hairs on her upper lip was distinctly visible. Ned Stocking was right about that much at least and judging by her tone of voice he was right about Tam's character as well. 'But it must have been an accident,' she said.

'They took against me from the word go.' The faint moustache twitched. Yes, Tam was the hostile one.

They reached the chapel and Sir Repton lifted the latch and pulled open the door.

'Either way, I don't think it's got anything to do with Sir Repton and Part of the Union,' Laura said.

The dank smell emanated from the gloomy interior was reminiscent of the previous plumbing incident. It was a pity that this unfortunate coincidence was only fuelling Repton's delusions. 'Surely State of the Union was insured to flood the bog garden.' Laura turned to Tam. 'After all it was you that hired the contractors.'

Tam gave short exhalation of air from her nose and turned to Sir Repton. 'And all this when we've only just seen the back of the Woldham police over the gypsy business.'

'I don't know what to say. It's terrible luck.' Sir Repton looked about the chapel.

A thin layer of mud coated the pink and green polka dot runner leading to the altar and to either side Laura could see that the original floor tiles were now uneven.

'I'm sure we can get a new carpet. It wasn't very expensive.'

This was the newly identified Pom.

'Robert won't like that one bit.' Her sister turned and marched out.

'I had better placate her,' Repton said. 'I'll ring my insurance people... again,' he called, as he hobbled after her.

Laura and Pom were left surveying the scene in the chapel. Pom walked up to the altar and began to rearrange the minaret candlesticks, placing them closer to the Perspex cross.

'I met a friend of yours the other day,' Laura said.

Pom turned to her, 'Who was that?'

Laura sat down on a pew and beckoned to her. 'Jez Abelson, or do you prefer to call him by his real name?'

'Dear Ned.' Pom walked back down the aisle. She sat down beside Laura and as she did so, Laura could just discern the little mole on her neck where the top of her shirt was unbuttoned.

'Did you meet him with Repton? I do hope he's not too shocked. Ned's such a poppet. His Elvis at the Rock and Roll wedding in December last year was amazing. And we've had so many requests for him since he did Tom Jones, even though he hates doing it. Say's he much prefers Michael Buble and Ollie Murs. He's so talented. I'm sure Repton will come round to him.'

Laura noticed a slight flush on the girl's cheekbones. It was a funny thing that twins could suddenly appear so different. The hardness that Pom lacked made her the prettier one by far.

'He said you were at RADA together.'

'For a short while. I wasn't cut out for it though. I kept forgetting it was just acting. I was in tears the whole time when I had to play Gretl von Trapp in *The Sound of Music*. So sad! Then Tam changed her mind when she met Robbie.'

'Robert Hanley Jones, you mean. But wasn't he an actor once, what happened there?'

'He had some problems with stage fright. He'd hoped he would get over it but sadly Repton's wife Matilda said the company couldn't keep parts open for him indefinitely. But it all kind of came full circle when they needed money to keep Mount Cod going and Robbie suggested they make it a wedding venue. Amazing really.'

'Does he like weddings?'

'Totally. Loves everything about them. Except having one himself.' Pom laughed.

Parker was sniffing at a sodden book on the floor.

'Robbie's not married?' Laura bent forward and picked it up.

'Married to his work. He's got a new venue in Northumberland. Fantail Hall, such a cool name. Says it'll open up a whole new market in the North. He's recruiting staff at the moment.'

'So that's why your sister said he'd be so cross. All the bother of dealing with an insurance claim here, when he's so busy up there.' She read the title, *Hymns Ancient and Modern*.

Pom crossed her arms and hunched her shoulders in the chill of the chapel. 'I don't want to seem disloyal to my sister, but agreeing to the lakeside wedding was a mad idea in the first place. I should have stood up to her.'

Laura clenched the hymnbook. Pom was such a nice girl and so delightfully indiscrete.

'The lakeside ceremony went okay but then the bride fell out of the boat even though the water was only about two inches deep, so Tam had to take her into the house to have a bath and change. I know we're not meant to go upstairs but she was covered in mud. Tam found her Lady Matilda's old silk nightdress that was still in the cupboard. Then the bride came down screaming at me that she'd seen a ghost. She was probably drunk.'

Laura turned the hymnbook over noticing there was something stuck to the back of it. It was another, thinner volume. 'Where was Tam?' She peeled off the slimmer volume, looked at the cover then put both books down beside her.

'Cleaning the bath I should think. Luckily they all had fun in the end and the bride said she loved the nightdress so we let her keep it.' Pom giggled. 'What's that?' she asked.

'What?'

'That other thing stuck to the hymn book.' Pom pointed.

Laura hesitated and then picked it up and flicked through the pages. 'It's a Libyan passport.' The photograph of a man stared out at them. She closed it and held it thoughtfully in her hand.

'Honestly people are careless,' Pom said. 'I'll put it with the rest of the lost property. I'd better be getting on anyway; we've got the plans for Friday to finalise.'

Laura handed her the document and they got up and walked out into the warm sunshine.

'Luckily it's a family of Sikhs from Birmingham,' Pom continued. 'So they don't need the chapel.'

Laura left her outside the State of the Union office and hurried through the backdoor her mind abuzz. All the little things she had learned about Tam were coalescing like tributaries into a river and that river led out to a sea of suspicion. Feeling slightly dizzy at the speed at which her thoughts had progressed, she put her head round the kitchen door. There was no sign of Cheryl or Sir Repton so she carried on and found him in his office, his head resting on a mass of papers on his desk.

'The assessors will come out tomorrow,' he said, without raising his head. 'Tam says she will deal with them. In the meantime the Christians will have to go back to using the church in Chipping Codswold. Oh weary with toil, I haste me to my bed.' Sir Repton lifted his arm up and checked his watch. 'Even though it's only twelve o'clock.'

'I think you'd better come back with me. Mind you, what the nutritionist from Age Related Inconvenience will have told Edward Parrott, who knows. There may be nothing to eat at Wellworth Lawns either. Poor Alfredo will go mad if he interferes with the menus again.'

As they walked up to the house, they saw Edward Parrott wearing a pair of yellow rubber gloves, and Mimi's boyfriend, Tom standing by the ramp at the side of the steps to the front door.

'But don't you need it for the wheelchairs?' Tom asked.

'It's the wheelchairs that are the problem. Like the mobility scooters, they promote inactivity. Residents must be encouraged to walk.' He turned to Laura and Sir Repton. 'Now Lady Boxford here is a prime example of one fighting the malaise of the aged. And Sir Repton, a walking stick I see? Make sure that you do not succumb and find yourself any more reliant – the Zimmer frame is the slippery slope, quite literally, that so often leads to a sedentary existence and then the inevitability of infection. Bed sores and other such pestilences. MRSA and it's curtains for the lot of us.'

Sir Repton tucked the stick under one arm. 'I'll do my best, Edward.'

'Coming to stay again?' the manager continued. 'Get the key to your old room from Mimi. Now Tom,' he turned back to the handyman. 'Get this ramp into the storeroom and then meet me in the recreation room. I want you to help unpack the treadmill that has arrived.'

Laura got Sir Repton settled back in and went to call on Strudel and Jervis. She followed Parker who followed Strudel from the kitchen into the sitting room.

'I'm certain Matilda's death is connected to Tam and the wedding business,' she said, as Strudel decided where to place the plate of flapjacks she was carrying.

'Matilda must have found out something,' Laura continued.

'Your feeling for the finding of clues is without parallel, but I am not seeing so much of evidence.' Strudel put the plate down on a table by the sofa.

'And what's more I think Tam may be having an affair with Robert Hanley Jones.' Laura carried on regardless. 'Do we know how old he is Jervis?'

'Fifty. She must go for the father figure, ' Jervis called out from where he was sitting at his computer. 'Mind you with fifty being the new thirty it's not so bad. Before you ask me, I haven't got round to researching Ned Stocking yet, I'm afraid,'

'But that would make Tam about two,' Laura pointed out.

'Yes, that analogy doesn't quite work does it? But it makes sense them having an affair; she's a director of his property company. Her real name's Tamara Fettes.'

'Interesting. And Pom, is she a director too?' Laura asked.

'Paloma? No, just Tamara.'

'My goodness you've been busy Jervis. Can you Google a place called Fantail Hall; it's going to be their next wedding venue.'

'Half a tick.'

Laura and Strudel gathered round the screen as Jervis brought up Google Maps and zoomed in on the house.

'I am feeling most sorry for these people in the north for having to be married in such a *fabelwesen*… a monster,' Strudel said.

'Strudel's taste in architecture is not one of her strong points, is it my love? Do you remember when we went round Blenheim and you said it reminded you of the Reichstag building.' Jervis snorted with laughter.

Laura leaned closer to the screen to get a better look. 'It must be Grade One listed,' she said. 'But it's got the same run down air of Mount Cod. Think how much it would cost to repaint all those window frames.' She had a brief memory of the days of Chipping Wellworth Manor before double-glazing and the never-ending bills for upkeep.

'Getting back to Robert Hanley Jones,' Jervis continued. 'Let me tell you an intriguing story I gleaned online about another of his wedding venues; Casswell Grange in Dorset. Look at this.' Jervis clicked and a headline flashed up. "Casswell's of Casswell Grange in Fatal Car Accident."

'It's from the *Daily Mail* about a year ago, not long after the old couple had signed up with Robert Hanley Jones.' Jervis got up, stretched and took a flapjack from the plate. 'Sad but not unusual I hear you say, but the circumstances are not clearcut. They were out for a jolly when their car breaks down. So they're being towed to a garage when a passing truck hits them. Bang. Lights out. But guess who's towing them at the time?' Jervis paced about, the flapjack in his hand.

Laura shrugged. 'I've no idea.'

'Robert Hanley Jones.'

She gasped. 'You're joking?'

'No way of telling where the fault lay. The truck driver was concussed although he claimed to remember the two vehicles coming out of a side turning without warning and trying to slam on the brakes. Of course it was inadmissible and Robert Hanley Jones swore it was a terrible accident.' Jervis took a bite of flapjack. 'Christ, Strudel.' He spat it out. 'Have you mixed up the salt with the sugar?'

Thinking it best to ignore the culinary mishap, Laura carried on. 'Are you suggesting the accident could have been engineered?' she said.

'Again, oh dear.' Strudel picked up the mess on the floor. 'But what are you saying of this engineering?'

'It's not impossible, but the upshot was that the family were forced to sell up. Inheritance tax planning a shambles. That's when I discovered old Mrs Casswell's maiden name was Laverack. Amazing the kind of stuff you can find on the *Daily Mail* website.'

'You mean a member of Matilda's family? I wonder if Venetia knew her?'

'A cousin I believe. *Debrett's* online is pretty handy too. But now we get to the crux. Guess who steps in and snaps up the house before it's gone on the open market?'

Laura nodded knowingly.

'Robert Hanley Jones?' Strudel said. 'Jesus wept, as my Ronny would have said.'

'Have you been checking the *Daily Mail* too? My poor love!' Jervis turned to Laura. 'I tried to keep it from her, but Strudel's getting pretty internet savvy.'

'There's a warrant out for my Ronny's arrest. They are tracking him down to a villa just outside Puerto Banus, but he is scarpering again.' Strudel sat down on the sofa next to Parker, who was snoring loudly. 'It is all making my nerves most frayed, but this Casswell Grange is a scandal I am feeling in my bones.'

'I must tell Victoria.' Laura said. 'It may be too late to get Robert Hanley Jones on the Casswell case but I'm sure Vince will know what to do. We should tell him about Fantail Hall, and in the meantime I believe a little pressure on Miss Tamara Fettes will pay dividends.'

Chapter twenty-four

The air in the wedding planner's office was static with tension. Laura had persuaded Sir Repton to convene the meeting with Tam and Pom on the pretext that the insurance company needed certain facts to process the flooding claim.

It did not take long before Laura had launched in on the offensive.

Tam gripped the edge of the desk. 'And you are seriously suggesting that I had something to do with Lady Willowby's death? This is preposterous,' she said.

Laura kept her mind firmly focused on Tam's upper lip. 'Matilda found out that you were in league financially with Robert Hanley Jones and having successfully dispatched the Casswell's, you and he intended to get your hands on Mount Cod and that meant getting rid of Matilda.'

'The Casswell's? What's this about?' Sir Repton said.

Laura hadn't filled him in with all the details.

'Repton, tell your friend that she's completely mad,' Tam protested.

'But for my own part it is all Greek.'

'Leave the talking to me, Repton.' Laura returned her attention to Tam. 'So having got rid of Matilda, you had to finish the job. But here you took a more pragmatic approach. Frightening Sir Repton with your fake apparitions would, you believed, hasten his departure, one way or the other.' Out of the corner of her eye, she spotted Parker sniffing a crate on the floor. 'And further; by appearing as the ghost in front of the bride, you were insuring the haunting of

Mount Cod became public knowledge thus further devaluing the property.'

She could just make out the label on one of the bottles. 'Finding your name on the list of directors of Robert Hanley Jones' property company,' she continued, 'was all the evidence I needed.' Her heart raced faster as she realised it was Suffolk Mead.

'Tell me it's not true,' Pom said.

Tam turned sharply to her sister. 'That may be true but the rest is all a slanderous lie.'

'You mean you're on the board of JHJ?' The colour was draining from Pom's face.

Laura shifted in her seat, drew up her shoulders and turned to Pom. 'Oh yes, your sister and your so-called boss, have been intentionally and systematically devaluing Mount Cod so that they could buy it cheap and turn it into a care home. But Lady Willowby found out.'

'Robert Hanley Jones? Turn Mount Cod into a care home?' Sir Repton cast around for assistance.

'There's nothing wrong with care homes,' Laura said. 'Now you sit quietly, I haven't finished yet. My friend Jervis has done a fair bit of research into Robert Hanley Jones. The Casswell's; a tragic accident? My foot. And Matilda would have known about it.'

'Known what?' Sir Repton asked.

'Known about Robert Hanley Jones towing the poor old couple in their car into the path of the oncoming truck. Oh yes, Matilda saw through it. Watched as the family had to sell up; they were her cousins after all. That's the reason Tam had to act.'

'Her cousins?' Sir Repton said.

'You should take the *Daily Mail*, Repton, that's how she knew.'

Tam turned to him and began to laugh. 'Do you really expect anyone to believe her insane ramblings?'

Laura tried to keep calm, she knew the dangers of losing

her temper but she could feel an uncontrollable urge to shout. She took a deep breath and lowered her voice an octave. 'You deliberately tried to cover your tracks by implicating Sir Repton. Making out that he was careless; leaving his wife in precarious situations, losing his keys so that any amount of people had access to the house.' Laura delved into her handbag, pulled out a lipstick and continued, somewhat inadvisably. 'Yes you, Tam, were the one who intruded into her bathroom on that fateful day.' She could feel her voice rising but there was no stopping her. 'You,' she continued. 'Who had openly discussed euthanising your own grandmother with her. The flagrant cheek of it.'

'We took my grandmother to Dignitas in Switzerland. She had motor neurone disease.'

'That means nothing. You drowned Matilda in the bath. Then hid the nightdress she was wearing as she applied her makeup, only to replace it in her cupboard when it was dry. And then you gave it to that bride. '

Buoyed by her own eloquence, Laura got up and walked over to the crate. 'But the serving wench conceit was a step too far, and I can prove it.' She picked out a bottle and held it up, the label clearly visible. 'This is proof if ever it was needed. Suffolk Mead.'

Tam clenched her fists on the desk. 'You are demented.'

Sir Repton cowered.

Laura could see Tam's knuckles whiten.

'If you must know,' Tam spat the words out. 'The gypsies ordered that without telling me.'

Tam's curt riposte cut Laura short. She looked at the bottle but was not put off. 'We'll see what the police have to say about that,' she countered wildly. 'And there's no doubt in my mind that those mushroom spores Robert Hanley Jones planted in the cellar were a part of your plan.'

Tam's jaw dropped. 'What are you talking about now? Those are rare cepes we're going to use for a canapé recipe.'

'Cepes? You can't fool me. You planted them to make it

look like dry rot. Come on Repton, there's no point hanging around here.'

'Do sit down, you're making my neck ache and I keep dropping stitches. I have to watch the needles when I'm knitting,' Venetia said, as Laura paced up and down.

'Thank goodness I managed to persuade Repton to go and rest; he'd only have muddled things up. Phil Sandfield should be here anytime now.' She glanced out of her sitting room window half expecting to see him tramping over the lawn.

'You're very confident,' Venetia said. 'It doesn't happen like that on Inspector Morse. Normally he listens to an entire opera and then what with driving that old car of his, he probably has to stop at the garage and get his gaskets fixed.' Venetia put down her knitting. 'You say you left a message at the station switchboard?'

'Yes, the woman said he was coming out this way. What is that you're making?'

Venetia held up the fat wooden needles and loosely woven purple square. 'It's going to be a picnic rug. I got the idea from Kirsty. After I've finished knitting it, I have to boil it for some reason. I can't quite remember why. I expect I'll end up giving it to Parker for Christmas.'

'What a kind thought, I used to love a picnic.' Glyndebourne flashed into Laura's mind. *Cosi fan tutte* with Tony and... who had the other chap been? She was just trying to remember when she heard a knock. She got up and opened the door. Phil Sandfield stood in the corridor, greasy cap in hand. Beside him, a young woman in uniform.'

'Afternoon Lady Boxford,' he said. 'You remember WPC Lizzie Bishop don't you?'

Laura could hardly forget the Inspector's heavily mascaraed assistant. 'Come in, Inspector, Miss Bishop. I knew you wouldn't let me down. I've a lot to tell you.' Laura introduced them to Venetia and offered them a seat.'

Venetia's tucked her elbows in and continued knitting as Lizzie Bishop sat down on the sofa next to her. 'My feet are killing me,' Lizzie said, slipping off her shoes and wiggling her toes.

'I'd prefer to stand thank you, Lady Boxford,' Phil Sandfield said.

'As you wish, I'll get straight to the point. I expect you've heard of Sir Repton Willowby of Mount Cod.'

'That's why we're here.' Lizzie Bishop rubbed her calves.

'If you wouldn't mind Lizzie.' Inspector Sandfield coughed and held his belly.

'Has he rung you as well? How silly of him, I told him I'd do it. Did he tell you about the wedding planners?'

'Miss Tamara and Miss Paloma Fettes.'

Laura sat down. 'Tam and Pom, exactly.' Parker jumped up on her lap and she began to stroke him.

'I believe that they are commonly known as such.' Inspector Sandfield nodded.

'Good, so you are abreast of the situation?'

'I have received a complaint, if that's what you mean.'

'From Sir Repton?'

'Not from him, no, Miss Tamara has lodged a complaint of some seriousness in regard to yourself. You are not actually under arrest but I'd like you to accompany me down to the station for questioning.'

Venetia put down her knitting. 'Under arrest, that's more like Morse.'

'Inspector Sandfield, ' Laura gave a little laugh 'Phil. I hate to have to say this, but I think you may have got the wrong end of the stick.'

Lizzie Bishop reached into her pocket and took out a notepad. She flicked through the pages. 'Warped moral compass… Libellous defamation of character.' She looked up. 'And I believe you accused her of…' She looked down at her notes again. 'Yes here we are, your precise words were, "You've been posing as the ghost of an eighteenth-century serving wench in order to emotionally terrorise Sir Repton."'

'Emotional terrorism?' Venetia's eyes glistened.

'It's the accusation of murder that's the nub of it,' Inspector Sandfield interjected. He turned to Laura. 'So if you'd like to accompany us? Leave the dog with your friend if you don't mind.'

There was no answer when Laura tried to call Strudel and Jervis so she had to get Edward Parrott to come and collect her from Woldham Police Station.

'I'm afraid I shall have to inform your granddaughter,' he said, puffing air freshener from a can round the interior of his car.

'I don't think that will be necessary.' Laura fanned the air.

'I would not be doing my duty as manager of Wellworth Lawns if I did not inform the proprietors of potential criminal activity amongst the clientele.'

'Oh really Edward, this is too much. Vince – Mr Outhwaite will not take kindly to time-wasting.'

'On the contrary, Lady Boxford, I think he would be most anxious as to your welfare. What light it may shed on the wording of the prospectus I do not know. At present, there is no specific need to divulge a criminal record, but this may be an oversight.'

Laura sat pondering this as they returned to Wellworth Lawns.

The manager drew up in the driveway and took out a sachet of wet wipes as Laura undid her seatbelt and opened the car door. 'Inspector Sandfield let me off with a caution,' she said. 'So I haven't actually got a criminal record.'

'Not yet, Lady Boxford, but the Inspector was clear in his analysis of events and I can't take any chances. From what he said, you have had mental health issues in the past. In old people, weak in mind and limb, it can be a small step from minor depression to full on violence. In such a setting as Wellworth Lawns this kind of thing could prove transmittable.'

Laura was too agitated to collect Parker and she made straight for Mulberry Close. 'As if the Inspector's caution wasn't enough,' she told Strudel and Jervis. 'He told Edward Parrott that I should be watched closely. Then that wretched Parrott said he'd make sure Doctor Todhunter was informed.'

'Try to be calm.' Strudel stroked Laura's arm.

'How can I be calm? Inspector Sandfield disregards all the evidence I put before him and, not for the first time, accuses me of being mad.'

'Valerie Todhunter. Have you had dealings with her?' Jervis asked.

'Not yet.'

'She is to be avoided in my opinion. Much too liberal with laxatives, Strudel can vouch for that.'

'She should be warning a person of the strength and immediacy of such things. But what about Vince; is Mr Parrott going to tell him?'

'I don't know yet, I'll have to ring Victoria later when I've composed myself. And on top of everything else have you seen the poster he's put up in the hall?'

'What is this?' Strudel asked.

'It's got a picture of a Zimmer frame on it and a sign that reads, "Beware of machines that disempower. Keep fit if you want to avoid the forthcoming pandemic."'

'Pandemic? What bloody pandemic?' Jervis huffed.

'We would never be getting Hilary St Clair onto the dance floor without her Zimmer frame,' Strudel said.

'Strudel's right,' Laura said. 'Modern technology has given us untold freedom. Parrott's wholly misguided and for some reason he's becoming obsessed by contagion. He even wiped the seat of the car where I had been sitting with one of those antibacterial tissues after I got out.'

'But this could play into your hand,' Jervis said. 'When you ring Victoria, you must tell her about him. It smacks of misconduct to me. Vince will soon forget about Inspector Sandfield and Tam's harassment charges. He'll be far too busy finding a replacement for Mr Parrott.'

'Positive thinking Jervis. That's what I like about you.' Laura felt her pulse rate slacken. 'And I'd quite forgotten to tell her about his dodgy CV, being a stage manager and all that.'

Strudel clapped her hands. 'This is calling for a stiffener.'

'Snifter, my love, but I'm afraid I've drawn a blank with Ned Stocking's birth record. I'll do some more checking online.'

'Jervis, you are not signing up to more ancestry services are you?'

'Fair point Strudel. Remind me to cancel the subscription after the free trial. Give me a couple of days Laura.'

Chapter twenty-five

Two mornings later, as Mimi was dusting in Laura's bedroom, Jervis rang. Laura picked up the phone.

'I've identified Vince's helicopter on the live air traffic app on my phone,' he said. 'He's traded up. It's an AgustaWestland AW 109. Heck of a beast; you should be able to see it any minute. I hope Parrott's battened down the wheelie bins.'

Laura's granddaughter had said she would be making a visit soon, but the present situation had precipitated an earlier than expected arrival. Now Laura beckoned to Mimi as they heard the thud of the rotors overhead. They rushed to the window. Laura picked up Parker so that he could see the branches of the trees swaying every which way as the great machine lowering to the ground on the lawn outside the front door.

'Mr. Parrott he no telling that old thing I think.' Mimi pointed to the figure of a man in the adjoining formal garden who appeared to have been swept into a rose bush.

'Oh dear, it looks like Sir Repton,' Laura said, as the rotors whirred to a standstill. 'But I think he's all right.' She watched as he scrambled up. 'Mind you, Sybil Thorndike doesn't look too happy.' The dachshund had been blown into another bush, her flowing tail entangled in the barbs.

They watched as the pilot ran to the scene. Edward Parrott followed him and together they went to the aid of Sir Repton and then extricated Sybil Thorndike.

Vince and Victoria, both immaculately dressed as usual,

joined them and the whole party walked back to the front door and out of sight.

Mimi turned to Laura. 'Soo elegant Mrs Outhwaite and Mr Outhwaite too!' She put her hands to her cheeks. 'I wishing my Tom is dressing suit time. He always wearing dirty overalls.'

'I wonder how long Vince and Victoria will be with Mr Parrott?' Laura said.

'I best get going. Him in very bad mood this morning. He saying Alfredo no more pastries them fat old things.' She waved as she shut the door behind her.

'Oh dear,' Laura said to Parker. 'That does not bode well.' Still, she thought with a smirk, the manager had made a fool of himself not having warned poor Repton of the arrival of the helicopter.

Victoria had said that Vince hoped to have finished with Mr. Parrott by half past twelve as he had booked a table down the road at Swinley Court for lunch. It wasn't that he didn't like Alfredo's cooking, it was just that the wine cellar at Swinley Court was far superior to that of Wellworth Lawns – there being no takers of the Grand Crus since Monty Babbington passed away.

To while away the time, Laura went next door to see Venetia.

'I'm watching Helicopter Heroes Down Under,' she said above the blare of the TV. 'I saw Victoria arriving; that's what reminded me.'

Laura decided to take Parker for a walk.

She was returning through the hall – no sign of the poster – when the door to Edward Parrott's office opened and Victoria emerged, a serious expression on her face.

'Hello Darling,' Laura called out.

'Granny.' Victoria came running over and hugged her. 'Let's get out of here.' She steered Laura past the reception desk. 'That man Parrott's very odd. He thinks you've contracted a form anxiety disorder. He's found some American medical research that's convinced him it could be contagious; he mentioned the Waco siege murders. He was contemplating having Dr Todhunter put you in isolation.'

'What?'

They reached the front door.

'Vince, ever the diplomat, managed to chill him out. Said he'd make sure you stayed away from Mount Cod. The quid pro quo was him being allowed to install a hand sanitiser in the lift when it's repaired.'

'But he doesn't believe in the lift.'

'Vince put him straight on that one. He's got to put the ramps back too. And Vince has increased Alfredo's budget, so no more rationing.'

Sir Repton was standing on the steps outside the front door, Sybil Thorndike in his arms. 'Most kind of your husband to invite me to join you for luncheon, Mrs Outhwaite,' he said.

Laura felt a slap on her rear.

'It was the least we could do,' Vince said, from behind her.

She turned to see her grandson-in-law. Vince was sporting a very dapper check suit that Laura knew would be from Savile Row. He smiled, his perfect teeth glinting – he really was good looking, but then what would you expect of Victoria's husband?

'Mornin' Laura.' He kissed her on the cheek. 'While the circumstances of our introduction were not as I would have wished, I'd a mind to ask Sir Repton anyhow. There's things it would be prudent to discuss.' He gave a conspiratorial wink. 'Right let's get this show on the road.'

They walked over to the helicopter and climbed in. The rotors whirred and as the helicopter lifted off the ground they could see Gladys running out onto the lawn waving her arms about.

'Oh dear,' Sir Repton said. 'I believe I may have had a prior engagement.'

'So, where shall we start?' Vince lifted his glass of Chateau Montrachet. 'I think a toast to the continued freedom of the lovely Laura.' He took a merry swig. 'And to Inspector Sandfield and the leniency of the law.' He raised his glass again.

'I feel we will prevail with a little more evidence,' Sir Repton said. 'Laura has at least set my mind at rest that it was the young lady, Tam who was masquerading as the serving wench.'

Laura didn't like to tell him that with the benefit of hindsight she realised that she hadn't really any proof of this.

'Yer whatty what?' Vince took a mouthful of foie gras. 'The pair of you would be well advised to keep your scatter-brained accusations to yourselves.' He turned back to Laura. 'I've got you out of one lot of mischief. Don't make me have to do it again. For once I concur with Inspector Sandfield, there are no questions to answer in regard of Sir Repton's late wife.'

Laura gulped.

'Now we've cleared that one up, I'd like to get down to the serious matter of State of the Union.' Vince turned to Sir Repton. 'I reckon you'd be best off axing the wedding business at your gaff asap.'

'Why so?'

'My people have been looking into this Hanley Jones bloke and they don't like the cut of his jib. You could find yourself in a heap of trouble if you continue to be associated with him.'

'But if I cut my ties now, Tam may reiterate her charges and press for further action against Laura. At the moment she has accepted my explanation that Lady Boxford was on the wrong medication for an ear infection.'

'What?' The piece of Melba toast Laura was holding snapped into pieces. 'On top of the apology Inspector Sandfield made me send her?'

'I'm afraid it was the best I could come up with.'

Vince took another mouthful of foie gras. 'It's up to you. All I'm saying is he might be leading you to believe things are hunky dory but I'd watch out he's not vandalising your assets. Granted he's making you a bob or two on the weddings, but I'd check your profit margins Repton.'

Sir Repton's eyes widened.

'You think it's all good news because you've got a slap-up toilet facility with Dyson hand dryers in what was once a perfectly decent library.'

'Gunroom,' Sir Repton muttered.

'But how's that going to help you when the time comes to sell up and move into Wellworth Lawns for good and proper?' Vince paused for a moment. 'And then you notice your oak panelling's done a bunk on account of being a fire hazard.'

'Vince wanted antique panelling for the villa in Ibiza.' Victoria twisted one of her long blonde tresses. 'You've no idea how expensive it was.'

'Worth every penny though.' Vince smiled at her but then his face became serious again. 'You mark my words Repton, that Robert Hanley Jones is a right sharp nazzart.'

Sir Repton looked to Laura. 'What does he mean?'

'Politely speaking, a scoundrel.' Victoria turned to Vince, fluttering her eyelashes 'Please darling, you were doing so well.' She had put a lot of effort into lessening the impact of his Yorkshire dialect, not that she was in any way a snob.

'I thought you might have known the word,' Laura said, remembering that Sir Repton too had had elocution lessons.

'Scoundrel, whatever,' Vince continued. 'But from what we saw at Fantail Hall, it's typical of the man.'

The waiter came to take away their plates and a few moments later the main course arrived. Vince brought the plate in front of him a little closer. 'You just can't beat a lobster thermidor.'

'But Vince, you mean you've been to Fantail Hall already?' Laura said.

'Bought it.' Vince picked up the crackers and snapped a claw open. 'Always fancied a grouse moor. Gamekeeper'll have to change his ways mind you. Shocking lack of heather.'

'Bought it?' Laura said. 'But what about the owner's and the wedding business?'

'As luck would have it they'd not signed the contract with Hanley Jones and when I pointed out the missing gates that were pictured on the cover of the brochure, they were more than pleased to take my offer.'

'The poor dears hadn't been down the main driveway in years. They used a track that led directly to the village,' Victoria said.

There were so many similarities to Mount Cod. Laura thought for a moment. 'But haven't you done rather the same as Robert Hanley Jones; taken away their most valued possession?'

Victoria explained that Vince was allowing them to live in a farmhouse on the estate. 'They couldn't be happier. The Hall was draining them financially and emotionally.'

'Whole thing's turned out grand as it happens and I've got my legal team talking to the Yorkshire Met. If Hanley Jones isn't facing charges by the end of September you can call me a mushy pea.' Vince took a slug of wine. 'You name it; theft, entrapment, sharp practice... sabotage, felony, larceny... Mark my words, they'll have him.'

Vince's pilot made the short detour back to Wellworth Lawns, dropping off Laura, Sir Repton and the dogs before returning Vince and Victoria to Leeds.

Laura left Repton to make his peace with Gladys and went up to her room. She was undecided as to what to do. Victoria had implored her to keep out of trouble until an investigation into Robert Hanley Jones was underway.

'I really should lie low,' she said to Parker.

As a diversion, she sat down and opened a volume of the Brigadier's diaries. She had tired of 1959 and had skipped through 1960 when the poor man had plainly succumbed to some unidentifiable illness. When the entries were not rambling incoherent nonsense they were indecipherable.

Hoping he had been able to get himself away from Lake Tanganyika, she began to flick through 1961.

March 1. Terrible infestation of ants. Men have gone hunting. Prayed with the womenfolk after dinner, their plight is bad. Marjani has had twins. Says she was relying on the Pampas grass method. Must speak with local witch doctor.

She moved on to April.

Men returned from hunting but have gone again. Much praying with the womenfolk. Kadicha has come to me. She says she is with child again. Witch doctor has filled her head with nonsense. These people do not listen.

Contraception was obviously a problem in the area. Laura put the diary down and closed her eyes. She had not seen him as particularly devout. Perhaps it was some sort of undercover operation his regiment had sent him on, with him posing as a missionary? Who knew? And why should she care when Robert Hanley Jones and Tam were still at large.

She may have got it wrong about the mead, but that didn't change the essence of the case. Tam and Robert Hanley Jones were in it together. They'd engineered the car crash at Casswell Grange. They'd managed to get rid of Matilda and all they had to do was frighten Repton into selling up. Even if Fantail Hall was now out of the equation, Tam was still most definitely in it, whatever the others said. All it needed was one small push and Laura felt sure Tam would show a chink in her armour. She checked the time again. Vince's lawyers might take months to galvanise the Yorkshire Police. Laura rang Venetia and then Sir Repton and asked them both to join her in the lounge.

'There is one thing I need to clear up,' she said. 'Did either of you know Matilda's cousin from Casswell Grange?'

'She doesn't ring a bell. There are a mass of Laveracks in Dorset,' Venetia said.

'What about you Repton?' Laura asked.

'I met them once at a family reunion; a frightful affair. I had no idea of the tragedy of this Casswell Grange branch though. Matilda certainly didn't inform me.'

'You know why?' Laura wasn't waiting for a reply. 'She probably read the court report; it was bound to have been in the *Daily Mail*. She suspected Robert Hanley Jones and she knew the danger Tam represented but she was silenced before she could say anything.' She turned to Sir Repton. 'We have to catch Tam out. Lay a trap for her at Mount Cod. The trouble is I must not be seen.'

'You could go incognito,' Sir Repton suggested.

'What a good idea.' Venetia said. 'Like on *Undercover Boss*. You could pretend to be a wedding guest.'

'Infiltrate a wedding?' Laura thought for a moment. 'I'd never get away with it but you on the other hand...'

'Count me out,' Venetia said. 'I'm sorry Repton, but until you've dealt with that ghost I'm not going near Mount Cod again.'

Sir Repton leant across and patted Venetia's arm. 'But we've solved the problem of the ghost; it's Tam.'

'I'm not convinced. What about sending in Gladys.'

'Gladys. Venetia you are a genius. We'd have to give her strict instructions. No drinking on the job. Gladys can put away a fair amount.'

'Talking of putting things away,' Venetia said. 'I've been meaning to tell you, the police are threatening to put Angel away if she refuses to do her community service for letting all those dogs out in the middle of Woldham.'

'The hounds?'

'She'd be in with a lot of smackheads I expect. Still it might teach her a lesson.'

'Smackheads?' Sir Repton's brow furrowed.

'Heroin addicts,' Venetia said. 'I know all about them from *Neighbourhood Blues*. Urinating and leaving their faeces in people's porches.'

'What on earth induced you to watch that?' Laura asked.

'I thought it was a programme about gundogs – I was going to ring and tell you. But the spaniels were hunting for the smack. They sniffed it out behind the fireplace.'

'A fireplace...' Laura thought for a moment. 'Now that is a possible way to prove Tam's involvement. I wonder if Gladys could pretend to be an antique dealer?'

Chapter twenty-six

Laura sat in Gladys' room watching as she tossed items of clothing out of her wardrobe into a suitcase on the floor.

'Gladys will you stop and listen. You're invited to Mount Cod for a reason. Will you take that boob tube off.'

'Where have I put that sequin sheath dress?' Gladys pushed the coat-hangers to one side. 'Here we are.' She pulled the pink top off over her head revealing, yet again, her ample and, not unnaturally aged chest. She grabbed the purple sparkly dress and stepped into it. 'How's this?' she said, admiring herself in the mirror. 'I think it looks just the part.'

Laura closed her eyes. She was beginning to rue the decision to involve her friend, but Repton had been all for it.

'Yes,' Gladys continued. 'Perfect for a disco.'

'I'm sure you're right, but you mustn't let the wedding party cloud your judgement. You are only pretending to be a guest. Now stop and tell me, what is the main objective of you being there?'

'I'm...' Gladys skipped over to her dressing table and picked up a plastic gardenia. 'What about this?'

'No. Your main objective is?'

Gladys sighed. 'To try and interest Tam into selling me the fire surround in the ballroom.'

'Good. And who are you?'

'I'm an architectural salvage expert from Brighton and a distant cousin of the bride.'

'Well done.'

'But there's no reason why Repton and I can't have a little fun at the same time.' Gladys picked up a lipstick from a bowl on her bedside table.

'I've told you, Repton won't be at the party,' Laura said.

'Of course he'll be at the party. It's in his house after all.' Gladys began applying crimson to her lips.

'We'll have to go through it again once we get to Mount Cod. Now come along, put the sequin one in the suitcase if you must, but personally I think you'd be better off with the dark blue dress. It's so much more…demure.'

Finally they managed to get the suitcase shut and Gladys dragged it down the passage. 'This lift business is a damn nuisance,' she said. Laura made a mental note to find out why it still hadn't been fixed, as Gladys bumped the case down the stairs into the hall where Sir Repton was waiting.

'I'll bring the car round,' Laura said. 'We'll never get Gladys' case across the gravel.'

'Fancy your poor cook finding out her great aunt was so ill,' Gladys said.

'Unfortunate indeed.' Sir Repton poured the tea he had brought in on a tray to the sitting room.

'And having to leave before she'd done the shopping.' Laura picked up a piece of fruitcake. 'This is stale.'

'I'm sure I could dust down my baking skills. Do you like a Victoria sponge Repton?' Gladys leaned over and touched his hand. 'But what will you do for supper?'

From the direction of the ballroom they could hear voices and banging. Cheryl had informed them on her way out, that the bride and groom were mad about the Tour de France and wanted yellow painted bicycles to be hung from the walls.

'I know,' Gladys continued.' I'll smuggle out some food for you two while I'm at the party.'

'No, you mustn't do that,' Laura said. 'Repton and I will rustle something up from the store cupboard. More pilchards, I suppose.'

'Perhaps we should adjourn to the public house again?'

'What? And leave Gladys here? I don't think so.'

Gladys was admiring her nail varnish. 'It's called Midnight in Marrakesh,' she said.

'Most exotic, my dear.' Sir Repton inched a little closer to her on the sofa.

From her chair beside them, Laura frowned; this love-bird nonsense was proving tiresome.

'Oh Repton, It's wonderful to be here at Mount Cod at last,' Gladys said. 'I'm so looking forward to this evening. Could you really not come and join in the fun? I'm sure Laura wouldn't mind having pilchards on her own.'

'Don't even think about it Gladys.' Laura walked over to the window. 'How many times have we told you? All you have to do is mingle in the crowd, then go to the bar and ask for Tam. Make an offer for the fireplace. Gauge her reaction, then come back and report to us. You shouldn't be gone more than an hour.'

They had seen the guests arriving. Kevin the gardener, now dressed in formal attire, had directed the cars onto the dry grass at the top of the park. As they heard the chatter of voices on the lawn, they unlocked the ballroom doors and Gladys slipped in to join the wedding party.

'I hope she'll be all right,' Laura said, as she and Sir Repton made their way to the kitchen to fix their meagre repast.

'I think she'll do magnificently. Her gown was most becoming.'

'Purple sequins? I just hope she doesn't stand out too much.'

Repton reached into the cupboard for a can of pilchards. 'Oh dear,' he said.

'What is it?' Laura joined him and together they surveyed the empty shelves. 'But there were at least twenty – not two weeks ago.'

'Cheryl and Lance must have availed themselves of them while I was at Wellworth Lawns.' Sir Repton walked to the fridge and pulled open the door.

He peered inside. 'At least the hens are laying.'

Laura nudged him out of the way. 'I'm sure I remember how to scramble an egg,' she said.

As they sat down at the kitchen table to eat, they could hear the strains of the band coming from the direction of the party. Laura's thoughts returned to Gladys' frock. It must once have been quite soignée, but now the dress had been stretched to the limit over Gladys' frontage. Time had also taken its toll on the garment and Laura had had to cut off several loose strands of cotton with her nail scissors.

When they had finished washing up, they returned to the sitting room and tried watching TV, but the noise from the party was too distracting. Every so often the sound of cheering and clapping reverberated through the walls as the speeches were made. Gladys must have decided to wait for them to finish before she went on her mission.

'Shall we watch a DVD?' Sir Repton's sallow cheeks flushed as he admitted he quite often put on an old movie of himself and mimed the words when he was on his own. 'I know *Eyeless in Gaza* backwards,' he said.

'I don't remember there being a film of *Eyeless in Gaza*,' Laura said.

'It was not the success it should have been and the leading lady, whose name escapes me, was hopelessly wooden, but a fine piece of cinematography nonetheless.' He was going through the alphabet trying to remember the actress's name when they heard the band strike up. It was an old Frank Sinatra song.

'Oh no, it's Jez Abelson,' Sir Repton said.

'You mean Ned Stocking. I'm surprised we haven't heard from him. He must have been busy with his auditions. But where is Gladys?' Laura looked at the clock on the mantelpiece.

All they could do was sit and wait. Laura could hardly stop

herself from humming along when they could clearly hear the timeless classics; "Love and Marriage", "Strangers in the Night", "Fly Me to the Moon". Apparently Ned knew them all.

They could hear cheering now and then hoots of laughter. Laura sighed and looked at the clock again. To her astonishment saw that it was half past eleven.

'Wherever is...' Laura did not complete her sentence because at that moment they heard a loud knocking on the front door. Sir Repton jumped up. 'Gate-crashers, I shouldn't wonder. I'll go and see them off.'

Laura waited behind the open sitting room door and peered into the hall through a crack in the hinges. Sir Repton heaved open the front door and Tam walked in with Gladys clinging to her arm.

'Yours I presume and I bet I know who's behind this.' Tam shoved Gladys forward. 'Laura Boxford.'

From behind the door Laura involuntarily held in her stomach. She could feel a hot flush rise up her neck.

'First this woman tried to sell me your fireplace and then she tried to dance with Jez,' Tam continued. 'He misguidedly helped her up onto the stage thinking she was someone important. When the bride and groom realised she was nothing to do with either of them, they quite rightly wanted her out, but when the groom's father tried to get her down off the stage, she tried to assault him. She's left half her dress on the dancefloor. You can sweep it up in the morning. Here, take her away.'

Gladys flopped into Sir Repton's arms.

As Tam disappeared, Laura ran out from where she was hiding and took Gladys from him while he shut and bolted the front door. Then together they dragged Gladys, trailing sequins, back into the sitting room.

'Oh Reppy, he was just like you,' she slurred and fell onto the sofa, legs apart, as the final threads covering her bosom fell to the floor exposing her sturdy brassiere.

'This has been a total failure,' Laura said.

The next morning, Laura and Sir Repton busied themselves making breakfast in the kitchen as they waited for Gladys to appear.

'Quiet night?' Laura asked. She was feeling thoroughly jaded herself.

'Nothing could be further from the truth.' Sir Repton poured oats into a saucepan on the Aga. 'She came into my bed while I slept.'

'She can't have done,' Laura said. 'I could hear her snoring in the room next to mine. She kept me awake for hours.'

'Rosalind?' He added milk and stirred the mixture

'Of course not, Rosalind does not exist. It was Tam.' Laura stopped to think about why she had been so convinced the ghost was Tam, but couldn't remember. 'Anyway I thought we'd got that clear,' she continued. 'It's Gladys I'm talking about.'

'I had believed it to be true that it was Tam but I fear you are wrong, I'm afraid. For it was definitely Rosalind. Her vile and putrid breath awoke me in the pitch black of night.' Sir Repton spooned the porridge into two bowls and brought them to the table. 'I was powerless to move. Somehow I found a strength deep down in the furthest recesses of my organs and beseeched her to go henceforth from my chamber and it was only then that I gained some peace of a sort.'

Laura sprinkled on some sugar. 'You frightened her away?'

'Mercifully, yes.'

'But do you really think a ghost would have been put off like that?' Laura's night had been disturbed, but she must have managed some sleep during which time Gladys had attempted a spot of corridor creeping. 'No, on this occasion it was definitely Gladys. It's hardly surprising her breath was bad after the amount of alcohol she'd consumed. I wonder how much she will remember?' Laura couldn't stop herself from laughing. She dug her spoon into the thick glutinous mess as Sir Repton brooded.

They were finishing their coffee when Gladys strolled in, apparently unabashed.

'Get me some of that,' she said sniffing the air. 'Black with plenty of sugar.'

'Porridge is what you need.' Laura opened the bottom oven of the Aga, and retrieved the saucepan. She dolloped some into a bowl and placed it in front of Gladys.

As she was pouring the coffee, Laura heard the sound of whistling. The tune was distinctly familiar: "You Make Me Feel So Young". There was a short knock on the back door and a voice call out, 'Anybody here?'

Ned Stocking walked into the kitchen. 'Good morning,' he said. 'I thought it would be all right to let myself in.' He turned to Sir Repton, 'I'm so sorry, Father, I meant to be in touch sooner.'

Sir Repton staggered backwards, staring open-mouthed at the young man.

Laura almost cricked her neck, she turned so fast to see Gladys' reaction, but Gladys was in a state of bemused adoration and the word had passed over her. 'Now I remember, Darling Jez.' She leapt up from her porridge and embraced Ned Stocking.

So Gladys remembered something of the night before, Laura thought, but perhaps not all.

'Steady old girl.' Ned gently disengaged himself and Gladys sat back down.

Laura turned her attention to him and was surprised to see that he was clean-shaven. Without the beard, there was a curious likeness between him and Sir Repton but something was not right; Laura could not put her finger on it.

'I missed the last train so I stayed the night at the girl's flat in Stow after the party,' he was saying. 'I came over with them just now. Pom said she thought it would be OK if I popped in and then I thought I'd better check up on your guest. Gladys made quite an impression last night.'

They heard the back door slam and Cheryl walked in.

'What's all this then?' She fixed her gaze on Ned.

'Hi Cheryl,' he said. 'Well, I'd better be running along. I've got to get back to London and Pom's waiting to take me to the station.'

He certainly was in the thick of it; the twins and now Cheryl. Laura studied him. Was it the plumpness of his cheeks that made her doubt Repton's paternity?

'You couldn't give me and Lance a lift,' Cheryl asked.

'Both of you?' Sir Repton said.

'Lance has invited me to a gig up in town and you did say we should have a day off. You should have told me earlier that you'd be here, but either way I put it in the diary.'

'The diary?'

Cheryl walked over to the windowsill. She picked up a week-at-a-glance diary and flapped it in his direction. 'And the Land Rover's got a flat battery,' she continued. 'I was going to call a taxi.'

'But...' Sir Repton interjected feebly.

'Don't worry we'll get it fixed when we get back.'

'I should think there'll be room,' Ned said. 'I'm sure Pom won't mind.'

'Neat.' Cheryl took her mobile from her pocket as she headed for the back door.

Ned turned to Sir Repton. 'So,' he said. 'I'll see you next week. I'm back here doing Abba with some mates and I might have some news on your stone eagles by then.'

'My eagles?' Sir Repton perked up. 'How so?'

'I've got a friend in the props department at Pinewood Studios who deals in ornamental statuary as a side line. There's not a lot he doesn't get to hear about. Well, cheerio for now.' He waved and followed Cheryl out.

Having digested all this information and seeing that the catering at Mount Cod appeared to have run its course, Laura decided they would be better off getting back to Wellworth Lawns.

'I fear I maybe putting a strain on my friendship with Edward Parrott with all my comings and goings,' Sir Repton said.

Gladys took a noisy slurp of coffee. 'If he gets shirty, you can always bunk up with me.'

Laura eyed Sir Repton and noticed that he did not seem unduly agitated by her last remark.

There was no trouble getting Sir Repton's old room back and once they had deposited Gladys and her less bulging suitcase in her room – the sequin dress had been consigned to the bin – Laura suggested she and Sir Repton take a walk in the garden before lunch.

Remembering the scene of the helicopter landing, Laura directed them away from the rose garden and up the hill at the back of the house towards the old pet cemetery.

As they ambled along the path, Laura asked him again about Ned. 'You and he are uncannily similar,' she said. 'Are you sure there is nothing you are hiding from me about Jezebel Stocking?'

'Splendid larch trees.' Sir Repton carried on walking.

'Are you avoiding the issue?'

He halted. 'There is something that has been encumbering my thoughts.'

'Yes?'

'There was a particular occasion…'

'Shall we sit down?' Laura beckoned to a fallen tree trunk. She knew it well but now wasn't the time for memories of Tony and the head groom, Barry.

'You know I'm broadminded,' she said, as Sir Repton took his place beside her. He cleared his throat and she waited as a fat wood pigeon flapped down and began to strut about. Parker growled and he and Sybil Thorndike ran after it.

Finally he found his voice. 'It is not something I am able to divulge without a deal of personal humiliation.'

Laura watched as the pigeon took flight. 'Get on with it

Repton. Nothing can be that bad at our age.' Laura picked up a twig.

'The fact is, I believe I may have been the victim of date rape.'

'What?' Laura let the twig drop to the ground.

Sir Repton took a deep breath. 'It was at a time of my life that I am not proud of. I was in the habit of hard carousing and would often frequent a small dining club in Islington.' He paused.

'And?'

'On this occasion I awoke shortly after dawn outside a newsagent's shop on Upper Street.' He ran one hand over his grey stubbled chin. 'The proprietor was about to start his delivery round and I wished him good morning. He was not a cordial man in particular and carried on with his work. I asked him if I could avail myself of his telephone as I found I had no money about my personage.'

'What did he say?'

'Even after all these years I still remember his words clearly. "Sling your hook you dirty loser," he said.'

'How very unhelpful of him.' Laura waited for Sir Repton to continue.

'So with no other course of action open to me, I found a telephone box and reversed the charges. Matilda was not best pleased at having to make the journey to collect me.'

'What did you tell her had happened?'

'She was not worried about my whereabouts as I often stayed out after the show and she tired easily of my thespian friends. I'm afraid it had happened before.'

'How very long suffering of her.'

Sir Repton's waxy cheeks grew pink.

'So how does this relate to Ned Stocking?'

His brow was glistening. 'Thinking back, I remembered that Jezebel had a small flat in the Islington area. And then I recalled what happened at the theatre the next evening. It was the last night of the run you see. Jezebel was playing

Lady Macbeth to my... Scottish Lord. She was nothing if not punctilious about learning her lines.'

Laura crossed her legs. 'And?'

'It was during the third act. If you recall Lady Macbeth attempts to pacify her husband for the murders he had committed. "What's done is done," she says.'

Laura crossed her arms. 'And?'

'Instead of just saying those words, Jezebel added, *so there!*'

'A bit off the cuff, I see. Was there any reaction from the audience?'

'Those philistines? They wouldn't have noticed. And to be fair I myself was so enraptured by the part I was playing that I pretty much dismissed it as a minor aberration. But you see, now it takes on more significance, don't you think? What's done is done. *So there.*'

'So what you are saying is that you may have been with Jezebel the night before and have no recollection about what occurred between the two of you.' Laura let the words sink in. 'But why would she drug you?'

'I cannot but presume that she was desperate to carry my child. And now I think about it, we would often celebrate after the show in my dressing room with a glass or two of champers, she could have slipped something into my glass.'

It was hard to imagine anyone wanting the child of the frail old stick sitting beside her, but back then he had been something of a matinee idol. 'Didn't you keep up with her after the run had ended?'

'I never saw her again. You know what an actor's life is like.'

They sat in silence for a while listening to the pigeon coo from the branches above them. Laura could only suppose the ludicrous date rape charge was a vain attempt on Repton's behalf to make himself look less like a drunken Lothario living a life of seduction and debauchery, but the fact of Ned Stocking's assertion remained.

'The only way to be sure,' Laura said, 'is a DNA test. He

won't go for it if he's not who he says he is and if he's not who he says he is, he's going on my list of suspects.'

'You mean Matilda?'

'If Ned is having an affair with Pom as I believe, then he must know what's been going on. He could easily be involved in the whole thing. Don't forget, Pom was only taken aback when she found out Tam was a director of the property company, but that's not to say she didn't play a part in the death of Matilda and therefore knew about her sister masquerading as the ghost.' It was all suddenly making sense again in Laura's mind and it did occur to her that Ned Stocking could have been playing the role of the ghost – he was also an actor after all, but she kept this to herself. 'If on the other hand, he is your son,' she continued. 'He wouldn't want your position as owner of Mount Cod jeopardised by Tam and Robert Hanley Jones.'

'But – '

'No more buts Repton, either way it's vital we find out who he really is.'

Chapter twenty-seven

Jervis was tasked with finding out how to get a DNA test done and the next day he invited Laura and Sir Repton over to discuss his progress. As they were making their way to Mulberry Close with Parker and Sybil Thorndike on their leads, they happened to see Gladys walking ahead of them through the gate into the field.

They waited out of sight for some minutes; Sir Repton said he didn't want to upset her by appearing to ignore her but at the same time they both agreed that it was too complicated to involve her at the present time. When they finally came out from their hiding place behind a garage, they could see Gladys striding up the hill in the distance.

'She's probably looking to see where to plant her fastigiate oak,' Laura said.

'She mentioned this tree to me. What is the meaning of it?'

As Laura rang the bell, she explained about Gladys's memorial.

'Oh dear,' Sir Repton said. 'I told her Matilda thought them very suburban in a parkland setting and was keen to have the one at Mount Cod chopped down.'

Jervis opened the front door and ushered them into the kitchen where Strudel was busy wiping down the draining board, a bright pink and blue floral apron covering her peach coloured dress.

'Kettle's just boiled,' Jervis said. 'I'll fill the pot.'

'Another dry day?' Laura asked.

'Christ no! We've modified the rules.' He looked up at the cuckoo clock on the wall. 'Nearly four; only an hour before the yardarm goes up.'

'Please do sit,' Strudel said. 'I have this morning made a stollen cake.' She flicked off the cloth that was covering a plate the middle of the table revealing a brown mound covered in icing sugar. It had looked pretty solid to Laura but as Strudel cut into it, the cake sagged and a gooey mass of raisons oozed out.

'About the DNA test,' Jervis handed Sir Repton a mug. 'Dr Todhunter will do it privately for £99.'

Sir Repton took the piece of cake that Strudel offered him.

'She recommends the split kit pack,' Jervis continued. 'One half with her, the other half she sends to the preferred doctor of the alleged child.'

Sir Repton nodded studiously, his mouth full.

'You simply go into her surgery in Woldham and she takes a saliva swab.' Jervis put his teaspoon in his mouth and mimicked the procedure so that one of his cheeks stuck out. 'She bottles it up, gives it a barcode and bingo; results back in ten days.'

'Jervis is making you an appointment for tomorrow morning at 10.30.' Strudel handed Laura a slice of cake.

Laura took a tentative bite. It could definitely have done with more time in the oven.

'I tell you what Repton, I can run you down there if you like,' Jervis said.

Sir Repton's mouth was full again, so he nodded in the affirmative.

'Good, we've sorted that out,' Jervis said. 'But you are still no further on with your investigations; the Gladys ruse was a bit of a failure, I gather. Tell me, out of interest, were there any unnatural occurrences on the night of the party?'

'Laura has convinced me that Rosalind was, in fact, Tam in disguise. She duped us in the manner of the finest stage performance. Oh unhappy times,' Sir Repton moaned, as a dollop of cake he was holding dripped onto the table. 'My buttocks clench like a warhorse when I think of the moments leading up to Matilda's death.'

Laura was impressed. 'You've no idea what lengths Tam will go to,' she concurred.

'I'm sorry but not entirely convinced,' Jervis said.

'No, neither am I.' Sir Repton wiped the mess up with his handkerchief and put it back in his pocket.

'What?' Laura glared at him and forced down another piece of cake.

'The answer of course is an exorcism. In fact, I don't know why we didn't think about that before,' Jervis said.

Sir Repton's eyes lit up. 'I could ask Canon Frank to assist us.'

'That old charlatan?' Laura huffed.

'You must keep an open mind,' Jervis said. 'Don't forget, you weren't there when we had our encounter with… well with whatever it was.'

Laura gave a placatory nod. Why not let them have their exorcism and be done with it.

'I'm sure Frank won't charge – he's a friend after all,' Sir Repton said.

'Charge you? Don't be ridiculous,' Laura said. 'Not after the debacle of the séance, and we never got to the bottom of him kipping down uninvited. I'd say he owes you big-time.'

Sir Repton sat deflated like a puffball someone had trodden on and Laura felt suddenly sorry for him. 'We need more witnesses,' she said. 'Why don't we invite Gladys and Venetia too? Make a party of it.' And afterwards, they could get back to the real problem of exposing Tam.

Laura rang Sir Repton's room the next afternoon to see how he had got on with Dr Todhunter.

'We didn't need the split kit,' he said, 'because quite coincidentally Ned appeared last evening when I had left you and he took me to dine in Woldham. Very cordial of the young chap, I thought. We had an excellent pie at The George. So then I met him in Woldham this morning when Jervis dropped me off and we went to see Dr Todhunter together.'

'So you killed two birds with one stone, or rather one DNA kit.'

'Funny you should say that. You see that was the reason Ned had come to see me. Stone birds. He's tracked down the eagles from the roof of Mount Cod to an antique shop in South Audley Street. He had a picture of them on his phone. They're definitely the same. He's contacted the police.'

'So he came down from London to tell you this?'

'I think he had an ulterior motive. You see, he's in love with Pom.'

'What did I tell you?'

'I was most moved. It was the first true paternal feeling I have had. I must change my will.'

Laura listened as Sir Repton blew his nose. He had all but convinced himself. Again Laura remembered that it was Angel's inheritance that had been her motivation for becoming embroiled in the first place. 'Let's not jump to any conclusions,' she said. 'Didn't Jervis say it took ten days to get the results?'

'How shall I pass the time?'

'Where's Gladys?'

'She has gone to a clinic in London to have her varicose veins done.'

'Gladys going private, I can't believe it. Well, in that case, you'd better have dinner with Venetia and me.'

They had hardly sat down for the meal before Venetia began regaling them with tales of her televisual experiences.

'I watched a thing about junkies in Canada last night,' she said, taking a mouthful of bread roll.

'Not more drug addict programmes?' Laura said.

'You can't avoid them but I thought it was a cookery show with a girl called Molly but that turned out to be the name of the drug. It's a pity about these people because they all love cooking but they're so off their heads they never get round to it.'

'On the subject of cooking, Canon Frank says we must only have a light repast the night before the exorcism. He will be with us the day after tomorrow, as there is no wedding that day. I have informed the others. Jervis is going to collect him.' Sir Repton turned to Venetia. 'I'm sorry you won't join us cousin.'

'No fear.' Venetia huffed.

Mimi appeared carrying bowls of consommé.

'A light repast?' Laura wondered what had happened to Alfredo's delicious croutons.

'It might prove something of a problem,' Sir Repton mused. 'What with Strudel and Jervis, ourselves, and the Canon we will be quite a number and I don't imagine Cheryl will want to make us all luncheon. I expect we will be done by then.'

'Who knows but we should take some provisions.' Laura took a spoonful of soup. She supposed it was another of Mr Parrott's health directives and wondered what had happened about Vince's order that Alfredo's budget be increased.

'Frank said we must not wash our hair between now and then and we must desist from the use of scented products,' Sir Repton continued.

'I wonder if Canon Frank is the best man for the job?' Laura said. 'Perhaps we should have asked Reverend Mulcaster? Anyway, I have a hair appointment tomorrow morning.'

'And we must leave the house empty the night before in order that Rosalind feel secure in her domain.'

Mimi returned with the main course.

Laura looked at the small piece of white fish surrounded

by elegantly positioned florets of grilled cauliflower on the otherwise empty plate. She was reminded of the fashion for cuisine minceur but could not remember who had said life was too short it.

'I'll have to speak with Victoria about this,' she said. 'But as for leaving Mount Cod empty the night before, that's completely unnecessary and having us around has never put her off before. Even saying the name of the house was an affront to the plate in front of her. 'No, we must go there tomorrow afternoon,' she continued. 'There will be things to do; the shopping for one and making sure all the rooms are open; the attics for example. We'll pick up proper fish and chips in Woldham on the way.'

'The attics. I hadn't thought,' Sir Repton said. 'That could indeed take some time, I agree.'

'I wish you hadn't mentioned chips,' Venetia said.

'Will you not change your mind, dear cousin?'

Venetia shook her head and scraped the remains from the butter dish onto her cauliflower. 'Not even chips could tempt me back.'

Chapter twenty-eight

Having an exorcism? Lawks a mercy Lady B,' Dudley put on a pair of turquoise rimmed glasses and grabbed the hairspray. 'You'd better have plenty of this in that case.'

As he shook the can, his young assistant Kelsey came over.

'By the way Lady Boxford, I remembered you wanted to know what the man was like who was having dinner with that Cheryl woman of the, "Sun-in" foul up,' she said. 'Well me and Billy was walking down the High Street the other day when we saw her. She was on the other side of the road with him.'

'You saw him?' Laura said.

'Yeah. He was wearing a check shirt and baggy cargo pants. I reckon he used the "Sun-in" on his hair too. Terrible brassy yellow it was.'

That's Lance, Laura thought, putting Parker on his lead. There was definitely more to Cheryl and the handyman's relationship than met the eye.

She put a couple of pound coins in Kelsey's gratuity box and headed back to Wellworth Lawns.

By the time she had collected Sir Repton and Sybil Thorndike, it was late afternoon. He said he had tried calling both Cheryl and Lance but neither had responded, so they decided to pick up an Indian takeaway in Woldham on their way. Laura had a special place in her heart for Chicken Tikka and unlike fish and chips; it would keep warm in the Aga.

As they drove past the lodge there was no sign of the Land Rover and when they got to the house it was all locked up. Sir Repton knocked on the door to Cheryl's flat but there was no reply.

'Really, those two are the limit,' Laura said, as they let themselves in and set about preparing for the next day.

Their primary task was to check the attics, of which there were two, Sir Repton informed her.

The first was reached via a steep uncarpeted staircase next to the scullery off the kitchen. It led to a small landing. They picked up the dogs and ascended a further and even more precipitous set of creaking, uneven boards that led to three interconnecting rooms. They lay empty and had plainly not been used for many years. Laura tiptoed over a layer of dead flies through the narrow, low doorways. In the furthest room were two garret windows under the eaves.

Beside her, Parker sneezed and the last rays of sun illuminated a myriad of dust particles that danced in the light as she looked down onto to the stable block.

'This may have been Rosalind's room,' Sir Repton said, peering out of the other window. 'I can picture her hurrying with her corsets. Her poor chillblained fingers pulling the laces tight as she listens to the clatter of horses hooves below. And then again of course it could have been a window like this from which the poor child defenestrated.' He pressed his forehead to the pane of glass.

'I thought you said that the old house burned down?' Laura said. 'Anyway, come on, we'd better look at the other attic.' She turned to go but noticed a wooden ladder in one corner leading to a trap door in the ceiling. 'Where does that come out?' she asked.

'It takes one up onto the roof, but we don't use it anymore. There is a newer one in the other attic. I'll show you.'

They descended and passed through the kitchen and back down the corridor leading to the hall. Then they went up the main staircase and carried on down the passage past

Flamborough Head. Laura had only glanced at the tapestry hanging at the end of the passage on her last visit but now Repton drew it aside to expose a door. He opened it, revealing the staircase to the second attic. As they reached the landing above, the heel of Laura's shoe snagged on the threadbare magenta Axminster. She pulled at the shoe as she surveyed a series of closed doors to left and right.

She opened the first door to reveal a bathroom. Next to it was a single toilet. Further investigation revealed three small rooms. The first was filled with packing cases. The second had a single bed covered with a patchwork quilt of faded pinks and blues. They opened the last door. Inside was what looked to be a sitting room. Two tatty armchairs covered in floral cotton sat facing a tiny fireplace. Over the back of one was draped a white bath towel. A further two wooden chairs tucked under a small pine table stood against one wall. On the shelf above the fireplace stood a row of books held up at each end by plaster bookends in the form of ancient Egyptian cats.

Laura walked over to inspect them. She glanced at the spines. A copy of the Bible and *The Complete Guide to Fasting* jostled with some Barbara Cartland's, a set of Adrian Mole books and a Ladybird book of farmyard animals. 'Whose are these?' she asked.

'Matilda allowed her niece to stay here.'

Laura picked up a small patterned tin resting on top of the books and opened it.

'There was a period in her life,' Sir Repton continued, 'when Angela did not get on with her mother; our dear cousin Venetia. Then, when Angela followed her religious calling, she agreed with Matilda that she no longer required this refuge. Now it is only used as access to the roof.' Sir Repton opened what Laura had assumed to be a cupboard.

A narrow set of steps wound up to another trap door. Sir Repton picked up Sybil Thorndike and climbed up. He pushed on the door. 'It won't open,' he called to Laura.

'Let me have a go.' Laura replaced the tin. 'Come down. We can't both fit up there at once.'

With Parker yapping at the bottom of the steps, Laura leaned her head to one side and gave the door a good shove with her shoulder. It swung up and landed on the lead roof with a bang. She climbed out and stood in the evening breeze surveying the park and gardens. Sir Repton joined her, breathing heavily as the dogs yapped below.

'Splendid up here don't you think?' He puffed. 'And even more so if young Ned is right and we manage to get the eagles back.'

They clambered back down, shutting the door behind them and went back down to the kitchen to heat up the curry. As they were finishing eating, the telephone rang. It was Gladys. Judging by Sir Repton's expression, she was conveying good news.

'She's come back,' he said, putting the receiver down.

Laura held a poppadum in her fingers. 'I'm amazed; varicose veins can be very painful.'

'She said she couldn't miss the exorcism.'

'Good,' Laura said, as she halved the remaining bhaji and gave it to the dogs. 'I'm sure tomorrow will be a resounding success but we must be up early to make any last-minute adjustments. At least we are now sure that we have full access to all the rooms in case Canon Frank wants to go walkabout.'

'I fear that Rosalind's resilience may outwit the Canon. In fact, I can feel her presence creeping up on me now.' Sir Repton glanced furtively from left to right.

It was true an unnatural quiet had descended on the kitchen. Even Parker was alert.

'Don't be ridiculous,' Laura said. 'Let's go and watch the *News at Ten*.'

When Sir Repton had asked her which room she would like, Laura had chosen Flamborough Head. She was interested to see how comfortable it actually was, and the thought of a nice hot soak in the generously sized bath the next morning clinched it.

She closed the curtains, unpacked her things and made Parker cosy in his bed on the floor beside her. She was determined he should not join her in one of the twin beds – it would be too much of a squash. She was about to fold up the bedspread but looking at the thin quilt underneath, had second thoughts – It really was like *Britannia* but she was not taking a summer sailing vacation in the Med and the last thing she wanted was to wake up cold in the middle of the night. She turned on the bedside light, before putting off the main ones, then got into bed and opened the Brigadier's diary. She had moved on a couple of volumes in the hope of a change from his missionary phase and she now opened 1965. To her surprise he was living in Orpington. He had plainly moved recently and there were some nice descriptions of the hen house he built to house his Buff's. His life had taken a very different turn and he made constant reference to the lateness of trains and the fact that the High Street had, yet again, had to be widened. He had also joined the Orpington Photographic Society.

Laura was falling into a soporific haze at his suburbanite ramblings when, on September the 17th, something quite startling happened. There had been no mention of her in all the pages Laura had ploughed through, so it came as something of a shock when she read, *"Iris fairly hit the roof last night in bed. Must cover tracks better in future."*

Laura put the diary down on the bedside table. What's all that about? As she plumped the thinning feather pillows, Parker took the opportunity of jumping up beside her. She shooed him down and listened as he scratched at his bedding in a disgruntled fashion.

Iris? The Brigadier had never mentioned anyone called Iris. Laura felt a moment of pique. But then again their histories were so long that it would have been impossible – at least in Laura's case it would have involved a lengthy list – if they had divulged to one another the entire antics of their private lives. She sighed, pulled up the thin quilt and closed her eyes.

Soon, by association, she was dreaming of being on the royal yacht. Despite having freshly read the Brigadier's diary. It was her first husband Tony who was accompanying her on the night-time voyage. They had had a delicious dinner with the Queen and Prince Philip and were now in their cabin.

'It's awfully cold in here,' Laura said.

'Damnably,' Tony agreed.

Laura was beginning to shiver when they heard a knock on the door. 'I'll give you one guess as to who that is,' Tony said, grabbing Laura round the waist and falling with her onto the bed.

'The purser,' Laura giggled. 'He should keep us warm.'

'Come in,' called Tony. She heard the slam of a door. He'll wake the whole ship, Laura thought, as a man's voice called out, "Keep it down."

She woke with a start. It wasn't just the dream; her room was like an icebox. She pulled the bedclothes up around her chin. As she rubbed her arms she heard the voice again.

"Quiet please!" But it wasn't a member of the crew.

It was the voice of Canon Frank Holliday.

Chapter twenty-nine

Laura fumbled for the bedside light and flicked on the switch. She listened intently for the Canon's voice again, but all was silent. She was wondering if it had been part of the dream after all when she heard the distinct sound of a car door slam. Judging by the direction, it was coming from the stable courtyard. She looked at her watch. It was two-thirty. What was Canon Frank up to? Had Cheryl dumped him here again? But why not wait until the morning as expected; after all it was he who had insisted the house be empty before the exorcism.

She strained to hear if the back door opened, but all was quiet again. Where had he gone? She found her torch, turned out the light and got out of bed. The room was bone-chillingly cold. Reaching for her kimono she cursed Sir Repton.

The windows of Flamborough Head all faced onto the garden but in the bathroom, one faced onto the stable court-yard. She followed the beam of the torch to the window then turned it off as she gently pulled back one corner of the curtains. Below her, in the moonlight, she saw two battered white minibuses parked in the middle of the cobbles. Next to them was another car, dark, possibly green. She watched to see if anybody got out, but they appeared to be empty.

Laura flicked back the curtain and, turning on the torch, returned to the bedroom to find Parker curled up in a tight ball shivering on her pillow. As she approached, he lifted his head and wagged his tail.

'I'm going to see what's going on down there.' Laura pulled

the bedclothes over him. 'You wait here.' She put on her sheep-skin slippers and made for the door. Having second thoughts, she returned and scooped up the short wool jacket she had been wearing earlier. 'I shan't be long,' she called out, shutting the door behind her and heading off down the passage.

Downstairs the temperature was curiously warmer and she made directly for the room by the kitchen where she had found the Canon on her previous nocturnal investi-gation. It was empty. She carried on to the back door and was surprised to find it still locked. Perhaps he wasn't in the house? She took the key from where it hung on a peg on the wall and unlocked the door. She pulled her coat on and headed into the yard. Peering into the driver's window of one white van, she noticed the keys were still in the ignition. She walked over to the other one; it was the same. She tried the door of the car but it was locked. She looked around. A crumpled piece of paper and an empty crisp packet lay in one corner of the yard near the small wooden door that led into the garden. She picked them up and put them in her pocket. Then she opened the door and crept round the side of the house, stopping occasionally to listen for the sound of footsteps. She got all the way to the laurel bushes that screened the path to the chapel. A cloud scudded over the moon and their great dark masses loomed eerily in the night sky. As a child she used to love to play and make dens in the roomy interior of such bushes but now she wondered who or what could be lurking there. She listened in the silence again.

And then she heard it. Coming from the direction of the chapel. A kind of murmuring of voices chorused together.

Skirting around the laurel, she tiptoed up the gravel path. The voices were louder now. As she reached the door, she heard Canon Frank Holliday from within. Laura put her ear to the door. 'Do you take…' There was a pause. 'What is her name?'

What did he think he was doing and how extremely unprofessional not to have even found out the name of the bride. But more to the point, how dare Tam and Pom start conducting weddings in the middle of the night without even having the common courtesy of telling Repton? It was too much. She grabbed the handle of the door.

Laura heard the voice of a young girl. 'My name is Megan.' The accent was redolent of the Welsh valleys.

'Thank you Megan,' said the Canon. 'Do you... What is your name?'

There was another pause and then a male voice called out, 'Mah nem is Andwele.'

Laura was reminded of the streets of Cairo.

'Andwele,' the Canon continued. 'Do you take Megan for your lawful wedded wife?'

'What he say?'

What kind of people were they that had not bothered to acquaint themselves with the order of service?

Laura heard a fourth voice now. 'Listen mate, just say "Yes."' It sounded like a London accent.

Really this was an outrage. Laura burst open the door. She stood stock still. The chapel was filled with people. A sea of dark-haired men turned in their pews on one side of the aisle and on the other side a corresponding amount of pale young girls.

Canon Frank looked down the aisle from where he was standing at the altar. 'Lady Boxford, you shouldn't be here,' he said.

The as yet unmarried couple turned their heads.

'Shit,' said a man standing next to them. He ran up the aisle towards Laura. Before she had a chance to think, he had reached her. She saw his pockmarked face and then his outstretched arm as it swung at her, fist clenched.

The next thing Laura knew she was being held upside down in a fireman's lift. She hoped her nightdress and kimono hadn't risen up. 'Tony', she called out as the blood rushed to her head.

The man with the London accent was speaking. 'Take the van back to the house now. The others'll follow. I'll see you this evening,' he said.

'Veery well,' came the reply very close to her ear.

Then her mind went blank.

'You want the marriage certificate?' Was the next thing she heard and then, 'Is that wise?'

Laura knew that voice; it was the Canon.

'Shut it Frank,' the first man said.

What did it mean? Laura was falling sideways. Her head hurt too much.

She heard a car door slam before passing out.

She could feel her head pressed against a cool pane of glass. She opened her eyes. In a haze she saw headlights stream past and heard the steady hum of wheels going at speed over tarmac. There was a conversation going on beside her.

'I veery much like the look of thees.'

'Listen Andwele, We not coming all the way on the boat in Italy and in the Tesco van for you to go soft on this old white lady. Hell I feel thirsty just remembering that stinking truck filled up with Parma ham.'

It didn't make much sense to Laura and now she could feel pain in her chest and ankles.

'I tell you Balcha, theese is one big good idea I have,' the voice continued.

'You are one hundred per cent off your head. You can't keep her. You heard what Liam said.'

Again Laura wondered what it meant but her need for sleep was overwhelming.

When she next awoke she saw a row of shops illuminated by street lighting. They seemed to be closed and there were no people on the streets. It wasn't the familiar high street of Woldham that was for sure. She passed out again.

'Hey Lady, maybe you like nice egg shakshuka. You want to try?'

Laura's eyes flickered. The dawn chorus of blackbirds outside was deafening. She felt as if a Tibetan monk was banging a gong inside her head. She touched it to make sure it was still attached to her neck. Relieved that this was the case, she further investigated and felt a lumpy cushion behind her. 'Were is Mimi?' she asked.

'No Mimi, my name Andwele.'

Laura looked up as two eyes stared down at her, dark and clear as a mountain tarn. She was taking in the man's smooth bald head when his brow unexpectedly creased into deep lines like a ploughed field and he flashed a row of pearly white teeth.

'Are you new here?' she asked the smiling face. 'Someone has taken my pillow. Would you be so good as to see if you can find it?'

'Hey, Balcha. She ees waking.'

Laura heard the sound of thudding feet and soon beside the first face another appeared in her limited field of vision. This was a much bigger man altogether. A neat black beard and short-cropped fringe framed his face accentuating his wide forehead.'Where's my husband?' Laura asked.

The first smaller face popped into view again.

'She is veery nice beautiful lady. Too much good. Wait there lady, I like to take a selfie to send back home.'

The man jumped up and was temporarily out of view.

'You are one hundred per cent crazy Andwele. You know what Liam said. You can't keep her if we want to stay in England.'

'Don't say that Balcha, it is making me afreed.'

Laura sat up with a start. 'Wait a minute? Where's...' Of course Tony wasn't there. How could he be, he'd been dead for ten years. But where was she and who were these people?

Her brain blurred again

Chapter thirty

Laura lay on her side eating a bowl of rice pudding with a cheap metal spoon. 'This is very kind of you, Andwele, but could you tell me why I am here?' she asked.

'I don know why you give her food.' The man Balcha said, from where he was lying against a long sagging curtain under the window.

'Are you forgetting you are Christian?' Andwele pulled down his brightly coloured sleeveless golfing jumper. 'She ees hungry and she has got the right to know what's going on.' He shuffled a little closer to Laura on the mattress and sat cross legged beside her. 'You reeceived a hit on the head when you came into the church unexpectedly in the middle of the ceremony.'

'I don't know why you are telling her all this.'

'Leave it to me, Balcha.'

Laura looked about the sparsely decorated room as the man called Andwele elucidated further and she pieced together the events she could remember.

She felt her eye with one tentative finger. 'So this man Liam finds girls from Wales for you to marry so that you can stay in the country?'

'That is so,' Andwele confirmed.

And Canon Frank Holliday officiates. Laura picked at a loose thread from the grubby blanket covering her legs. 'But isn't it against your religion?' she asked.

'Like I said, we are Christian men. Many times they try to kill us in our country. You people have no idea. Is veery bad. We have to escape and now we stay here for the papers Liam will bring.'

'One hundred per cent we get the wedding certificate.' Balcha glared at Andwele. 'When you do as Liam said.'

Laura turned to Andwele. 'What have you got to do?'

Andwele shook his head mournfully.

Balcha took a mobile from his pocket and looked at it. 'Is now twelve-thirty. She already been here long enough.' He got up from the floor and walked out leaving Laura alone with Andwele.

'He's quite right.' Laura made to get up. Her head reeled and she took a deep breath. 'I'm most grateful for your hospitality Mr. Andwele, but I really should get a move on.' Her knees quaked and she toppled sideways.

'You stay there lady, Andwele is thinking.'

She heard a dog barking on the street outside. In a moment she was reminded of Parker. She bent her head down as she tried to get more oxygen to her brain. It was all flooding back. She put her hand in the pocket of her coat and drew out the empty crisp packet and the folded piece of paper. Opening it out, she realised it was a service station receipt. No help at all. Laura could feel her chest thumping. But no, she calmed a little. Repton would have found her missing and rung Strudel and Jervis.

'Where exactly are we?' she asked.

Andwele shrugged his shoulders. 'Many streets in Brixton Town.'

Laura took another deep breath to quell the panic. Jervis would ring Victoria. She and Vince would know what to do.

As Andwele sat deep in thought, Laura crawled over to the window and pulled herself up. Looking out, she half expected to see Vince's Range Rover, but the leafy street was empty, and there was no sign of the barking dog.

She heard the sound of voices coming from downstairs.

'Who else is here?' she asked.

Andwele seemed to cheer up. 'Many my friends from the village,' he said.

As far as she could make out from him, there were possibly thirty men staying there. All had travelled illegally from Libya via Italy and then by boat across the channel landing at dead of night in Hastings. It had been a harrowing and dangerous journey. Many had drowned in the Mediterranean.

'Me and Balcha, many times we are hanging on one plank of wood in the sea before we are picked up and put in the detention centre. Then those damn Italians giving us pizza, pizza, pizza. It blockiing you up like nobody business. Maybe we thinking they do this because there is only one toilet.'

'That's terrible,' Laura said. 'But you are safe now.'

Andwele gave her another mournful look. 'Not without the marriage certificate.' He clarified the situation. 'I am veery sorry Lady, but Liam say I must kill you and he is coming tonight to check.' Tears began flowing from his eyes. 'There is no two ways about it, as far as I can see.'

Laura eased herself down from the window and crawled back to the mattress. She took Andwele's hand. 'As a matter of fact there is,' she said. 'You see I happen to be single.'

'Boxford. Hmm.' Andwele toyed with the word.

'That's my surname; my first name is Laura.' Laura was beginning to feel better. Her headache had subsided. It was now like the sound of raindrops pattering monotonously on a plastic gutter and it acted as a distraction from her reservations about arranged marriages but either way, needs must.

'Boxford.' Andwele rolled the word out slowly. 'This is too much good.'

'Mr. Andwele Boxford Akadigbo.' Andwele grinned.

'It doesn't work like that. We'd be Mr and Mrs Akadigbo.' Laura felt she was done with real marriage; the Brigadier would surely have been her last foray into matrimony, although the thought of Mr. Parrott calling her "Lady Akadigbo" did give her pause for thought. She was not sure how the manager would take to the idea of Andwele at Wellworth Lawns but it was something that would have to be sorted out at a later date.

'But we maybe having a problem here, Laura.' Andwele had his troubled look again. 'If I am married to you, I am becoming the bigamist.'

'I'm sure that is something that can easily be resolved. Canon Frank Holliday will just have to cancel the registration of your marriage to the Welsh girl.' Laura remembered Canon Frank's startled expression as she had entered the chapel that night. The fact that he was embroiled in all this illegal activity was something else she would have to stop and think about later, but at the moment she needed him in his official capacity and he was in no position to refuse her.

'We should leave immediately,' she said 'He can cancel your first marriage and marry us at the same time. Have you got any money? We'll have to call a taxi and then there's the train fare. I normally use my pensioner's railcard, but I've left it in my handbag.'

'Hell Boxford.' Andwele put his hand in his pocket and drew out a wad of cash. 'Many times I got plenty money.'

'Well, that's good. So now all we need to do is get back to my home and find the Canon.'

Andwele thought about this. 'So I am coming live with you? Then I get a job; pay the taxes like the proper British citizen. This is making me veery happy.'

'Good. Now go and tell the others and we'll be on our way.'

Andwele returned some minutes later with Balcha. Balcha said it was bad juju not to celebrate Andwele's change of fortune and wish him well on his departure from them.

It occurred to Laura that time was of the essence. Liam had only given Andwele until that evening to get rid of her and it was already late in the afternoon.

'I think we've just about time for a quick one before we hit the road,' she said.

As they went downstairs Balcha called out to the others. They went to the kitchen and Balcha opened the fridge and took out some beers.

'We have my village-style wedding celebration,' Andwele said, winking at Laura and rubbing his hands together. 'You and me as King and Queen.'

'One hundred per cent.' Balcha gave the thumbs up.

'I don't want you to get the wrong end of the stick here Andwele,' Laura said, as they went into a living room strewn with mattresses. 'This will be purely a marriage of convenience. No conjugal rites involved. Do you understand me?'

'Many times, and you no bringing the cattle to the feast, but no point missing out on a good time eh?'

Despite still being in her nightdress, Laura got into the party spirit. There was some sort of ceremonial display that Laura didn't understand but the beer hit the spot and what with the general conviviality of the occasion, it was seven-thirty by the time Laura looked at the cheap plastic clock above the door. Horrified, she took another slug of beer – it really wasn't bad – and shook Andwele who had passed out on a mattress.

'Wake up,' she shouted above the din of the music.

Then she heard a loud hammering on the door.

Liam?

She jumped up and tried to push through the crowd of men into the kitchen. There must be a back door somewhere.

She heard the sound of splintering wood. The drunken men would not let her pass. She was trapped.

She heard a voice.

Her heart missed a beat. He's going to kill me.

Chapter thirty-one

'Granny, thank goodness we've found you.' Victoria said.

Laura felt her knees give way as she sank to the floor.

Vince barged through and grabbed her under the arm. 'Come on Laura, We've got your handbag in the car.'

'My handbag?' What a long day it had been. It really was her bedtime.

'Let's get out of here.' Victoria took Laura's other arm and together they jostled their way to the open front door.

The fresh air hit Laura like a smack from Nanny.

'Hey,' she could hear Andwele call out as he tried to push through the revellers. 'Where are you taking my wife?'

Vince bustled Laura off the pavement and into the back seat of his car. Victoria got in beside her and Vince sped away.

'Thank goodness you're alright,' Victoria said. 'But what did that man mean when he said "my wife"?'

'I can't imagine. He must have been drunk. They were celebrating something,' Laura said.

'Your captivity I suppose. How terrifying for you Granny but they haven't forced you into marriage too?'

'Heavens no.' she gulped.

Laura awoke to a gentle tapping on the door. She sat up smartly. It took her a few moments to remember she was in Vince and Victoria's comfortable flat in Chelsea.

'Cup of tea Granny?' Victoria asked. 'I hope you slept well?'

'Oh, the joy of proper linen.' She let her head fall back on the soft down pillows.

Victoria put the cup on the bedside table. 'You'll have to borrow my sunglasses to cover your black eye,' she said. 'Vince is cooking devilled kidneys; it's his latest thing. The smell is truly frightful at this time of the morning.'

Laura felt her eye tentatively. It was sore. There were a million questions she wanted to ask but this news was too important. 'Devilled kidneys. How delicious.'

'I'm sure he'll do you some, but have your tea first and then a nice bath. I've ordered you some clothes from Harrods. Vince's chauffeur, Charlie is collecting them. Actually, I think I just heard the doorbell. It'll be him, hang on.'

Victoria returned with two large carrier bags. She pulled out the tissue paper wrapped contents and held up a dark blue dress with matching jacket. Around the neck of the dress was sewn a row of spangled beads.

'I can't wear that,' Laura said. 'It's far too smart. People will think I'm going to Ascot.'

'We are.' Victoria unwrapped another parcel and held up a matching set of underwear. Normally Laura wore samples that Vince sent her from the lingerie company "Foundation Rocks", that he'd made his fortune from but the ones Victoria now held up were in a class of their own. She felt a flush coming to her cheeks.

'Oh good,' Victoria said. 'I can see you like them. There's nothing better for support than a Rigby and Peller bra and you've been so brave going without, Granny.' She delved into the bag again and fished out a pair of Wolford tights. 'Did I tell you Vince is into racehorses now? He's got a runner in the King George. Typical Vince, after he'd dealt with that man Liam and we'd found out where you were and dropped Canon Frank at the tube station, Vince made us stop at his bookmaker in Shepherd's Market. He said it was on the way to Brixton. I was furious.'

'Canon Frank? A runner in the King George and Queen Elizabeth Stakes? And Liam; how does Vince know Liam?'

Victoria took a pair of shoes out of a box and handed them to Laura. 'We found Canon Frank wandering around in the garden when we got to Mount Cod. He'd been out cold in the chapel all night. He said Liam knocked him out too.' She got up and headed for the door. 'I'll tell you about it at breakfast. Have your bath and then come along to the kitchen. I must wash my hair.'

Laura lay in bed sipping her tea. This mass of information was really too much for her. And now Ascot… and that must mean it was Saturday… and that meant Liam would have found her gone and poor Andwele; what about him? Laura leapt out of bed and went to run her bath. There was much to do and so many unanswered questions but one of the main ones was, where was Parker?

'Don't worry Granny, we left him with Repton,' Victoria said. 'He's fine. I called Repton earlier – I think I may have woken him up.' She took a small spoonful of manuka honey and added it to her hot lemon water. 'He's probably exhausted, what with two dogs and Gladys Freemantle staying. Gladys said she could cook but she didn't look too practical to me in all that tight clothing.'

Laura sprinkled smoked paprika over the plate of kidneys in front of her. 'Repton should never have let Cheryl and Lance get so out of control.'

'Bit late for that.' Vince turned on the tap of the sink where he was standing in his apron.

'You know them too?' Laura asked.

'Ee aye Luv, you've got a bit of catching up to do.' Vince rolled up his sleeves and began washing up the frying pan. 'They'd been conning old Repton in more ways than one.'

'You don't have to do that darling,' Victoria said. 'Myah will be here later.'

'I'm not a great believer in Myah's washing up skills.

Hoovering, now you can't fault her on that.' Vince picked up a tea towel and began to dry the pan.

'Perhaps Myah has a Filipino cousin that we could send down to Mount Cod to shake those two up a bit?' Laura said.

'Cheryl and Lance have gone, Granny.'

'Gone where?'

Victoria put a hand on Laura's shoulder. 'They've disappeared. The police are trying to track them down. You see Liam is Cheryl and Lance's son. They were married.'

'Liam? The man who wanted me bumped off was Cheryl and Lance's son?'

'What do you mean "bumped off"?' Victoria stared wide-eyed at her grandmother.

Laura took a bite of kidneys. 'He was going to have me killed.'

Victoria gasped. 'We had no idea you were in that much danger.'

'Heck I'd never have stopped off at the bookie's if I'd known.' Vince opened a cupboard to put the pan away.

'More toast Granny?' Victoria asked.

'No thank you dear, but where is he?'

Vince returned to the sink. 'Best you don't worry yourself about the finer details of what happened to young Liam, he'll be safe in custody by now.' Vince began wiping the draining board.

If Liam hadn't made it over to Brixton, then Andwele was safe. Relieved, Laura loaded up her fork.

'Suffice to say,' Vince continued. 'With the help of Frank Holliday – dark horse him – he'd learned a trick or two in Northern Ireland from when he was chaplain in the Maze – we got what we wanted from the boy.'

Laura looked up; half a kidney perched on the end of her fork. 'What?'

'Not half handy his knowledge of waterboarding turned out to be.'

'Oh Vince,' Victoria said. 'You didn't waterboard Liam did you?'

'Honestly my love, what kind of a person d'yer think I am?' Vince flapped the dishcloth.

'But how did you know where to find Liam in the first place?' Laura asked.

'Canon Frank confessed to the illegal weddings when he realised you'd been abducted,' Victoria said. 'He was being blackmailed by Cheryl who knew about some affair he'd had.'

'Sang like a canary he did. Fear of defrocking I suppose, anyway he knew exactly where Liam would be, so we got him in the helicopter and got Charlie to meet us at Battersea.'

Laura took a deep breath. Canon Frank had confessed to the illegal weddings but did he know Liam was intending to have her killed? In the back of her mind she felt that there was something she had forgotten about that night. She was about to ask why he hadn't been arrested too, but Vince was now on a mission.

'Come on you two ladies,' he said. 'Get yer arses in gear on or we'll miss the first race.'

Vince was chatting with Charlie the chauffeur, about the fitness of his horse, in the front of the Range Rover, while Laura and Victoria sat in the back.

'Oh yes, Golden Pom-Poms is a beauty; just you wait 'til the filly comes romping home.' Vince rubbed his hands together as they crossed the Chiswick flyover.

'What a name to call a horse,' Laura said to Victoria.

'She's called Golden Pom-Poms after Vince's new range. Hasn't he sent you a set?'

'I don't think so.' She was momentarily distracted by the name of the horse, as she recalled Tam's sister. 'But let's get back to the story. How did you find out I was missing in the first place? Do please start at the beginning.'

As the car sped past Heathrow, Victoria opened up the

armrest between them and chose a pale blue nail varnish from the selection. 'Jervis called us. Repton rang him after he went to check on you when you didn't come down. He found Parker and your handbag and that's when he knew there was something really wrong.'

Laura gripped the trusty black crocodile bag to her chest.

'By the time we got to Mount Cod, Jervis, Strudel and Gladys were there.' Victoria blew on one fingernail. 'They'd gone to collect Canon Frank for the exorcism you'd laid on – and that's another story isn't it?' Victoria gave her grandmother a knowing look. 'Anyway when they found he wasn't at home they carried on to Mount Cod.'

The carphone rang.

'I'll finish telling you later,' Victoria said.

'Vince? I can get you eleven to four on…' came a voice.

'Slap on fifty big ones,' Vince said, as they drew into the member's car park.

Victoria slipped on her shoes and went round to the back of the car. Laura joined her as she lifted the lids from two hatboxes.

'Which would you prefer?' she asked.

Laura looked at the two creations, she was still thinking about the Canon's story. He must have known her life was in danger. 'I can't possibly wear either of them,' she said.

'Rubbish.' Vince elbowed her out of the way. He picked up a pink feathery tricorn, eyed Laura up and down and handed it to his wife. 'This'll go better with your shades,' he said, putting a white cake-like hat on Laura's head.

'But I can't wear dark glasses all afternoon,' Laura said.

'Easier than explaining,' Vince said, as they walked through the car park milling with people. 'Anyway you'll just look rich and a bit mad like all these other people.'

There were various friends and business acquaintances already waiting in Vince's box and soon the champagne was flowing. Then lunch was served.

Laura found herself sitting beside a Frenchman who said he was the silkworm farmer who supplied Foundation Rocks. As she ate her lamb cutlets, he entertained her with stories of how Vince had tried to engineer the output of the worms so that they produced even softer silk. 'For one whole season he had me feeding them Jacaranda leaves that he had sent from Cuba.'

'Did it make any difference?' Laura asked.

'No. The worms are refusing to eat them.'

The pudding arrived and Laura turned to Vince's old friend and accountant, Bernard, who was sitting on her right. He had just received the bill from Vince's racehorse trainer and was not best pleased, but as Laura knew him well, she quickly steered him onto safer ground. He had taken up tennis.

'That's good,' Laura said, lifting the damask tablecloth and revealing Bernard's shoes – he had only ever worn trainers, even with a suit. It was one of his little idiosyncrasies that Vince had learned was best ignored.

Laura and Bernard discussed the predictable nature of the Wimbledon finalists and it was not until the waiter standing behind her asked her if she would like more pudding, that she was diverted. I know that voice, she thought, and looked round.

Dressed in a dark suit, holding a bowl of Îles flottantes surrounded by berries, was Ned Stocking.

'Ned,' she called to him.

'I beg your pardon?'

Laura lifted her dark glasses.

'Christ, Lady Boxford, that's a corker.'

'Long story but what funny places you crop up in.'

'All in a day's work for the jobbing actor. Nice to see you.' Ned continued round the table and then went out to the kitchen closing the door behind him.

She managed to catch up with him as he was clearing away the coffee. Most of the guests were waiting outside on the balcony for the first race.

'I haven't had a chance to speak to Repton,' she said. 'Have you had the DNA results?'

'Any time now.'

Laura heard the race being announced, Vince didn't have a runner but she was reminded of his horse. 'Have you spoken to Pom about it?' she asked.

Ned looked disconsolate.

'Is something wrong?'

'Pom and I aren't seeing each other any more.' He stacked the coffee cups on a tray.

'Why, what's happened?'

Ned turned away from Laura and picked up the tray. 'It was when I told her I was going to the police about the stone eagles. Repton wanted to buy them back but they've got a huge price tag on them. Anyway I told Pom that Repton had been so happy when I'd told him I knew where they were.' Ned put the tray back down. 'He and his wife Matilda had bought them together from a house sale in Halifax shortly after they were married. I said to Pom, I know it's nothing to me, but Repton and Matilda were obviously very much in love.'

'Why should that have anything to do with you and Pom?'

Outside, a cheer rose up.

'I don't know. She started to cry and said she couldn't see me anymore.'

People were coming back in.

'I'll have to go, they'll be wanting tea any minute,' Ned said.

'We'll speak again soon, I'm sure.' Laura kept her eye on him, as he hurried out with the tray, wishing she'd had time to ask him more.

She watched the next two races with the silkworm farmer. He didn't really understand the finer points of racing and kept asking questions. Obviously he was most interested in the jockey's attire.

'I am hearing that in cold weather they wear ladies stockings underneath their jodhpurs,' he said, as they walked down to the paddock to look at Golden Pom-Poms where Vince was giving the jockey some last minute advice. The young man nodded his head in earnest, the gold bobble on his blue silk helmet – Vince liked continuity of marketing – bobbing up and down.

'Don't pay any attention to him,' the trainer said. 'Just do what we discussed last night.' The trainer launched the jockey up into the saddle. 'Now tuck your shirt in laddie. Look smart!'

'And these tops they are wearing, they are silks?' the Frenchman continued, as he and Laura walked back up to the box. Laura tried to concentrate on answering him but her mind was elsewhere. So much had happened in such a short space of time. Her brain was one swirling mass of Higgs boson microparticle possibilities; Canon Frank, Lance and Cheryl, Liam, Tam and Pom, Ned Stocking... Stockings... Silks? 'Silks?' she said, as Victoria joined them. 'They're barristers.'

'So the jockeys are all coming from the legal profession?' The Frenchman took off his top hat and scratched his head. 'This is a custom of Ascot I have not heard before.'

'Granny, are you filling Monsieur Garel's head with nonsense?'

His head? My head? Laura wondered if she had any aspirin in her bag.

Victoria turned to the Frenchman. 'You'll have to excuse her; she's had a tiring couple of days. Now come and watch the race, Golden Pom-Poms is down at the start.'

The rest of the afternoon became something of a blur. The heady smell of horse sweat in the winner's enclosure as Vince threw the Foundation Rocks rug on Golden Pom-Poms. The horse stamping its hooves and shaking its head as the stable girl held onto the reins. The crowds jostling around them as Vince was interviewed by the press and made jokes about Golden Pom-Poms' vital statistics and the likelihood of the filly's stable companion, Underwired, being a contender for the St Leger.

Before she knew it, Charlie was opening the car door for her and she sat down wearily next to Victoria.

'That was fun, wasn't it Granny?' she said. 'Frankly, I didn't think Golden Pom-Poms stood a chance.'

'Frankly, my love, you should have more confidence in your husband's choice of racehorses,' Vince called out. 'I hope you put some money on Charlie?'

'Certainly did Mr Outhwaite.' The chauffeur flicked the indicator and they headed back to London.

Laura turned to Victoria. 'So how did the Canon know where to find Liam?'

'Goodness, Granny how your mind does dart about, but honestly I don't know. We were just so relieved and the Canon seemed so sure we were on the right track and there was not a moment to lose.'

'So what did Liam say when he saw the Canon?'

'I wasn't there. Vince told me to go and sit outside in the car.' Victoria tapped Vince on the shoulder. 'Didn't you darling?'

'Back on that are we?'

'So what did you manage to get out of him?' Laura asked.

'Half the little creep's life story and a bit more once we'd took the sponge out.'

'Taken darling,' Victoria corrected. Vince's accent still tended to broaden when he was excited.

'Told us how you'd barged in on 'em in t'chapel. He'd had this idea of marrying illegal immigrants while he'd been studying psychology at Lampeter University. Hence his ready supply of young Welsh girls. They were all too willing to do it for the cash to help pay their tuition fees and they'd be divorced by the time they'd graduated. Tidy plan though I say it myself.' Vince chuckled.

Laura looked out of the window as the car came to a halt in traffic outside the Brompton Oratory. 'But how did Liam know where to get the men from?' she asked.

'Failed his first year exams and got a job in London with a property developer. Came across some Russians needing residency,' Vince said. 'Started small. Got himself a bent vicar and he's thinking this is a piece of...'

'Vince!'

'By that time he's living in a flat in Peckham. That's when the jammy tyke realised how easy it was to sub-rent. And then the Afghans started to arrive and after that it snowballed. But then some churchwarden starts to smell a rat. Needed new premises. Needs a new vicar. That's where Mount Cod comes in. So much handier for the Welsh connection.'

'I don't suppose you remember much of the evening do you Granny?'

Laura raised her sunglasses. 'I must admit it's hazy.' She felt her eye. 'But perhaps Matilda found out about what Cheryl's son was up to and that's why they had to get rid of her.'

'That's enough of that,' Vince said sternly. 'Leave it to Inspector Sandfield.'

Laura sat in silence.

'I think for once, Vince is right,' Victoria said. 'Anyway, when I spoke to Repton earlier, he said the Inspector had had a call from the police in Ludlow. Repton's Land Rover was spotted in a farmyard nearby. Cheryl and Lance have been found hiding in a grain silo and they've taken the Canon in for questioning.'

Chapter thirty-two

'Being abducted and getting engaged to a Libyan gentle-man,' Venetia said. 'And then Ascot, oh Laura, you have all the fun. The only thing that's happened to me is that I've managed to restyle my raincoat into a miniskirt. I got the idea from the sewing programme on BBC 2.'

'When did you last wear a miniskirt, Venetia dear?'

'Perhaps I could turn it into a mac for Parker?'

Laura looked at the pug as he lay curled up beside her on the sofa. He had been in the darkest of moods since she collected him from Mount Cod. Having greeted her with his usual enthusiasm he had quickly trotted off to join Sybil Thorndike in her basket.

'He's not speaking to me since I removed him from his love nest,' she said.

The dogs were not the only ones who were insepara-ble. Sir Repton was almost totally distracted by Gladys Freemantle and seemed not to fully comprehend the mag-nitude of Laura's ordeal. Gladys was now ensconced as acting cook and companion. Whether the relationship had developed further was something that Laura and Venetia had speculated on and concluded that it was not in any-body's interest to dwell on the matter. But there was some-thing that Laura found just a tiny bit irksome about the situation, so she hastily turned her mind to other matters, despite Vince's warning. But it was hard work keeping Venetia up to speed on the developments at Mount Cod and occasionally she even felt that perhaps the bump to her head she had received had had a lasting effect on her own powers of concentration.

'As I see it,' she said. 'It could still be either Tam or Cheryl and Lance who killed Matilda Willowby. But then again I haven't entirely discounted Canon Frank Holliday. I must find out what Inspector Sandfield's charged them with. Of course he wouldn't have a clue that they could be murderers as well.'

Laura could still feel her black eye throbbing and she rested her head on the back of the sofa. 'Of course it could have been Ned Stocking... bumping off his father's wife... revenge is a prime motivator when it comes to murder, but I'm not so keen on that idea.'

'Who are all these people? I thought you said it was Repton? I've always thought there was something rum about my cousin.'

'You're right, he really should remain in the picture.'

'There was a case on *Crimestoppers* only the other night about a man who murdered his wife. But then it turned out she had cancer and she'd asked him to do it. Have you thought about that? Matilda was ill after all.' Venetia made a grab for the TV remote but Laura got there first and put it out of harm's way in a drawer of her desk.

'Matilda had diabetes. She was hardly in a terminal condition. Oh dear, I'm feeling very muddle headed again. No, It's got to be Tam; frightening her to death because Matilda found out something about State of the Union.'

'State of who?'

'The wedding business. Do try to keep up Venetia.'

'I can't. I can feel withdrawal symptoms coming on. What time is it? Couldn't we just have the TV on in the background. I'm sure I could multitask and listen to you at the same time.' Venetia made a lurch for the drawer. 'Who did you say the other suspect was? I'd say it was a member of the family, it generally is. Repton, he's your man.'

Laura relented and gave her the remote.

Venetia flicked the TV on. Briefly they saw horses galloping down to the finishing line before Venetia changed channels and settled contentedly in front of *Come Dine With Me*.

The few frames of racing were enough to remind Laura of Ned Stocking again.

'I must get hold of him,' she said. 'What was it that had kyboshed his romance with Pom so effectively?'

'Crab pancakes?'

'His cooking?'

'But one of them is a vegetarian. Look. How idiotic of her,' Venetia pointed at the screen.

Laura tried to take an interest. The contestants were looking round their hostess' bedroom as she prepared the main course.

'How untidy young people are,' Venetia commented. 'Just like Angel. I never could get that slut to keep her bedroom tidy. She's a most unhygienic girl. I remember once I found a fish finger under her pillow. She'll be out soon I shouldn't wonder. Back on the streets collecting donkeys again. That girl really is a case.'

Case? Laura weighed up her options and found she didn't have any. She heard the telephone ring and got up to answer it.

'Ladyship?'

'Hello Mimi. How are you?'

'I downstairs in reception. There is man here wanting see you. He saying he is your fiancé but he no Brig time coming back, I sorry to say.'

'Mrs Boxford Akadigbo!' Andwele clasped Laura to his chest. 'Greetings from Brixton, from where I have come to be with my wife. All our friends are sending greetings, but they are also sad since Liam has disappeared with the wedding certificates.'

Laura extricated herself from his embrace. 'Oh dear.'

'But Ladyship...'

'Not to worry Mimi, I'll take Mr Akadigbo into the lounge. Could you by any chance have a cup of tea sent in for us?'

Laura took Andwele by the hand and steered him away from the reception desk.

'I believe Canon Frank Holliday is living in this vicinity, and what a very lovely vicinity it is,' Andwele said, as Laura sat him in a chair in the far corner of the room. 'I think maybe we could make him a visit so that he can conduct the ceremony for us as you had suggested?'

Laura followed his gaze as he looked around. Topsy Reynolds had made a rare foray downstairs and was sleeping in a chair beside the fireplace. Otherwise the room was empty.

'Veery nice, veery nice.' Andwele nodded appreciatively as he felt the fabric of the chair.

'Of course I will honour my side of the agreement,' Laura said. 'But it will take a little time to organise. In the meantime I'm afraid you cannot stay here, Andwele. Remember our little arrangement was only for the purpose of letting you remain in England.'

'But we are being evicted from our home in Brixton. I am once again a poor refugee.' Andwele fell to his knees. 'I beg you to show mercy upon me.'

'What about all the others?'

'They have set up a business in the town of Diss on the Suffolk border. But I am no good at car washing and soon enough they will end up in a detention centre if there is still no sign of Liam.'

Laura heard the clank of china and saw Alfredo making his way over to them, his chef's hat perched at a jaunty angle on his head, a tray in his hands.

Laura waved and beckoned him over. 'Hello, Alfredo, this is terribly good of you. Are you very short-staffed in the kitchen?'

'Faking hell Lady B, it's always the same,' he said, putting the tray down at their table. 'If it was for anyone else but yourself, I'd have refused point blank.'

'We must have words with Mr. Parrott, this can't go on.'

'Holy Zaragosa, don't get me started on Senor Parrott. I mean I'm only half way through preparing onions for the coq au vin when he comes in and says I can't have any wine. Says I use too much alcohol and you'll all get gout and give it to him and then we'll all get sepsis and die in agony. Man's a faking lunatic.' The chef took a step back and, seemingly for the first time, noticed Andwele, still on his knees at her side.

'This is Andwele Akadigbo.' Laura introduced them. She could see the look of consternation on the chef's face. Explaining the situation would have meant the tea going cold, but then an idea came to her.

'I wonder,' she said. 'Could Mr. Akadigbo and I possibly have a word with you in private in the kitchen. Shall we say in about half an hour?'

Andwele was most impressed by the kitchens at Wellworth Lawns. He admired the stainless steel work surfaces and looked in awe as Alfredo opened the cold meat store to get out the chickens.

'This is a veery fine bird,' he said, patting a fattened carcass that Alfredo held out for him. 'Why you no let me make the top class tagine for the supper with my wife?'

'Wife?' Alfredo frowned.

Laura sidestepped the issue. 'Do you enjoy cooking Andwele?'

'Many times I am complimented on the fine taste of my couscous.'

'Alfredo, you did say you were short-staffed.'

'Holy Santander Ferries, I'm run off my feet Lady B, can't you see?' Alfredo chose a meat cleaver and jointed a bird with lightening dexterity.

'How would you like it if Andwele here was to join you? You see I am indebted to him and he is at present in need of employment.'

Alfredo looked at Andwele and handed him the knife. 'Show us what you're made of then.'

Andwele grinned. He put the chicken down and sliced it clean in half.

Alfredo nodded appreciatively and turned to Laura. 'When can he start?'

Alfredo said Andwele could stay with him for the time being in the staff cottage in Woldham.

'What about Mr. Parrott?' Laura asked.

'Fak, as long as Andy here washes his hands and keeps his whites clean, old Parrott will be happy. I swear that man's got OCD. Where he doesn't keep a wet wipe is nobody's business.'

Laura told Alfredo she would have a word with Vince about the manager and left the two men in the kitchen.

It had been time consuming but she felt she had contained the situation. She would have to stand by her word to Andwele or there would be a problem with his wages. The sooner she got hold of the Canon the better.

Laura took Parker upstairs for his dinner. As she was opening a can of dog food for him the telephone rang. It was Sir Repton.

'My dear Laura,' he said. 'Such news I have. The DNA test has come back and now I have a son and heir!'

'I'm very pleased for you. You must give me his phone number so that I can congratulate him.'

'Indeed, indeed but I am calling to invite you to a celebration. Ned is coming to stay and I should be most pleased if you and Jervis and Strudel and my dear cousin Venetia would join Gladys and I here for luncheon on the Sunday after next. I've decided to forgive Canon Frank, so he will be coming too.'

'That's big of you under the circumstances.'

'He's too old a friend to desert and the Bishop has secured him bail.'

Laura was bemused by his magnanimity but she returned to feeding Parker, who in his impatience, had taken to turning in ever decreasing circles at her feet, puffing and spraying saliva on her shoes. Then she sat down to ring Ned Stocking.

'Funny old world isn't it,' he said.

'But you must be thrilled.'

'I'm afraid the delight has been tainted by something.'

'Is it Pom?' Laura asked.

There was a hesitation at the end of the line. 'I suppose it's only a matter of time before it come outs,' Ned said finally. 'Tam has been taken into custody with Robert Hanley Jones. They're facing charges of fraud and of course all the weddings have been cancelled.'

Chapter thirty-three

It was too important a conversation not to be shared immediately and while Venetia would have been Laura's first port of call, she knew that to interrupt her in the middle of her early evening schedule would be a bad idea, so she rang Strudel and Jervis. They invited her to join them for a vodka martini. Putting Parker on his lead she hurried downstairs and strode over to the bungalows.

Jervis let her in, a cocktail shaker in his hand. 'Go through, he said. 'Strudel's in the sitting room, I'm just getting some more olives.'

While Jervis went to the kitchen, Laura and Parker joined Strudel who was relaxing with her feet up on the sofa in a multicoloured crepe de chine kaftan and matching turban. 'You must forgive me Laura,' she said. 'I meant to wash my hair earlier but we had a crisis. It's our first divorce and the husband is blaming Ancient Eros for not telling him of his wife's addiction to online gambling.'

'But when I went through her paperwork I discovered she hadn't even got an email address.' Jervis said, as he came in with the olives.

'Like me, a Luddite, you mean?'

'We don't expect people in their eighties to be computer literate – and she's ninety-three – that's why we have the paper registration form.'

'So she must have learned from him,' Laura said.

'Exactly. I would have told him to bugger off it weren't for the fact that he's a retired solicitor.'

'Eventually we calmed him down and Jervis is explaining about a firewall.' Strudel patted her turban. 'But my wash and set went out of the window.'

'You look simply gorgeous as you are my love, but Laura, what's the hot news?'

Laura told them about the arrest of Robert Hanley Jones and Tam.

'Christ that makes five of your suspects in custody doesn't it?' Jervis laughed.

'I fail to see what's funny,' Laura said. 'Anyway the Canon's out on bail.'

'Well I'd say this latest news puts those girls squarely back in the frame for Matilda's murder.' Jervis stabbed an olive with a cocktail stick and dipped it in his martini. 'Sir Repton must be heartily relieved.'

'But that's not the end of the story,' Laura said. 'Pom, the nice twin, has had a nervous breakdown and been admitted to The Priory.'

When Ned had told Laura this, she had listened as his voice cracked with emotion. The poor girl had gone to visit her sister and discovered that Tam was secretly engaged to Robert Hanley Jones and they were planning to run away together. As if her sister's perfidy were not bad enough Tam had admitted to being party to his deceptions. She blamed Pom for her arrest saying she must have told Ned Stocking about the stolen eagles from the roof of Mount Cod.

'It's a tragedy for Ned. Pom refuses to see him. She feels too bad about the things that have happened and now that Ned is proven to be Repton's son, it makes matters even worse. Ned says it may be months before she recovers.'

Laura was a little anxious when Strudel invited her to stay and share their supper but at least she was prepared, knowing topside to be invariably tough and she asked for a small amount as Jervis sawed through the grey lump of meat.

'So what are you thinking about Cheryl and Lance?' Jervis eyed a piece of beetroot and turned to Strudel. 'You haven't pickled these have you my love?'

Strudel's lower lip quivered.

Jervis sighed. 'Pass me the Rennies, they're in the drawer behind you.'

'They are capable of anything,' Laura said, taking a sip of Riesling to help wash down a piece of beef.

'Your abduction was truly shocking.' Strudel reached across the table and squeezed Laura's hand.

'Thank you Strudel, but let's not go back over old ground. I'm trying to forget that episode. The thing is someone really needs to see Inspector Sandfield about it all. Of course I can't.' Laura turned to Jervis and gave him a pleading look.

'But Laura, I can't go blundering in with no real evidence. What about Canon Frank, is he back in the picture?'

Laura reached for her glass. She didn't like to lie to her friends. If Canon Frank were involved, it would have to come out later. For now she needed him until the Andwele business was concluded. '… I don't think so,' she said.

'You should speak to Sir Repton,' Jervis said. 'See if he can remember anything, anything at all that might be put before the Inspector as useful.'

'Good thinking, Jervis.' Laura put her knife and fork together looking at two last pieces of beetroot on her plate. 'For example if the so called hauntings had stopped since Lance and Cheryl have been in custody, that would be something.'

'Do not be reminding me of this. It is a subject on which we cannot agree.' Strudel got up to clear the plates. 'Jervis, we have a bowl of mandarins in the fridge and some condensed milk that my cousin has sent me from the Aldi in Badmunchensden with the bottle of Gewürztraminer. We shall celebrate with it and give thanks for the progress we have made and the safe return of our friend.'

The next morning Laura stayed in her room. She was still feeling a little tipsy when Mimi brought her up a sandwich at lunchtime. She had a vague recollection of dancing to a Nina Simone song in bare feet in Jervis and Strudel's carpeted sitting room. It had been a fun evening.

She was about to ring Sir Repton when she changed her mind; she'd visit him instead. It was overcast but still warm; a little ride out in the car with the windows down would clear her head.

As the lodge came into view, an idea came to her. Why had Lance and Cheryl lied about being married? She parked outside the front of the house and got out.

The front door wasn't locked so she walked in. She could see through to the kitchen and decided that that kind of chaos was best avoided. She carried on to the living area. A huge flat screen TV hung above the fireplace dominating the room. In front of it was placed a low-slung L shaped sofa on which the remnants of a meal still sat on dirty plates. She could imagine the two of them lounging on it while carrying out their deception.

Upstairs, the bed lay unmade, a trail of clothes scattered on the floor. The wardrobe door was open, hanging half off its hinges so that a brightly coloured silk dress on a hanger caught her eye. She checked the label. Of course, the fabric was a give away, she should have known it was by Pucci. But what was it doing here in the lodge? Could it have been Matilda's? Laura's pulse quickened and then slowed again.Even if it was, there could be a perfectly innocent reason for it being there.

She rifled through the rest of the dresses and found they were all from well-known high street stores; Laura wondered what, if anything, was in Cheryl's flat in the stable block.

'Come on, let's get out of here,' she said, as Parker emerged sneezing from under the bed, a tangle of cobwebs caught on his snout.

She drove up to the stable yard and still thinking about the dress, climbed the rough stone steps that led to Cheryl's flat. The door at the top was unlocked and she let herself in. It was as if no one had ever been there. Sir Repton had obviously never bothered to check because there wasn't even a bed. No wonder the Canon hadn't been able to stay there.

She walked back down and rang the back doorbell. There was no answer so she opened it and called out. The sound of the radio was coming from the kitchen where she found Sir Repton and Gladys sitting at the table reading recipe books.

'You've no idea how easy it would be to burgle you,' she said.

'Laura,' Gladys said. 'You nearly gave me a heart attack. We were planning the menu for our luncheon.'

'You two seem to have got things sorted out remarkably well.' Laura turned to Sir Repton. 'Has Gladys seen off Rosalind as well?'

'Golden lads and girls all must,

As chimney sweepers come to dust.'

'Oh Repton,' Gladys pulled a hankie from her pocket. 'That was lovely.'

'You mean she's gone?'

'It would appear that Gladys has indeed seen her off.' Sir Repton's watery eyes glazed over as he took her hand.

She left them discussing summer pudding having first asked him for the Canon's address.

Chapter thirty-four

Laura headed back to Woldham and edged her way down Campden Road in second gear, looking at the house numbers. She needn't have bothered as she saw Canon Frank in his front garden. He was up a ladder in a smart set of dark blue overalls, pruning a rose.

She drew up, put Parker on his lead and got out.

He only noticed her as she opened the wicket gate and called out, 'Hello Canon.'

The secateurs fell from his hand, landing with a thud not far from where Parker was sniffing some exceptional aroma on the lower branches of a purple flowering hebe. Laura picked them up.

The Canon hurriedly descended the ladder. 'Lady Boxford, You have been in my prayers. I had hoped to come and see you but I thought you might not be too keen under the present circumstances of my bail conditions. '

'Well, I'm here now and there's something I'd like to talk to you about if now is convenient?'

'Of course, come in and have a cup of tea.'

She handed him the secateurs and followed him into the house.

Despite the plain 1960s' facade, the interior of the house was a charming hotchpotch of tasteful knick-knackery. They walked through the hall past a console table with a floral arrangement of which Constance Spry would have been proud. Next to it was a miniature rendition of a chapel under a glass dome. It looked familiar.

'Is that Eton College Chapel?' Laura asked.

'A memento of my time as chaplain.' The Canon showed her into the sitting room.

'What a varied life you have led,' Laura said.

'I've had plenty of time in which to accomplish it. Please make yourself comfortable while I put the kettle on.'

While he was out of the room, Laura wandered around. Tall narrow bookshelves interspersed with Victorian watercolours lined the walls. Over the fireplace hung a gilt mirror the quality of which was immediately obvious; the top section was painted in oils depicting a bucolic scene.

Chaplain at Eton and the Maze, she thought. Perhaps they weren't so very different? But then St Botolph's… it was quite a career.

She walked over to the fireplace. On the mantle shelf stood a collection of Staffordshire greyhounds. She turned and looked out of a pair of French windows that led into the back garden. Roses rambled and clematis trailed in a profusion of colour around a circular area of lawn and along the back wall the doors of a Gothic style loggia stood open revealing a daybed covered in a multitude of brightly coloured cushions. It all looked most inviting and so unlike Sir Repton's broken-down sunroom.

'What a lovely garden,' she said, as the Canon returned. He placed the tray he was carrying on a low table and proceeded to pour the tea from a well polished silver teapot.

She sank down onto a soft, dark blue sofa. It was all so unexpectedly delightful that it seemed a pity to have to start a conversation of such an unpleasant nature. Still, she'd better get on with it.

'So you've been charged with conducting fake marriages?' she said.

The Canon's eyebrows slumped as he nodded in affirmation.

'I imagine you will plead coercion to the charge. But there's more to it than that. You see I also know that you knew the real danger I was in and that, Canon...' She took a sip of tea. The aroma of Lapsang, warm and smoky, filled her nostrils. '... makes you an accessory to attempted murder; rather different to merely being coerced into arranging false marriages don't you think?' There, she thought, that's got him.

The Canon glared at her, his eyebrows like two moles about to bump into each other. 'Steady on there, Lady Boxford. I tried to stop Liam Wilkes. That's why he knocked me out.'

'Oh.' Laura hadn't thought of this and it rather scuppered her line of attack. 'I'm so sorry,' she said, regrouping her thoughts. There was only one way forward and that was to grovel. 'Alright then I'll come clean Canon. The real reason why I'm here is that I find myself in a somewhat delicate position as a result of my abduction and I need your help.'

'Obviously I am deeply ashamed of my part in the whole sordid misadventure. I'll pay for it no doubt.' He sat down in a battered leather armchair. 'But in the meantime I will be of any assistance I can. Please tell me how?'

'When I was forcibly confined in Brixton, I had to make a pledge to marry one of the men that you had already illegally married in the chapel that evening. Liam Wilkes was himself blackmailing the men. He said he would not give them the wedding certificates that you had issued unless one of them, Andwele Akadigbo, got rid of me. So I struck a bargain for my freedom but before there was time to honour it, I had been rescued.

'Now Mr. Akadigbo has come to Wellworth Lawns – I have managed to get him work in the kitchen there but it is only temporary and he cannot stay. So you see I must honour my pledge to him.'

The moles took off, transformed in an instant back into birds in flight. 'Is this not a bit drastic?'

'As I said, I am an honourable woman and after all he could have killed me.'

'I'll write you out a marriage certificate now, this very minute.' The Canon jumped up and pulled open a drawer of his desk. 'How do you spell his name?' he said, taking out a pad of paper.

'You'll make sure his name is removed from the previous paperwork?'

'Of course. Inspector Sandfield has yet to gather all the evidence and I still have not finished filling out the certificates.'

Another man down on his knees, Laura thought as the Canon began filling in the form at a low table in front of Laura.

'You mean Liam didn't have them?

'I would have sent them to him. How do you spell his name?'

Laura hoped she had given him the right spelling 'So what about all those other men you married that night?' she continued.

'They can stay here legally I suppose. It is indeed a bad business.'

'But really Canon, how on earth did you ever get involved?'

'I'm afraid the Wilkes family are consummate black-mailers and unfortunately I became the recipient of their nefarious ways.' He handed her the completed form.

'The truth is that when Senora Diggory came to Woldham she was in a state of grief at the loss of her husband,' he continued. 'My wife and I took on the role of comforting her but unfortunately I let the situation get out of control and found that I was attracted to her in a physical sense. She was not averse to my attentions and before very long we were embroiled in a liaison of a sexual nature.' He looked up, still on his knees. Laura could only assume it was a position he was well practiced at from years of prayer.

'We made every effort at discretion but Cheryl Wilkes happened to be passing through the back of the churchyard one morning – I had no idea that it was a shortcut to the hostel where Lance was temporarily residing having been in prison for robbery. They were trying for a reconciliation at the time.'

'Lance had been in prison?'

'Yes, that's why Cheryl had taken the job at Mount Cod. She was most incensed when he took the job of gardener and was given the lodge. But over time they got back together.'

'So what happened that morning in the churchyard?'

'She caught us in flagrante. Threatened to tell my wife and the Bishop. Shortly after Senora Diggory left Woldham with a man she had met while attending an Anglo-Spanish culinary event in Birmingham. But the damage for me was done.'

'And when was this?' Laura said.

The Canon finally got up with a resounding crack of his knee joints, the confession over, 'Oh some years ago now. But Cheryl waited for her moment and I was trapped.'

Their eyes met. Laura felt a little faint but managed to compose herself. She hoped he hadn't noticed. Was this the sort of Rasputin effect he had had on Senora Diggory and... 'Tell me,' she said, 'did Matilda Willowby find out any of this?'

'Lady Willowby?' Canon Frank sat back down in the leather chair. 'Not as far as I know but I was only brought in after her death. Cheryl made her move on me when the vicar Liam had found in Pontypool turned tail.'

'So Matilda could have found out what Cheryl and Lance were up to?'

The Canon ran his fingers through his virgin white hair. 'That's true, but what are you saying?'

'I'm saying, Frank – may I call you Frank?'

'I insist!'

'I'm saying that it is not impossible that Cheryl or Lance or even Liam may have murdered Matilda. Don't you think it's suspicious?' Laura fiddled with her bracelet. 'I mean she may have gone into a diabetic coma but from what I've heard about her, it seems unlikely. She may have been missing one toe but she was still strong as an ox as far as I know.' She looked out at the warm early evening sunshine. 'Shall we go into the garden?'

Canon Frank opened the French windows. 'Now you say it, I'm beginning to think... She was most punctilious with her medication.' He walked out in front of Laura absently.

She followed him onto the lawn.

'I well remember on one occasion when I was reading a passage from Leviticus to her, that she stopped me in order to check her blood sugar levels. And if she wasn't in her boudoir, she liked to position herself at the top of the stairs with a loudhailer in order to command operations.' Canon Frank stepped into the loggia and began puffing up the cushions on the daybed. He gestured for Laura to take a seat as he eased himself into a Lloyd Loom chair beside it.

Laura had a sudden idea about actually lying down on the daybed but decided against it and sat instead as Parker jumped up beside her. 'So, what if she had found out about the Wilkes'?'

The Canon leant forward. 'So they have to silence her?' With his elbow on one knee, he rested his chin in his cupped hand.

'Then after they've killed her, Cheryl starts the ghost business. That's why she and Lance had to pretend they weren't married. So that she could be in the flat, close enough to put on her nightly show and frighten Repton into submission. Making him, half out of his mind and so incapable, he was completely reliant on her and Lance. Do you know there hasn't been a so-called haunting since the evening they disappeared. The evening of the last weddings you conducted.'

The Canon remained silent as he swatted away a fly buzzing above his head, and then he said, 'Did you think it could have been me?'

'You were on my list, yes. But then so was Repton himself. Actually, he could theoretically still be in the frame.'

'You're not serious are you?'

'I don't know.' It was as if they had turned a corner and now Canon Frank was on her side. A gentle gust of wind shook the climbing rose above them and a flurry of petals landed on the ground. Laura told him about her other suspects.

'But I still think Cheryl and Lance have the best motive and the wherewithal to play at haunting.'

'So what will you do?'

Laura heard the sound of whistling coming from a neighbouring garden and Parker growled beside her. 'It's more of a case of what you can do,' she said. 'I was going to send my friend Jervis, but now I think it would be better if you went.'

'Went where?'

'To see Inspector Sandfield. It could also help your case.'

Canon Frank's pale cheeks coloured. Laura went on to tell him about Kelsey's boyfriend seeing Cheryl wearing a large diamond ring and of her finding the Pucci dress in the lodge.

'I wouldn't think Lady Willowby was the kind of person to lend her clothing out to her employees,' Canon Frank said. 'But you say Sir Repton had no knowledge of the ring?'

'He couldn't remember.'

'All the same, I agree this sounds like a matter for Inspector Sandfield.'

'Excellent,' Laura said. 'I feel we have achieved a lot this afternoon.'

Chapter thirty-five

First thing the next morning, Laura went down to the kitchens.

'Look Andwele,' she said, holding up the marriage certificate.

Andwele put down the knife beside the bunch of mint he was chopping and took the piece of paper. Tears began rolling down his cheeks. He clasped her to him. 'Boxford, this is indeed too much good.'

How had it happened that this new husband used the same nomenclature as her late departed fiancé, the Brigadier?

'But I stay here in Wellworth Lawns,' he continued. 'Alfredo, he is my friend and I am teaching him many of my country's favourite dishes.'

Laura realised she was going to have to tell either Vince or Edward Parrott about her marriage to Andwele or he would lose his job. But then she had a better idea. She had seen Bernard, Vince's accountant at Ascot. He would understand the delicacy of the situation. She called him in the office in Leeds.

'Don't you worry Laura,' he said. 'Your matrimonial arrangements are nobody's business but your own. I'll simply tell Parrott that Mr Akadigbo's papers are in order and that'll be an end to it. Between you and I how are things going at Wellworth Lawns?'

Laura told him about the continuing short supply of food and Edward Parrott's obsession with cleanliness.

'This situation can't go on,' Bernard said.' I've just had another invoice for wall-mounted hand sanitisers. Sixty-five of them.'

'I'm not going to Mount Cod with that murderer, and I don't trust Gladys' cooking,' Venetia said, as Laura walked her down the stairs for lunch. The problem of the lift being permanently out of order was now beyond a joke. Some of the residents had been stuck in their rooms for weeks. Mimi was fraught with having to bring up trays to the inhabitants of the second floor who had set up their own dining club on the landing. Sometimes, Venetia said she had joined them, as the stairs to the second floor were carpeted and not nearly as hazardous as the ones to the ground floor. There was also a fire door leading onto a small balcony up there that they wedged open and sat round on sunny evenings playing Happy Families.

'But I'm pretty sure Repton's not a murderer,' Laura said. 'I've told you before, it's that couple who looked after him. Inspector Sandfield will have to investigate after the Canon's spoken with him.'

As they reached the bottom of the stairs, Venetia felt safe enough to let go of Laura's arm and they walked side by side into the dining room and chose a table near the window.

'Talking of the police,' Venetia said, tucking her napkin into the collar of her shirt. 'Angel came to see me. She's out you know and she's found a donkey in a field somewhere that she wants to transport to Devon as all the local sanctuaries are full. I suggested she ride it there. She's lost a bit of weight while she's been in prison.'

Mimi placed their starters in front of them.

'What's this?' Venetia asked.

'Is Andy chickpea mealie. Alfredo leaving him in charge.'

'Who's Andy?' Venetia asked, as she popped the fritter into her mouth.

'He Ladyship's…'

Laura coughed.

'He is Alfredo's new assistant,' Mimi said.

'Well, tell Andy I'd like some more.'

'I so sorry Mrs Hobb. Mr. Parrott he still keeping tight eye on portion control and now he say vegetarian is best for health. He saying no vegetarian ever die of nasty diseases.' Mimi leant forward and whispered to them. 'I tell you he going way crazy with the hand washing and all that. Alfredo say his OCD headcase is danger to us and he need to see psychiatrist pronto.' Mimi nodded her head conspiratorially and went back to the kitchen.

'I'll have to talk to Vince,' Laura said. 'It's just that there are so many other things to do right now.'

'Like what? All I've got to do is try not to forget it's the last episode of *Benefits Britain* and I want to find out what happens to the man who says he can't feed his twenty-six children. It's truly shocking in this day and age.'

'Children, that reminds me, Repton 's lunch party is to celebrate his child.'

'Are you deliberately trying to confuse me now?'

'It's been proved that Ned Stocking is Repton's son.'

'I don't think Angel will be best pleased if she gets to hear about that. She's got some very detailed plans for converting Mount Cod into a cat refuge and feline veterinary centre.'

Mimi reappeared with the main course. 'Is aubergine and rice sausage,' she said.

Laura picked up her fork. 'How delightfully authentic.'

'But so little of it,' Venetia said. 'Thank goodness my Tesco biscuits are being delivered.'

'How have you managed that?' Laura asked.

'The second floor residents have formed an association. Reggie Hawkesmore says it reminds him of being back in the POW camp. One of his female friends orders for us online.'

Later in the afternoon, Laura returned from Dudley's Hair Designs. She walked into the hall pulling Parker behind her; he had become a rather reluctant companion recently and had been loath to leave the greyhound's basket at the hairdresser's. As she passed the reception desk Mimi called out to her.

'Ladyship, I having urgent message for you.'

'Goodness Mimi, what's happened?'

'Is Mrs Free. She coming back this morning. Now she calling me and asking where you are, because you not answering your phone. She say me when Ladyship coming she want see you soon as possible.'

'I'd better go and see what the matter is.'

Parker stood with his feet firmly planted at the foot of the stairs and refused to budge. Becoming exasperated, Laura picked him up and carried him until they got to the carpet on the first floor. They walked down the passage and knocked on Gladys' door.

The door inched open and Gladys poked her nose out.

'Thank goodness you've come, where have you been?' she said, opening the door wide enough for Laura and Parker to pass through. Then she closed it hastily behind them and made a rush for her bed. 'I'm sorry,' she said. 'But it's the only place I feel safe.'

'Whatever is the matter?' Laura asked, taking a chair.

'It happened last night.' Gladys clutched the bedclothes.

'What happened?'

'I was in bed in Grimsby. Something woke me. The door creaking I think. I called out, "Repton, is that you?" But he didn't answer. It was pitch dark. I tried to find the bedside light switch. I could hear his breath. It was coming closer. I fumbled trying to find my glasses and then I heard them drop onto the floor. I called out again.'

'What did you call out?'

'I called his name. But he didn't answer and I could feel the breathing coming closer. It was hot. Close by. And then I could feel his hand on the bedclothes and then. And then...' Gladys sobbed.

'And then what?'

'He felt my breast!'

'But Gladys,' Laura, who had been sitting on the edge of her seat, relaxed back into the chair. 'This sounds to me exactly the result you had been looking for. I can't see what the problem is.'

'No Laura. You've got it all wrong.'

'But what about your sexual awakening. I thought you said you wanted to get in as much as possible before it was too late.'

'But that was before.'

'Before what?'

'Before Repton. He was so much the gentleman. I could understand him wanting to wait until after we were married.'

'Has he asked you to marry him?'

'Not exactly.'

'What do you mean, not exactly?'

'Well, not in so many words. But I thought that he was leaving it until he thought a suitable amount of time had passed since his wife died. I was happy to wait. But then this happened. Honestly Laura I was in fear of my womanhood.'

'Good heavens Gladys, what did you do?'

'I screamed. It made him press harder on my bosom. And then his hand moved up... I felt it closing on my neck. I was petrified.'

Laura gasped.

Gladys fanned her face with her hand.

'So then what happened?'

'I found the lamp. I picked it up and hit him. It was made of brass.'

'What did he do?'

'Let go of my neck. Swore F.U.C.K, and ran out.'

'F.U.C.K?'

'You know what I mean. I don't like to swear.'

'So then what did you do?'

'What do you think I did? It was three in the morning. I didn't have much choice in the matter. But I did get up and put a chair in front of the door. I had to edge my way to the main light switch as the lamp had broken. Then I opened the curtains and waited until morning.'

'So did you see him then?'

'Yes, I was in the kitchen with my case ringing for a taxi. He came in all bright and cheery; said he'd never slept so well on account of taking a sleeping pill.'

'You mean he denied everything.'

'Yes.'

Had Repton's manly desires got the better of him after weeks of Gladys' relentless flirting? 'He must have been sleepwalking.'

'But Laura, it makes no difference if he was or not. Either way his intentions were... dangerous. Anyway I didn't exactly feel like discussing his nocturnal habits at that moment. I was just keen to get away from him.'

Or was he intent upon something more sinister? Laura could feel her thought processes spiralling but it was often this wildness that could precipitate a breakthrough. Had Gladys' takeover bid reminded him of Matilda's overbearing character? That same intolerance in his flawed character that had driven him to murder her. 'What did you say?' she asked.

'I told him while he'd been so heavily asleep the telephone had rung for me and that an old friend from the Hydrangea Society had had a heart attack and that I must go to her.'

Laura knew how heavily she relied on Strudel and Jervis and she knew she must tell them this latest news at the first opportunity. Gladys was reluctant to come with her so she and Parker hurried over to Mulberry Close alone.

They were in the kitchen bottling cabbage. 'What are we going to do about the lunch party?' Strudel asked. 'I cannot see Gladys being in attendance and who will do the cooking now?' She handed the jar to Jervis to screw the lid on and took off her apron.

'You'll have to do it my love, we've got enough sauerkraut here to feed an army,' Jervis said. 'But in all of this it doesn't seem to have occurred to you Laura, that Sir Repton may be perfectly innocent. I mean what possible motive could he have for attacking Gladys?'

'Psychopathic tendencies; you ask Venetia. I should have listened to her all along. And anyway who else could it have been?'

'I'd have thought that was perfectly obvious.' Jervis opened the cupboard and put the jar on the shelf with all the others. 'The ghost of course.'

'But Cheryl's in custody.'

'You don't get it do you?'

'Jervis, you must not be speaking to our friend in this most brutal tone. It is not her fault that she is not blessed with the kind of mind that is receiving the supernatural vibe.'

'We must put an end to all this,' Laura said. 'We'll have that exorcism after all. I'll call the Canon. We'll do it tomorrow afternoon and thinking about it, I'd better tell him to hang fire with his meeting with Inspector Sandfield. Cheryl wasn't the murderer. Repton was and the minute we've finished laying your ghost to rest, I'll go myself to the Inspector and dob in the wretched old thespian myself.'

Canon Frank was dismayed by the news of Gladys and more so having recently returned from his interview with Inspector Sandfield who had left immediately to interrogate Cheryl.

'Never mind that,' Laura said. 'It will be good practice for him.'

'But Sir Repton?' Canon Frank was genuinely shocked. 'Can we be sure? I don't like the sound of all this.'

'I know,' Laura realised she must placate him. 'It is most

distressing, but that is why the exorcism is so necessary. Repton must either be implicated or Vindicated. You must tell him the ghost may only be temporarily inactive and we must pretend we have no idea about Gladys.'

She watched as the Canon nodded his head, deep in thought.

'I think we should prepare ourselves for an overnight visit,' he said.

'But last time you said the ghost had to be left alone before the exorcism.'

'Different circumstances call for different methodology. It is now well past Sexagesima and her hormonal balance will be affected by the longer evenings.'

Not for the first time Laura wondered if she shouldn't have called Reverend Mulcaster instead.

By the end of the evening Laura had everything in place. Having agreed on the time with Sir Repton, Strudel and Jervis, she checked on Gladys, walked Parker and had supper with Venetia – 'I told you he was a murderer' – Laura retired to bed.

But her mind was still abuzz and she knew she couldn't sleep so she opened the Brigadier's 1965 diary. Having taken out her contact lenses, she put on her reading glasses and angled them firmly on her nose. The little satin ribbon marked the last page she had read. And then she remembered Iris. She studied the rest of September but there was no mention of her. Various numbers were jotted down that she assumed were to do with the Buff Orpington's egg-laying habits. Then the hens went off lay and the Brigadier was taken up with photography. He had taken a picture of a car crash in Orpington High Street that was published in the local newspaper. The driver had walked away but the paintwork on a lamppost had been damaged. The Brigadier was busy with these humdrum goings on and Laura was getting bored. She flicked to late November, scanning the page for

Iris' name. On the twenty-second she saw it:

'Iris left this morning. Bad business.'

Eyes wide, Laura turned back a page to see if there was a reason for Iris' disappearance. And then she found it. On the Friday before she read:

'Kadicha turned up. God knows how she found me? Alas the older child has died but the twins are now four years old. Very bonny but a shock all the same.'

Laura took off her glasses, flung the diary on the floor and turned out the light.

For hours it seemed, she lay unable to sleep. It was all very well her engagement to the Brigadier being based on the unspoken principle that the past was the past, but the idea that he had not told her of his offspring was, to put it mildly, not what she was expecting.

Parker shifted down the bed and snuggled in to her left ankle. She rolled over trying to distance herself from him but he followed her. Eventually she turned on the light and got up. She sat on the sofa thinking. Times were different then. Africa was a wild continent. He was far away from home. But then she remembered the other girls. She hunted round and found the 1961 diary. All that time when she thought he'd had malaria… She found the page. Marjani… Kadicha… Afi… And those were only the ones he mentioned by name. It was too much. How many children had he fathered?

Chapter thirty-six

Laura felt as if she had only just got to sleep when the phone woke her at 8.45 and Jervis told her to be downstairs at half past one. She wondered if she was going to make it through the rigors of a full blown exorcism at the hands of Canon Frank Holliday. He had said it could be a lengthy process and he was bound to be thorough.

By early afternoon, she was feeling a little better and she set out with Parker and her overnight bag.

'There you are Laura,' Jervis held the car door open for her. 'You'd better go in the back with Strudel,' he said. 'I don't think the Canon's knees will fit. Let me put your bag in the boot.'

Jervis drove down the drive and swung at speed onto the main road.

To Laura's relief, he slowed and stopped behind a bus. He waited. Minutes passed.

'Perhaps it's out of service,' she suggested.

'Fair point.' Jervis indicated, eased out and hit the brakes as a van behind hooted and overtook. As it passed them Laura saw a familiar black-clad arm appear out of the window as Angel Hobbs flicked them a V sign.

'Damn fool,' Jervis said, taking up pursuit as they passed the 30 mph sign on the outskirts of town.

Laura suggested a short cut and soon they were crossing the speed bumps of the narrow residential streets that led to Canon Frank's house.

Jervis turned into Campden Road and pulled up outside

his house where the Canon was ready waiting, a six-foot crucifix at his side and a small case clasped to his chest. 'That's what I call service,' he said, as Jervis leant over and opened the passenger door.

'I like to be punctual.'

'I meant not having to step down.'

Jervis got out. He looked at the tyres parked on the pavement and then at the cross.

'It's the one from Holy Trinity,' Canon Frank said. 'The Bishop recommended it for the job. Sometimes size is important if the spirit turns recalcitrant.'

'I don't think it will fit in the boot,' Jervis said. 'But don't worry it can go on the roof-rack, I always carry plenty of bungee ropes for this sort of occasion.'

Laura felt the car springs moving from side to side as the two men grappled with the religious artefact. Finally they returned to their seats and they resumed their journey.

Sir Repton was waiting at the front door, pacing up and down, his stick under one arm. 'But where is Gladys?' he said.

'I'm afraid Gladys is not feeling well,' Laura said. 'She sends her apologies.'

'Unwell?'

'Her friend died.' Laura thought it better to be final in this matter and they followed Sir Repton into the sitting room while Canon Frank brought in the crucifix. He propped it up against the tallboy and took a seat on one of the sofas. Strudel and Jervis sat opposite him and Laura took up her position on the tub chair. Sir Repton looked round and drew up another chair.

'So, let battle commence.' Jervis rubbed his hands together.

'I think we must get a few things straight before we begin.' The Canon took a large Bible out of his case, 'This act of exorcism is a holy rite. I suggest a prayer.' The Canon got to his knees.

'Christ, I can't do that, I'll never get up again,' Jervis said.

'A bowing of the head should be sufficient.' Canon Frank opened the Bible. 'Holy Father,' he intoned, and then read out a lengthy passage Laura was not familiar with. From early girlhood in her convent school, she had always found it difficult to concentrate on sacred texts, preferring instead to imagine the hairstyle each nun was concealing underneath their respective wimples. Now she clouded over almost entirely until she heard the Canon say, 'Amen.'

She raised her head as he got up and began to pace around the room.

'We must fix upon an object that typifies the spirit of...' He looked about him.

'Rosalind?' Laura offered.

'Yes, the serving wench. What do you think Sir Repton?' He walked over to the window and ran his hand down the brocade curtains.

'She's never come in through a window to my knowledge,' Sir Repton said.

The Canon continued round the room touching various objects. He picked up the lead tea caddy Parker had knocked off the tripod table on Laura's first evening at Mount Cod but Sir Repton shook his head. Next the Canon pointed to a Tibetan brass bell, and then he picked up a leather-bound volume of poetry and then a spelter statuette but none met with Sir Repton's approval. Having scoured the room for a second time his eyes alighted upon a pewter tankard from the mantle shelf. 'How about this?' he said. 'She liked a drink didn't she?'

Sir Repton shook his head again. 'Matilda's father won it for the high jump at his prep school, but I don't feel it's right.'

'What about upstairs?' Jervis suggested.

'Yes, I am agreeing. When she was strangulating me on the staircase, I was feeling a power coming from overhead.' Strudel put her hands involuntarily to her neck.

They trooped upstairs. Parker and Sybil Thorndike nudged one another playfully as they gambolled down the corridor. Laura followed as Canon Frank went into the bedrooms one by one. Things looked hopeful when they entered Matilda's boudoir situated off the main bedroom. Laura sat down on a satin daybed as the Canon fingered one of a pair of silver hairbrushes on the dressing table.

'Could it be this that Rosalind is using as her entry point from beyond?' he said.

Repton pondered. He picked up the brush. 'I can feel something,' he said, touching it to one cheek and closing his eyes.

'Well,' Laura asked. 'Is it her?'

'No,' Repton said and put it down again.

'What a pity.' Of course it's not you disingenuous old fool. Laura's feet were beginning to ache.

They moved on to Flamborough Head. This is a waste of time, Laura thought as the Canon suggested Rosalind could be manifesting herself through the heated bath rail. She trailed out after them as they discussed the possibility of Rosalind being the Persian rug at the end of the bed. She leant against a cupboard. The door creaked.

'What was that?' Sir Repton asked.

'It's just this…' Laura took hold of the cupboard door handle.

'That's it.' Sir Repton walked over sniffing the air. 'I can feel something definite. A power is emanating forth.'

Laura opened the door.

'Matilda's wheelchair.' Sir Repton took hold of the handles and wheeled it into the room. Canon Frank joined him.

'Seems incredulous to me,' Jervis said. 'It's old I admit, but it's hardly sixteenth century.'

'That is irrelevant according to the Bishop. Has there ever been an indication that Rosalind may have been infirm? These thing's work in mysterious ways,' he said, massaging one of the fake leather armrests.

'Not that I am aware of,' Sir Repton said.

'Never mind, I think we may be in business.'

'Would not, perhaps a tea break be assisting us before the next phase?' Strudel asked.

'No, no.' Canon Frank wagged a finger at her. 'We must fast. It is part of the process.' He turned his attention back to the wheelchair and raised his arms. 'I exorcise you, most unclean spirit. In the name of Jesus be uprooted and expelled from this... mode of transport.' He stood back and waited. 'The Bishop warned me this could be a tricky job. I suggest another prayer with some holy water. Sir Repton, do you have a bucket handy?'

'I'll go down and get one from the scullery,' Sir Repton said.

'I'll come too. We need the crucifix.' The Canon followed him out.

While they waited, Laura, Strudel and Jervis sat on the bed with the two dogs.

'The Canon's taking it damn seriously that's for sure, I'm impressed,' Jervis said. Sybil Thorndike growled as he lay back on a pillow. 'Bloody unpleasant dog that,' he said, pushing her off the bed.

They heard the sound of the crucifix being dragged along the landing. Canon Frank lugged it into the room and stood it upright against the cupboard. 'There'll be no escape for her with this,' he said, as Sir Repton followed him in carrying a red plastic bucket sloshing with water. 'Canon Frank thought the kitchen tap most apposite.'

'Nearest to the mains.' Canon Frank took the bucket from him. 'I sanctified it there and then. If I could trouble you for the utensil Sir Repton?'

Sir Repton handed him a stainless steel ladle and the Canon dipped it into the bucket and poured it over the wheelchair, exhorting Rosalind to quit the mobility equipment.

They stood in anticipation of what Laura was certain

would be the inevitable consequence of the absurd situation. It was. Nothing happened. Drips of water fell silently onto the Wilton carpet. The Canon tried again.

'In the name of the Holy Spirit I implore you Rosalind to evacuate this wheelchair.'

The inanimate object, the focus of all their attention stood like something from a Marcel Duchamp retrospective but again there was zero spiritual activity.

'The wheelchair is failing to respond. I think we may have underestimated the wench's cunning.' The Canon stepped backwards. At his feet, Sybil Thorndike snarled, drew back her gums revealing yellow teeth flecked with saliva. She snarled again and bit hard into the Canon's ankle.

'Hellfire,' he cried out, hopping about on one foot.

'Get that dog out of here,' Jervis shouted, running forward with a handkerchief and the bucket of holy water.

Laura snatched Sybil Thorndike off the floor before she had time for another mouthful. She handed the dog to Sir Repton. He patted her, but the dog continued to growl. He studied her. 'A countenance more in sorrow than in anger,' he said in a tone of doleful enlightenment.

'What are you talking about man?' The Canon sat down on the bed and pulled up his trouser leg. 'That vicious creature's drawn blood and it's my bad ankle.'

'I may have had an idea,' Sir Repton said. 'I think it could be that Sybil Thorndike is the conduit to Rosalind that we have been searching for. Her spirit of malcontent and desperation to communicate has infiltrated the hound, it all makes perfect sense.'

The Canon looked up. 'You may be onto something there.'

'Either way, it can wait. For now I think we should bandage up Frank then go downstairs and make a pot of tea – a biscuit wouldn't go amiss either.' Laura headed for the door. 'Repton, where's the first aid kit?'

'I'll fetch it and meet you in the kitchen.'

'Good plan,' said the Canon, as Sir Repton hurried out.

'But what about the fasting?' Jervis asked

'That was when we were concentrating on the wheel-chair. The dog is a different matter. We will start afresh after a brief respite.'

Chapter thirty-seven

Laura was feeling a good deal better after a couple of chocolate digestives – Gladys had stocked the place up well – and the colour had returned to Canon Frank's cheeks once Strudel had put antiseptic on his ankle and bandaged it up. Sir Repton furnished him with a walking stick and they returned to the sitting room where Sybil Thorndike had been shut in.

Jervis was dispatched back upstairs to collect the crucifix and holy water. He managed to get the bucket handle over one of the crossbeams thus getting both objects down in one go.

'Where d'you want it?' he asked, having put the bucket down.

'I think I'll conduct proceedings seated.' Canon Frank concertina'd himself into the tub chair and Laura fetched a stool for him to put his leg on. 'Let's have the cross on the floor to my left and the holy water on my right,' he said.

When he was happy with these positionings, he directed his gaze at Sybil Thorndike who was asleep in her basket. 'I'm loath to get too near that animal, I wonder if I can conduct the operation by proxy?'

'I shouldn't think so,' Jervis said. 'I tell you what, why don't we muzzle her?'

'Oh Jervis, this is most unkind,' Strudel said.

'I know exactly how to muzzle a dog, it's quite humane. I'll fetch another bandage.' Laura hurried back to the kitchen and returned with a length of crepe.

'Repton, wake her up and hold her tight in your arms.'

Sir Repton picked up the dog. 'Do you think she should go out first?'

'Bladders of iron these miniature breeds, I think she'll hold on.' Laura attached one end of the bandage to Sybil Thorndike's collar, wrapped it round her snout and attached the other end back to the collar. Sybil Thorndike looked up at her with wide watery eyes. She did not look like the incarnation of an eighteenth-century serving maid hell bent on murder. This is utter nonsense, Laura thought, not for the first time.

'Bring her to me,' Canon Frank called out from his chair. 'You're sure the muzzle is secure?'

'Quite sure,' Laura said.

Sir Repton carried the dog and stood in front of the Canon. By increments – the crucifix was repositioned leaning up against a bookcase behind the chair – and eventually with Sir Repton on his knees to one side of Canon Frank's prone leg, the dog was brought face to face with the mouthpiece of the Lord.

'I beg upon the Holy Spirit who will destroy with the breath of his mouth...' the Canon recited to the startled dog '... rendering Rosalind powerless by the manifestation of his coming.'

Sybil Thorndike whined and began struggling.

'Hold her tighter Sir Repton, this moment is of vital importance.' Canon Frank reached to his side and tried to get hold of the bucket. 'Jervis, hand me the holy water and the ladle.'

Jervis did as he was told and Canon Frank leant forward, dipped the ladle into the bucket and poured it over the dog's head. Sybil Thorndike whined furiously, struggled out of Sir Repton's soaking arms and ran from the room.

He leapt up with unforeseen agility, 'Canst thou not minister to a mind diseased?' he cried, chasing after the dog.

Laura watched with incredulity. She had never seen him move so fast.

'What was all that about?' Jervis asked.

'He is possessed of a need to follow the dog,' Strudel said, from where she was sitting on the sofa.

'Possessed?' Canon Frank sat back, still holding the ladle. 'I think we may have been metaphorically barking up the wrong tree.'

'What do you mean?' Laura asked.

'It's not the dog, I'm afraid.' He began to tap the ladle into the palm of his other hand. 'It is Sir Repton himself. Did you see his reaction to the holy water?'

'He got wet didn't he. That's why he let go of the dog.' Jervis said.

'Ah, but it was more than that. In my opinion he, or rather the incarnation of Rosalind, is, possibly temporarily, inhabiting him and as such was put in jeopardy by the presence of the Lord's water – if you see what I mean.'

Jervis looked at his watch. 'I'd say it was time for something a little stronger than the Lord's water. Where does he keep the whisky Laura?'

'Good thinking Jervis.' Laura pointed to the drinks cupboard. 'But I'm wondering how this is going to end.' She turned to the Canon. 'I suppose it means we must exorcise Repton.'

'Undoubtedly the answer.'

'But it's already six-thirty.'

'We must momentum not be losing,' Strudel said.

'Fair play but I'd still recommend a sharpener.' Jervis opened the cupboard door. 'Then we'll fix up something more solid to sustain ourselves with. You said it was all right to eat before the action didn't you Frank? Fried eggs on toast should do the trick and then we'll crack on. Out the ghost and… well we may just have to kip down here for the night, as you said Canon. I imagine the old boy will need looking after once he's had the she-devil extracted. Bit like a liver transplant I'd have thought?'

Laura walked over to the open door and looked out into the hall. 'Where do you suppose he's got to anyway?'

Eventually she found him lying on the daybed in Matilda's boudoir, Sybil Thorndike in his arms. The dog jumped down to greet Parker and they started to play.

'There,' Laura said. 'She's made a full recovery from her ordeal. She seems a little overweight... to ...that's what made her snap.' She seems a little overweight, I think Gladys may have been overfeeding her and perhaps that's what made her snap.'

It was not so easy to explain to Sir Repton the next course of action that the Canon intended.

'I suppose he must be right,' Sir Repton said. 'My chest feels tight, perhaps it's her corset?'

'I think what he means is that you may be nearest to her spirit and you might be the way to communicate with her,' Laura said. 'They all think it's worth a try. Why not come downstairs, Strudel's making us some supper. We thought we'd all stay on, if you don't mind. The Canon's keen to complete the task and he says we can drink, so actually it might be rather fun. A bit like playing charades at Christmas.'

'Except that it's only me that's the charade.'

Canon Frank managed to hobble to the kitchen where Jervis was busy knocking up Manhattans, while Strudel cooked the eggs.

'How's the leg feeling?' Laura asked the Canon.

'Fill me up Jervis and I'll be right as rain,' he said, draining his glass as Sir Repton hurried to the wine cellar and brought up a couple of bottles of Pomerol.

What with eating and then clearing up it was not until nine-thirty before they were back in the sitting room ready for round three, as Jervis put it.

'I do hope it's not going to turn into a boxing match with me as the punching bag.' Repton put his hand to his stomach.

'No, no,' Canon Frank assured him. 'I'm pretty sure she's

going to make a run for it as soon as I've rebaptised you. You have been baptised haven't you?'

Sir Repton nodded.

'You mean we've got to decamp to the font in the chapel?' Laura gave the Canon a stern look. He couldn't have the effrontery could he?

Canon Frank got the message. 'D'you think you could fit your head in the bucket Sir Repton?' he asked. 'It's only got to touch the water, not a full emersion.'

The Canon was sailing mighty close to the wind here, but Sir Repton didn't seem to have noticed the inference to Matilda's drowning.

'I may as well take communion while I'm at it,' Sir Repton said. 'Jervis could you get the port, it's in the cabinet over there.' He pointed to the drinks cupboard.

'Reservation of the sacrament, I like it,' Canon Frank said.

Jervis filled a glass and handed it to the Canon who agreed they could dispense with the body of Christ and consecrated it for Sir Repton. He downed the port then got on his knees again and sank his head into the bucket as the Canon urged him to reaffirm and give his life to Jesus. Sir Repton got up unsteadily from the bucket, his thin hair streaming water down his face and neck.

'That was most refreshing,' he said. 'But I think all the blood's going to my feet.'

Jervis caught him as he began to topple forward and sat him down on a sofa.

As Strudel patted his hair with a tissue from her bag, the Canon again exhorted Rosalind to leave. He closed his eyes. 'Be gone seducer, the desert is your home,' he roared. 'God has prepared hell for you and your angels.'

A deathly hush fell on the room. Canon Frank remained unmoving. Then he opened his eyes and looked about him.

After a minute or so, Jervis broke the silence. 'I say that was pretty steep,' he said. 'Perhaps we could all do with a glass of port. Do you think you've got rid of her?'

'I have an intimation of success but it's hard to be entirely certain. She may be lying dormant. I think this is a case for belt and braces.' Canon Frank delved into his pocket and brought out a matchbox. He opened it and held up a tiny yellow slither of something Laura could not identify. 'Have you got some Sellotape?' he asked.

'It's on his desk, I'll go and fetch it,' Laura said.

She returned some minutes later and handed the roll to Canon Frank.

'Come over here, could you Sir Repton. I'm going to stick this relic to your chest. It will keep the spirit at bay overnight. We may have to give her another session in the morning.'

'A relic, how very interesting,' Sir Repton said, unbuttoning his shirt and exposing his grey-haired chest. 'What sort of relic?'

'It's part of St Francis Xavier's toenail. I bought it when I was visiting the Basilica of Bom Jesus in Goa many years ago. Most fortunate timing as they only bring his body out once every ten years – immaculately preserved; charming lace mittens as I recall – he died in 1552.'

'How fascinating,' Sir Repton said, smoothing the tape. 'Ouch, it's rather sharp.'

'They keep him under glass these days, since a Japanese tourist bit off one of his fingers in the 1970s. But that reminds me, I took the opportunity to sanctify various objects and ingresses around the house that I thought the serving wench may have been using to obtain access. Did you mention you'd had a new convenience installed?'

'Yes the new miracle flush toilet, it's in the bathroom opposite Grimsby.'

'That's a nuisance. I don't think I'll make it up the stairs again tonight – I can feel my ankle swelling as we speak. I'll make myself comfortable in the old servants parlour.'

'Where I found you that night,' Laura said, giving him a meaningful stare. 'What did happen that night by the way?'

'I'd got the wrong month.'

Satisfied with this explanation, Laura picked up her bag. 'It's way past my bedtime. I'll take Grimsby if that's all right with you Repton. Then Strudel and Jervis can have Flamborough Head.'

'Oh yes, I am feeling so much more at home now that the Canon has safely sent the Fräulein packing.' Strudel stood up. 'Laura, I shall accompanying you be up the stairs.'

'That port's definitely gone to your head my love,' Jervis said. 'I'd better take your arm.'

As they went their separate ways, Sir Repton stood wishing them goodnight from the hall. He said he would shut Sybil Thorndike in the sitting room before locking the doors and turning off the lights before he retired.

Laura was too exhausted to even think about reading a book, which was lucky as since the revelations of the Brigadier's diary, she had nothing to read anyway.

'We must go to the library next week, Parker,' she said as he and she snuggled down and she turned off the light. 'There's nothing like a good Dick Francis.'

She wasn't sure what it was that woke her. Was it a floorboard creaking? She sat up and listened. If one of the others had had to get up in the night, she would surely hear a cistern flush. She lay back down and closed her eyes. And then again, this time the merest hint of a door being closed. Laura reached for her torch and got out of bed. She put on her kimono and crept to the door, her ears throbbing as she listened intently.

She was about to return to bed, thinking she was getting as paranoid as Sir Repton, when again, she heard something.

She turned off the torch. And then it came again. It was nearer now.

Right outside her door.

She tried holding her breath to stop the sound of her heart thumping.

Tap thud. Hadn't she heard that somewhere before?

She saw the handle of the door turn and it opened a fraction. A low beam of light illuminated the room.

'Lady Boxford,' Canon Frank whispered. 'May I come in?'

'What on earth…?'

'Shhh.' As he put one finger to his lips the torch beam flickered onto the ceiling but in the gloom Laura could just make out the stick and the bucket in his other hand. With a quick, tap thud, he was in the room and had closed the door behind him.

'What's going on?' Laura asked.

Again the Canon put his finger to his lips. 'There's someone in the house,' he said.

'How do you know?'

'I heard steps above my head in the servants parlour. It's not above any of these rooms so I knew it wasn't any of you. This may be our chance. I couldn't get the cross upstairs but I've brought the holy water. I think she might have been heading in the direction of Sir Repton's room.'

'What are you talking about?' Laura whispered.

'The ghost. I had a feeling the task was not complete but we may yet have another chance, if we're quick. There's no time to get the others, but I think you and I might just be able to catch her in the act.'

Was the Canon playing an elaborate hoax? There was only one way to find out. 'Come on then,' Laura said, putting her torch back on.

They set off down the corridor in the direction of Sir Repton's room. It wasn't the noise of the Canon's stick that was obvious but Parker's snuffling in front of them. His pace quickened. He was onto something.

They caught up with him. He had mounted the three steps and was sniffing hard at a crack in the bottom of the door. Then he began to whine.

'You go first,' Laura whispered.

Canon Frank opened the door and shone his torch

around the room. 'I can't see anything,' he said. 'She may have taken refuge in a cupboard.'

Laura stood in the doorway with him. She shone her torch at the bed. She could see the outline of Sir Repton. He was lying on his side facing away from them. 'Call him,' she said to Canon Frank.

'Sir Repton?' Canon Frank's voice was barely audible.

'Louder, he seems to be sleeping deeply.'

'Sir Repton.'

Still there was no response.

'Go nearer,' Laura said. 'Perhaps he took a sleeping pill.' She followed him into the room keeping a few steps behind him.

'Sir Repton,' Canon Frank called out again.

The recumbent figure remained prone. They went closer and stood at the end of the bed.

'Repton, wake up,' Laura said. She shone the torch at him. 'Give him a shake, Frank.'

Canon Frank walked round the foot of the bed. He gave Sir Repton's shoulder a nudge. Still Sir Repton did not wake.

'Turn on the light,' Laura said.

Canon Frank reached for the switch on the bedside lamp. The room was filled with a pale yellow gloom. Sir Repton remained motionless. Laura pushed past Canon Frank and reached for Sir Repton's shoulder. She pulled at his silk pyjama top, so that he rolled onto his back.

His mouth gaped a dark chasm, eyes wide open, hair dishevelled.

'Saints preserve us, he's had a heart attack.' The Canon crossed himself.

'I don't think so.' Laura picked up the pillow on the floor beside the bed. 'I'd say the old boy's been smothered.'

'We must call the police.' Canon Frank reached for the phone on the bedside table.

'Wait, turn out the light,' Laura whispered. She pointed to Parker who was scratching at a door in the far corner of the room. 'I think he knows something we don't.'

Chapter thirty-eight

By torchlight they crept to the door.

'Matilda's bathroom, it all makes sense,' Canon Frank said. 'Rosalind is returning to the scene of her crime.'

'What?'

'I've got the bucket ready. I may have to throw it at her. It's the only way.' He started reciting the Lord's Prayer as he opened the door.

Parker rushed in. Canon Frank shone his torch.

Laura saw Chinese wallpaper with birds of paradise covering the walls above a dado rail with oak panelling below.

She turned to the Canon. 'You mean this was where Matilda died?'

The Canon nodded.

'So she didn't use the bathroom next to her bedroom?' Laura stared at the bath. It stood in the middle of the room; a huge cast iron affair with ball and claw legs splayed out onto the carpeted floor.

'Cheryl brought her here every morning. I quite often had to help her get the wheelchair up the steps,' he said. 'Matilda loved this room.'

Laura's gaze followed the beam of her torch around the rest of the room. Beneath the window stood the basin and in one corner a loo was contained within a majestic gilt throne above which the cistern hung, a gold satin rope with a tassel acting as the flushing mechanism.

'Damn,' the Canon said. 'I didn't think to sanctify the water closet.'

'Don't talk nonsense Canon, but look, I believe there's another exit.'

Parker was snuffling madly at a piece of oak panelling on the far side of the room. Laura picked up a long-handled wooden back brush sitting in a bowl beside the bath and joined him. Below the dado rail was a small glass knob. She turned it, and the concealed door opened. Parker rushed out. Laura shone her torch down a passage. She tried to recall it from her tour with Sir Repton on the occasion of the first intended exorcism, but she'd lost her bearings.

She followed Parker. He had reached a thick velvet curtain. The hem lay in puddles on the floor and he could not penetrate it. Laura pulled it to one side and Parker rushed on. He stopped, sniffed the air and backtracked to another closed door. It was situated on a step and now Laura knew where she was.

'This leads to one of the attics and then up to the roof,' she said to Canon Frank, who had caught up with her. 'If we're not too late, we can trap whoever it is, but only if we have someone at the other end.'

'Where is the other end?'

'It comes out at the staircase next to the room you are in downstairs.'

'It's going to take me some time to get there.'

'Too long, but if I'm not mistaken, Flamborough Head is the other side of this door.' Laura pointed to another door on the other side of the passage. 'I'm going to wake Jervis. Stay here and secure the way.'

She opened the door and indeed found herself outside Flamborough Head. At that moment Jervis popped his head round the door.

'I thought I heard noises,' he said, tying his dressing gown cord.

As succinctly as she could Laura put him in the picture.

'Leave Strudel sleeping,' she said. 'We don't want to frighten her.' She explained where he was to stand guard and told him to arm himself with a stick from the umbrella stand in the hall. 'Don't put yourself in danger but turn on as few lights as possible. Just enough to identify the perpetrator, then be prepared to hide.'

'What happens if she flies straight through me?'

Laura was about to tell him to stop being ridiculous, but thought better of it. 'I'm sure Canon Frank would tell you to cross yourself. Recite a prayer or something. Now go. We'll give you a few minutes to get in place.'

Jervis turned on the landing light and trotted off in the direction of the main stairs.

Laura returned to Canon Frank and Parker, who had his front feet on the step to the attic and was snuffling noisily.

'As I recall, the staircase is very narrow,' she said, tapping the long-handled brush against her thigh. 'I shall have to go first.'

'I'll just sanctify this step.' The Canon ladled out some water. 'That should hinder her progress were she to attempt to overpower me here.'

As he said this, they heard a creaking coming from the top of the stairs above them.

'I think she may be on the move.'

'Jervis must be ready by now. I'm going up.' Laura opened the door.

Parker dashed on ahead, as Laura followed clinging to the bannister rope with one hand and brandishing the torch and brush in the other.

She heard a door slam shut above her. There was no point in secrecy now. She reached the top. Parker was at the door, growling. As Laura went to open it, she heard a thud. She flung it open and was about to reach for the light switch but the room suddenly illuminated. Above her the moon shone bright in the clear night air through the trapdoor to the roof. Laura looked at the ladder, then at Parker.

'That's the end of the chase for you, I'm afraid.' She turned back to the foot of the stairs where she could hear Canon Frank exhorting the ghost to quit the building peaceably.

'Canon Frank,' she called out.

His face appeared.

'There's no point staying there. Whoever it is, is on the roof. I'm going up. You'll have to take Parker. Go and find Jervis as quickly as you can.'

She rushed back and picked up Parker. Angry at being thwarted from his quarry, he wriggled in her arms. She managed to pass him down and Canon Frank. 'Will you be all right?' he asked.

'If I can fit through the hatch.'

Laura climbed the ladder. She peered out. There was no one to be seen. She got up onto the lead lined roof. Where did the other attic with the old ladder come up? Whoever this was, they knew their way around. She tiptoed over to the parapet where the stone eagles had stood. She looked down and hastily retreated turning in the opposite direction. And then she heard creaking and then the slam of wood hitting metal; it was coming from behind a tower of chimneys. She ran round just in time to see a wave of hair like the top of a chimney sweep's brush disappearing down a hole in the roof.

There was a shriek followed by the sound of snapping timber and then a loud thud followed some seconds later by footsteps running. Laura got to the hole. It was pitch dark. She shone her torch. The rungs of the ladder lay in a neat pile on the floor of the room below.

Laura ran back to the original opening and, as fast as she dared, descended that ladder. And then the stairs and out onto the landing. She rushed down the corridor to the main staircase, sped down the steps two at a time and then on through the hall to the green baize door. Her breath coming short and fast, she pulled it open.

'Grab the other arm, Canon,' she heard Jervis shouting. 'I can't hold on much longer.'

'I'm trying.'

Laura ran to the scene. The two men were grappling with a figure on the floor. Parker was standing close at hand growling in anticipation. Laura chose her moment. She raised the brush and brought it down with a mighty wallop.

'Awww.'

In that moment Jervis and Canon Frank managed to quell the assailant. Jervis straddled the face down upper torso pinioning the arms as the Canon lay across the writhing legs. A muffled 'awww' came from the now prostrate figure.

'Get some rope,' the Canon called out.

'Where from?' Laura asked desperately.

'The bungee ropes from the car,' Jervis said. 'I left them in the hall. But hurry, my thighs are on fire.'

Laura ran out. She found the ropes on the hall table and ran back.

'Bind the arms,' Jervis said.

Laura wound the elastic tight and hooked the ends together. Then she did the same with the legs.

A light flicked on and Strudel appeared in a floating coral pink gown, her hair in bright green spongy rollers. 'What is going on? I am waking to a terrible racket.'

'I think you can get up chaps,' Laura said. 'She won't be going far now.'

The body rolled onto one side and Angel Hobbs let out a tirade of abuse before Strudel put a stop to it by stuffing a roller in her mouth.

'Drag her into the kitchen while I call Inspector Sandfield,' Laura said.

She went to the sitting room where Parker had joined Sybil Thorndike who was sleeping on a sofa. She checked her watch as she waited for the operator to find out how long the police would be. It was three-thirty.

The operator came back on the line. 'I'm sorry but most of the force are out on a special operation tonight. You'll have to wait until we get reinforcements from Cheltenham. They'll be with you as soon as possible.' The operator apologised.

Laura put the phone down. 'That's outrageous,' She said aloud. 'They could be hours.' She went to the window and pulled back the curtain hopefully. To her surprise, she saw headlights coming up the drive.

'Silly man didn't know what he was talking about. They're here already,' she said to Parker, as she walked back through the hall.

She swung open the green baize door and heard shouting.

'Angel, we're here and we've got the donkeys. The cats are in the van. We'll bring 'em in.'

Canon Frank appeared at the kitchen door. 'What's going on?'

'Where d'you want the hay bales?' shouted another voice.

'Shove 'em in this passage. Angel, where are you?'

Laura saw the angular figure of Angel's friend, Rich. He was leading a donkey down the servant's passage.

'Hold on a minute,' Laura strode towards him.

'Oh hello, what are you doing here?' Rich said, pulling on the donkey's halter.

'I might ask the same of you.'

'We're moving in. This is the new sanctuary. Angel's organised it.'

'I think you may be premature in that assumption,' Laura said, as the sound of a siren could be heard. 'Now get that donkey out of here.'

'I've got the cats,' came another voice from behind Rich. 'I've let 'em out in the yard to stretch their legs. Plenty of ratting to be had.'

A large tabby strolled out from behind the donkey. Sybil Thorndike gave chase and as she and the cat disappeared out through the open back door, Laura saw the flashing lights of the police vehicles parked in the yard.

'Could be time to beat a retreat,' she said to Rich.

'You mean…?'

Laura heard a familiar voice coming from a loudhailer. 'We have you surrounded. Let go of the donkeys and come out with your hands up.' shouted Inspector Phil Sandfield, as he ran in.

Chapter thirty-nine

Laura thought long and hard about how she was going to tell Venetia. She decided it was better to be away from the lure of the television and suggested they take a walk around the gardens. In the end she need not have worried, Venetia, after years of frustrated parenting remained sanguine.

'Who'd have thought it, me, the mother of a murderer. She'll be away quite some time I'd have thought.' Venetia crushed a lavender head and held it to her nose. 'They might even make a biopic about her, although I don't suppose I'll be around to see it.'

'Don't be silly, of course you will,' Laura said.

'Do you think so?' Venetia dropped the lavender, taking more of an interest. 'Tell me what the Inspector said again.'

They sat on a bench looking over the rose garden.

'She tried denying Matilda's murder until Phil Sandfield showed her the tin I found in the attic. It contained two sets of false eyelashes and a lipstick. The lipstick had both Matilda and Angel's fingerprints on it.'

'That doesn't prove much,' Venetia said.

'I know but it was enough to make Angel crack. When Matilda refused to loan her any more money, I'm afraid your daughter simply lost her temper and pushed her, in her towel, backwards into the bath. She replaced the towel and took the wet one up to the attic where she used to stay.' Laura watched as Parker trotted between the bushes, Sybil Thorndike following him more slowly. 'As of Repton,' she continued. 'She said she'd gone to see him in the middle of the night to implore him to let the animals stay. Their previous home had been shut down under suspicious circumstances. She said she tripped and accidentally fell on him. I suppose she might get manslaughter for that.'

'Of course with her weight anything's possible.' Venetia's gaze followed the dogs. 'He let Sybil Thorndike get very fat didn't he?'

Laura studied the dog. Venetia was right. 'It was probably Gladys overfeeding her,' she said.

'But Angel must have been very light on her feet when she was pretending to be the ghost,' Venetia continued. 'What did she say about that?'

'Denied it.' Laura frowned as Sybil Thorndike lay down panting. 'But she had all that knowledge of the attics and staircases, it must have been her. They found a wind machine the photographers had left behind from the virtual wedding you got mixed up with.'

'Don't remind me.'

'The Inspector reckons Angel used it on the night Strudel and Jervis and I were staying, the night Strudel's scarf got tangled up in the banister and they all thought the ghost had created a tornado.'

'Very clever. I can see the re-enactment on *CSI*.' Venetia checked her watch. They had been away from a TV for some time.

Gladys was in her room sitting on a chair staring out of the window.

'All I can see is one long vale of spinsterdom leading down to a bog of sexless death,' she moaned.

'I'm sure Ancient Eros will sort you out with a new man,' Laura said.

'But until that fateful night I had a man of such perfection. I shall never be able to replace Repton, and to think how I maligned him. Accusing him of molesting me when all along it was…' Gladys gulped. '… Venetia Hobbs' daughter who had her hand at my throat.'

'To be fair on Angel,' Laura said, 'she did say it was a mistake. She took a wrong turning in the dark.'

'But what was she doing there at that time anyway?' Gladys asked.

Laura sat down on a chair opposite Gladys. 'She was hiding there most of the time after she got out of prison. She had nowhere else to go. Then she had the hare-brained idea of turning Mount Cod into an animal sanctuary. She had no idea about Ned Stocking.'

Laura leant forward and held Gladys hand. 'I spoke to Ned; he and Pom have moved in as caretakers until the will is formally read.'

'I thought she was in The Priory?'

'Ned has convinced her she was a blameless pawn in her sister's game. I'm so happy for them.'

'You are right of course.' Gladys blew her nose on a tissue.

'I was going to drop off Sybil Thorndike with them later,' Laura said. 'Unless you would like her?'

'No, I only put up with the dog because of him.' Gladys sniffed again and wiped a tear from her eye. 'I suppose I shall just have to go back to Mr. Parrott and reopen negotiations on the fastigiate oak.'

'That won't be necessary. Victoria rang this morning; she's arriving later with Vince. Edward Parrott's in custody.'

'Goodness Woldham police station's never seen so much action, but why?' For the first time Gladys looked her old self.

'Actually he's been remanded to Woldham hospital's psychiatric unit. Doctor Todhunter shopped him when Reggie Hawkesmore turned up at the surgery with rickets.'

'From malnutrition?'

'Edward Parrott was part of James Hanley Jones' care home master plan.

They knew each other from when they both worked in the theatre with Sir Repton. Their mutual loathing of

Matilda cemented their friendship. James Hanley Jones was getting him to run down Wellworth Lawns just like they ran down private houses so he could buy it on the cheap. Parrott's OCD behaviour was all part of a ruse that went too far.'

That afternoon Laura drove over to Mount Cod and delivered Sybil Thorndike. Ned and Pom met her hand in hand on the front door steps.

'I'm afraid she'll have to go on a diet,' Laura said.

'We're hoping to have a bit of a get-together to celebrate my father's life and the return of the eagles,' Ned said. 'There're arriving next week. The crane's booked. We thought we'd invite you, Aunt Venetia, Gladys, Strudel and Jervis and the Canon. All the people who helped dear father but sadly could not save him. The funeral will have to come later when the police release the body.'

'And have you thought what you are going to do with this place?' Laura looked up at the great stone porch.

Ned gazed at Pom. 'We've had a few ideas. Perhaps by the time we all meet we will have a clearer idea.'

Chapter forty

As it happened, the little party at Mount Cod had to be postponed and it was not until a month later that Ned Stocking invited them to a lunchtime celebration. It was partly in honour of Sir Repton, partly an unofficial announcement of the engagement of Ned and Pom, but mainly to welcome the new arrivals.

Sybil Thorndike had given birth to three healthy pughunds.

Parker was a disinterested father, mainly on account of Sybil Thorndike's maternal hostility to her former paramour, but he did not appear overly concerned.

'So, what are your plans after you are married?' Jervis asked Ned and Pom.

'We'd like to stay on here but I don't think that will be possible for a while. Pom is going back to drama school in London, so we will be based there for the time being.' Ned reached over and touched Pom's hand. 'We will rent out Mount Cod for a few years and then hope to escape to the country and start a family.'

Pom blushed.

'How charming.' Gladys began to weep silently.

'Delightful,' Strudel said.

'Escape to the country?' Venetia put her knife and fork down and looked at her watch. 'I might have to miss the pudding.'

'We have asked Canon Frank to marry us in the chapel here,' Ned continued.

Laura looked at the Canon. He was sitting opposite her at the table. His eyebrows were mid-flight larks ascending. They swooped in to land as he caught her gaze.

After lunch Laura dragged Venetia away from the TV and they all sat in the summerhouse and listened as Ned declaimed some of Sir Repton's favourite Shakespeare sonnets. Gladys became tearful again and Laura took her back into the house to freshen up.

'I'll wait for you in the sitting room,' Laura said, as Gladys went upstairs one last time.

The room was just as it had always been. The sofas; the table in the middle of the room where Canon Frank had broken his ankle on their first meeting at the séance; the gong and the fireplace where Repton's absurd turban had fallen.

Laura walked over to the window seat and felt the heavy damask curtains. She sighed and went to sit on the red velvet tub chair remembering her first evening at Mount Cod. Poor old Repton.

She looked around her again. On the little table to her side stood the lead tea caddy. She put it on the lap of her skirt and lifted the lid to inspect the sculpted head. In a curious way it reminded her of Andwele.

She heaved a sigh of relief that at least for the time being that secret was safe, but as she did so, she felt a sudden chill descend upon the room. She turned and looked out of the window. The sun was still shining outside. Where was Gladys?

She felt a coldness creeping through her bones, an arctic tightening of her shoulder blades. Her lips were numb. Her fingers, wrapped around the lid of the tea caddy had turned the same shade of leaden blue. Parker began to whine beside her. Then he ran from the room.

She wanted to follow him but something was stopping

her. The weight of the tea caddy lid seemed to be physically keeping her in her seated position. Her head fell back. She tried to move her hands but it was as if she was being turned to stone, ossified like a marble figure on the tomb of some ancient family, trapped forever in a dank mausoleum. She could see her features carved in an icy coolness where warmth would never penetrate, even in the sanctity of a holy place.

Her mind was wandering now. She thought she heard a distant voice. She wanted to call out to Gladys. What was the voice saying? She listened intently but a fog was descending. The fireplace was no longer visible. All around her was muffled in a miasma of frosted crystals. A deep hum had begun in the depths of her head. But it wasn't a hum. It was a voice. 'I'mm...' A tiny residue of warmth remained deep in her brain like the single seed within an over ripe furry apple. 'I'm here...'

'There you are Lady Boxford.'

She felt a weight lift. Her eyes focused as Canon Frank took the lid from her hands and placed it back on the base of the tea caddy.

She felt the warmth return slowly to her face and then her body as she lifted her head.

'My dear,' he took her hand gently. 'Are you all right?' His eyebrows burrowed. She smiled up at him as he took her by the arm.

With his assistance, she managed to get to her feet.

'The others are waiting for you outside,' he said.

'Where's Gladys?'

'She said she'd called out for you but as you didn't answer she assumed you were with us.'

They walked back out into the warm afternoon sunshine.

'I'm glad to see the colour coming back into your cheeks,' he said. 'For a moment back there I thought you looked like you'd seen a ghost.'